The cat's pajamas
& other stories

Other Works by James Morrow

Novels

The Wine of Violence (1981)

The Continent of Lies (1984)

This Is the Way the World Ends (1986)

City of Truth (1990)

Only Begotten Daughter (1990)

The Last Witchfinder (FORTHCOMING)

The Godhead Trilogy

Towing Jehovah (1994)

Blameless in Abaddon (1996)

The Eternal Footman (1999)

Short Story Collections

Swatting at the Cosmos (1990)

Bible Stories for Adults (1996)

For Mike
Keep embracing
the mutation!

The cat's pajamas
& other stories

Best wishes... **JAMES MORROW**

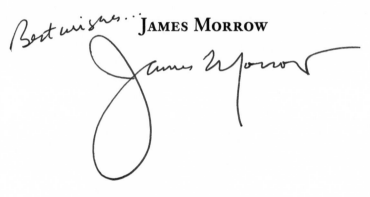

TACHYON PUBLICATIONS
SAN FRANCISCO, CALIFORNIA

TACHYON

the cat's pajamas & other stories

TYPOGRAPHY ✠ ANN MONN

TACHYON PUBLICATIONS
1459 18TH STREET #139
SAN FRANCISCO, CA 94107
(415) 285-5615
WWW.TACHYONPUBLICATIONS.COM

EDITED BY JACOB WEISMAN

ISBN: 1-892391-15-5

PRINTED IN THE UNITED STATES OF AMERICA
BY PHOENIX COLOR CORPORATION

FIRST EDITION: 2004

0   9   8   7   6   5   4   3   2   1

to my cousin
Glenn Morrow,
the brother I never had

Good Morrow to Our Waking Souls

By Terry Bisson

Want to know the real skinny about Voodoo Economics? Curious as to what the dead read for fun? Interested in sex as performance art?

You've come to the right place.

James Morrow is best known for his science-fictional fantasies, in particular the audacious Godhead Trilogy, which clothes the existential dilemma of the modern age, the Death of God (or of belief), in quotidian rags by providing the dear departed Deity with a *corpus delecti,* complete with gigantic nose hairs, parasites, and BO, to be disposed of and mourned by bereaved humanity.

The title itself, *Towing Jehovah,* is a deliberate and audacious mix of high and low, as if the Mother Church had subcontracted its funeral services to AAA.

R.I.P.

Heady, hilarious, horrific, *headlong* stuff.

Typical Morrow.

Towing Jehovah (Godhead #1) won a number of laurels, among them a World Fantasy Award nomination. The novel gave rise to an interesting discussion among the jurors (this writer among them), some of whom argued that Morrow's work, though clearly award-worthy, was just as clearly science fiction, not fantasy.

Huh? responded others. The central and (by a long shot) largest figure in the book was neither alien nor android but a Deity, the Deity, for Christ's sake (so to speak). The very nemesis, the archenemy of science: God, the Father, Himself, or at least his prodigious and venerable corpse! *Hello?*

As religion is manifestly fantasy, this eminently sensible position won. As did Jim, as did *Towing Jehovah* (World Fantasy Award, 1995). But the jurors' concerns were far from fanciful. For in fact the difference between SF and Fantasy, so often debated at dead dog parties as rockets vs. elves, more often comes down to a difference in style and tone rather than subject matter. Art direction, if you will. And Morrow's furniture, and therefore his tone, is almost always that of SF. The real world of tankers and tow-ropes, cereal boxes and oil slicks is always front and center. Moonlight and magic are at a minimum. Jerkins and goblets are there none.

So it is with the stories in this collection.

Morrow's short stories are as acclaimed as his novels, and show the same predilections and techniques, though in more compressed and often more vivid form. Short stories rely on voice rather than plot, and Morrow delights in assuming a professorial tone to describe the most outrageous events, thus becoming his own straight men. He astonishes the reader by refusing to be astonished, even when pint-sized aliens battle in Central Park, deserving infants are drowned in Holy Water, or newlyweds awaken to find their brains preserved in jars.

The tales in this volume are narrated for the most part with a repertory of Victorian flourishes and cadences. Morrow's tone is authentically (if deceptively) high, even as his adventures partake mightily of the low. Who else can speak of the "despairing throng" and at the same time let us know that they piss, they eat bran flakes, they communicate with Mars via harpsichords and dry cell batteries.

Dry indeed.

The drollery is as Victorian as the sensibility is modern, even post-modern. Morrow is after the biggest of Big Game, and for all their seemingly casual hilarity (and for the most part, they are funny as hell) these tales deal with the eternal, unanswered questions. They will rock your world. Sometimes slyly, sometimes directly.

"The War of the Worldviews" is perhaps the wildest, most original take ever on the oldest trope of SF, alien invasion; while for those with darker tastes, there is "Auspicious Eggs," set in the bleakest post-holocaust universe since Walter Miller's.

For every laugh there is an inhalation of brimstone. So be

warned.

Who else among modern SF writers (and Morrow, to his great credit, refuses to refuse the label) has worked so hard to sharpen the swords of satire? And had such fun doing it? His is a hard act to follow. Most of us are content with smaller targets than God and Man (not to mention Woman).

He is our Voltaire, casting a cold eye on both the follies of the day and the fashions of philosophy. He is our Swift, skewering his enemies with a smile.

He would be our Twain, except that we already have one. He is in fact our Morrow.

The war of the worldviews

One thing I've learned from this catastrophe is to start giving Western science and Newtonian rationality their due. For six days running, professional astronomers in the United States and Europe warned us of puzzling biological and cybernetic activity on the surfaces of both Martian satellites. We, the public, weren't interested. Next the stargazers announced that Phobos and Deimos had each sent a fleet of disc-shaped spaceships, heavily armed, hurtling toward planet Earth. We laughed in their faces. Then the astronomers reported that each saucer measured only one meter across, so that the invading armadas evoked "a vast recall of defective automobile tires." The talk-show comedians had a field day.

The first operation the Martians undertook upon landing in Central Park was to suck away all the city's electricity and seal it in a small spherical container suggesting an aluminum racquetball. I believe they wanted to make sure we wouldn't bother them as they went about their incomprehensible agenda, but Valerie says they were just being quixotic. In either case, the Martians obviously don't need all that power. They brought plenty with them.

I am writing by candlelight in our Delancey Street apartment, scribbling on a legal pad with a ballpoint pen. New York City is without functional lamps, subways, elevators, traffic signals, household appliances, or personal computers. Here and there, I suppose, life goes on as usual, thanks to storage batteries, solar cells, and diesel-fueled generators. The rest of us are living in the 18th century, and we don't much like it.

I was taking Valerie's kid to the Central Park Zoo when the Phobosians and the Deimosians started uprooting the city's power cables. Bobby and I witnessed the whole thing. The Martians were obviously having a good time. Each alien is only six inches high, but I could still see the jollity coursing through their little frames. Capricious chipmunks. I hate them all. Bobby became terrified when the Martians started wrecking things. He cried and moaned. I did my best to comfort him. Bobby's a good kid. Last week he called me Second Dad.

The city went black, neighborhood by neighborhood, and then the hostilities began. The Phobosian and the Deimosian infantries went at each other with weapons so advanced as to make Earth's rifles and howitzers seem like peashooters. Heat rays, disintegrator beams, quark bombs, sonic grenades, laser cannons. The Deimosians look rather like the animated mushrooms from *Fantasia*. The Phobosians resemble pencil sharpeners fashioned from Naugahyde. All during the fight, both races communicated among themselves via chirping sounds reminiscent of dolphins enjoying sexual climax. Their ferocity knew no limits. In one hour I saw enough war crimes to fill an encyclopedia, though on the scale of an 0-gauge model railroad.

As far as I could tell, the Battle of Central Park ended in a stalemate. The real loser was New York, victim of a hundred ill-aimed volleys. At least half the buildings on Fifth Avenue are gone, including the Mount Sinai Medical Center. Fires rage everywhere, eastward as far as Third Avenue, westward to Columbus. Bobby and I were lucky to get back home alive.

Such an inferno is clearly beyond the capacity of our local fire departments. Normally we would seek help from Jersey and Connecticut, but the Martians have fashioned some sort of force-field dome, lowering it over the entire island as blithely as a chef placing a lid on a casserole dish. Nothing can get in, and nothing can get out. We are at the invaders' mercy. If the Phobosians and the Deimosians continue trying to settle their differences through violence, the city will burn to the ground.

August 8

The Second Battle of Central Park was even worse than the first. We lost the National Academy of Design, the Guggenheim Museum, and the Carlyle Hotel. It ended with the Phobosians driving the Deimosians all the way down to Rockefeller Center. The Deimosians then rallied, stood their ground, and forced a Phobosian retreat to West 71st Street.

Valerie and I learned about this latest conflict only because a handful of resourceful radio announcers have improvised three ad hoc Citizens Band stations along what's left of Lexington Avenue. We have a decent CB receiver, so we'll be getting up-to-the-minute bulletins until our batteries die. Each time the newscaster named Clarence Morant attempts to describe the collateral damage from this morning's hostilities, he breaks down and weeps.

Even when you allow for the shrimplike Martian physique, the two armies are not very far apart. By our scale, they are separated by three blocks–by theirs, perhaps ten kilometers. Clarence Morant predicts there'll be another big battle tomorrow. Valerie chides me for not believing her when she had those premonitions last year of our apartment building on fire. I tell her she's being a Monday morning Nostradamus.

How many private journals concerning the Martian invasion exist at the moment? As I put pen to paper, I suspect that hundreds, perhaps even thousands, of my fellow survivors are recording their impressions of the cataclysm. But I am not like these other diary-keepers. I am unique. I alone have the power to stop the Martians before they demolish Manhattan–or so I imagine.

AUGUST 9

All quiet on the West Side front–though nobody believes the cease-fire will last much longer. Clarence Morant says the city is living on borrowed time.

Phobos and Deimos. When the astronomers first started warning us of nefarious phenomena on the Martian satellites, I experienced a vague feeling of personal connection to those particular moons. Last night it all flooded back. Phobos and Deimos are indeed a part of my past: a past I've been trying to forget–those bad old days when I was the worst psychiatric intern ever to serve an apprenticeship at Bellevue. I'm much happier in my present position as a bohemian hippie bum, looking after Bobby and living off the respectable income Valerie makes running two SoHo art galleries.

His name was Rupert Klieg, and he was among the dozen or so patients who made me realize I'd never be good with insane people. I found Rupert's rants alternately unnerving and boring. They sounded like something you'd read in a cheesy special-interest zine for psychotics. *Paranoid Confessions. True Hallucinations.* Rupert was especially obsessed with an organization called the Asaph Hall Society, named for the self-taught scientist who discovered Phobos and Deimos. All three members of the Asaph Hall Society were amateur astronomers and certifiable lunatics who'd dedicated themselves to monitoring the imminent invasion of planet Earth by the bellicose denizens of the Martian moons. Before Rupert told me his absurd fantasy, I didn't even realize that Mars *had* moons, nor did I care. But now I do, God knows.

The last I heard, they'd put Rupert Klieg away in the Lionel Frye Psychiatric Institute, Ninth Avenue near 58th. Valerie says I'm wasting my time, but I believe in my bones that the fate of Manhattan lies with that particular schizophrenic.

AUGUST 10

This morning a massive infantry assault by the Phobosians drove the Deimosians south to Times Square. When I heard that the Frye Institute was caught in the crossfire, I naturally feared the worst for Rupert. When I actually made the trek to Ninth and 58th, however, I discovered that the disintegrator beams, devastating in most regards, had missed the lower third of the building. I didn't see any Martians, but the whole neighborhood resounded with their tweets and twitters.

The morning's upheavals had left the Institute's staff in a state of extreme distraction. I had no difficulty sneaking into the lobby, stealing a dry-cell lantern, and conducting a room-by-room hunt.

Rupert was in the basement ward, Room 16. The door stood ajar. I entered. He lay abed, grasping a toy plastic telescope about ten centimeters long. I couldn't decide whether his keepers had been kind or cruel to allow him this trinket. It was nice that the poor demented astronomer had a telescope, but what good did it do him in a room with no windows?

His face had become thinner, his body more gaunt, but otherwise he was the fundamentally beatific madman I remembered. "Thank you for the lantern, Dr. Onslo," he said as I approached. He swatted at a naked lightbulb hanging from the ceiling like a miniature punching bag. "It's been pretty gloomy around here."

"Call me Steve. I never finished my internship."

"I'm not surprised, Dr. Onslo. You were a lousy therapist."

"Let me tell you why I've come."

"I know why you've come, and as Chairperson of the Databank Committee of the Asaph Hall Society, I can tell you everything you want to know about Phobos and Deimos."

"I'm especially interested in learning how your organization knew an invasion was imminent."

The corners of Rupert's mouth lifted in a grotesque smile. He opened the drawer in his nightstand, removed a crinkled sheet of paper, and deposited it in my hands. "Mass: 1.08e16 kilograms," he said as I studied the fact sheet, which had a cherry cough drop stuck to one corner. "Diameter: 22.2 kilometers. Mean density: 2.0 grams per cubic centimeter. Mean distance from Mars: 9,380 kilometers. Rotational period: 0.31910 days. Mean orbital velocity: 2.14 kilometers per second. Orbital eccentricity: 0.01. Orbital inclination: 1.0 degrees. Escape velocity: 0.0103 kilometers per second. Visual geometric albedo: 0.06. In short, ladies and gentlemen, I give you Phobos—"

"Fascinating," I said evenly.

"As opposed to Deimos. Mass: 1.8e15 kilograms. Diameter: 12.6 kilometers. Mean density: 1.7 grams per cubic centimeter. Mean distance from Mars: 23,460 kilometers. Rotational period: 1.26244 days. Mean orbital velocity: 1.36 kilometers per second. Orbital eccentricity: 0.00. Orbital inclination: 0.9 to 2.7 degrees. Escape velocity: 0.0057 kilometers per second. Visual geometric albedo: 0.07. Both moons look like baked potatoes."

"By some astonishing intuition, you knew that these two satellites intended to invade the Earth."

"Intuition, my Aunt Fanny. We deduced it through empirical observation." Rupert brought the telescope to his eye and focused on the dormant lightbulb. "Consider this. A scant eighty million years ago, there were no Phobes or Deems. I'm not kidding. They were all one species, living beneath the desiccated surface of Mars. Over the centuries, a deep rift in philosophic sensibility opened up within their civilization. Eventually they decided to abandon the native planet, never an especially congenial place, and emigrate to the local moons. Those favoring Sensibility A moved to Phobos. Those favoring Sensibility B settled on Deimos."

5

"Why would the Martians find Phobos and Deimos more congenial?" I jammed the fact sheet in my pocket. "I mean, aren't they just ... big rocks?"

"Don't bring your petty little human perspective to the matter, Dr. Onslo. To a vulture, carrion tastes like chocolate cake. Once they were on their respective worlds, the Phobes and the Deems followed separate evolutionary paths–hence, the anatomical dimorphism we observe today."

"What was the nature of the sensibility rift?"

Rupert used his telescope to study a section of the wall where the plaster had crumbled away, exposing the latticework beneath. "I have no idea."

"None whatsoever?"

"The Asaph Hall Society dissolved before we could address that issue. All I know is that the Phobes and the Deems decided to settle the question once and for all through armed combat on neutral ground."

"So they came here?"

"Mars would've seemed like a step backwards. Venus has rotten weather."

"Are you saying that whichever side wins the war will claim victory in what is essentially a philosophical controversy?"

"Correct."

"They believe that truth claims can be corroborated through violence?"

"More or less."

"That doesn't make any sense to me."

"If you were a fly, horse manure would smell like candy. We'd better go see Melvin."

"Who?"

"Melvin Haskin, Chairperson of our Epistemology Committee. If anybody's figured out the Phobos-Deimos rift, it's Melvin. The last I heard, they'd put him in a rubber room at Werner Krauss Memorial. What's today?"

"Tuesday."

"Too bad."

"Oh?"

"On Tuesday Melvin always wills himself into a catatonic stupor. He'll be incommunicado until tomorrow morning."

I had no trouble sneaking Rupert out of the Frye Institute. Everybody on the staff was preoccupied with gossip and triage. The lunatic brought along his telescope and a bottle of green pills that he called "the thin verdant line that separates me from my madness."

Although still skeptical of my belief that Rupert held the key to Manhattan's salvation, Valerie welcomed him warmly into our apartment–she's a better therapist than I ever was–and offered him the full measure of her hospitality. Because we have a gas range, we were able to prepare a splendid meal of spinach lasagna and toasted garlic bread. Rupert ate all the leftovers. Bobby asked him what it was like to be insane. "There is nothing that being insane is like," Rupert replied.

After dinner, at Rupert's request, we all played Scrabble by candlelight, followed by a round of Clue. Rupert won both games. At ten o'clock he took a green pill and stretched his spindly body along the length of our couch, which he said was much more comfortable than his bed at the Frye Institute. Five minutes later he was asleep.

As I write this entry, Clarence Morant is offering his latest dispatches from the war zone. Evidently the Deimosians are still dug in throughout Times Square. Tomorrow the Phobosians will attempt to dislodge them. Valerie and I both hear a catch in Morant's voice as he tells how his aunt took him to see *Cats* when he was nine years old. He inhales deeply and says, "The Winter Garden Theater is surely doomed."

AUGUST 11

Before we left the apartment this morning, Rupert remembered that Melvin Haskin is inordinately fond of bananas. Luckily, Valerie had purchased two bunches at the corner bodega right before the Martians landed. I tossed them into my rucksack, along with some cheese sandwiches and Rupert's telescope, and then we headed uptown.

Reaching 40th Street, we saw that the Werner Krauss Memorial Clinic had become a seething mass of orange flames and billowing gray smoke, doubtless an ancillary catastrophe accruing to the Battle of Times Square. Ashes and sparks speckled the air. Our eyes teared up from the carbon. The sidewalks teemed with a despairing throng of doctors, administrators, guards, and inmates. Presumably the Broadway theaters and hotels were also on fire, but I didn't want to think about it.

Rupert instantly alighted on Melvin Haskin, though I probably could've identified him unassisted. Even in a milling mass of psychotics, Melvin stood out. He'd strapped a dish-shaped antenna onto his head, the concavity pointed skyward–an inverted yarmulke. A pair of headphones covered his ears, jacked into an antique vacuum-tube amplifier that he cradled in his arms like a baby. Two coiled wires, one red, one black, connected the antenna to the amplifier, its functionless power cord bumping against Melvin's left leg, the naked prongs glinting in the August sun. He wore a yellow terrycloth bathrobe and matching Big Bird slippers. His frame was massive, his skin pale, his stomach protuberant, his mouth bereft of teeth.

Rupert made the introductions. Once again he insisted on calling me Dr. Onslo. I pointed to Melvin's antenna and asked him whether he was receiving transmissions from the Martians.

"What?" He pulled off the headphones and allowed them to settle around his neck like a yoke.

"Your antenna, the headphones–looks like you're communicating with the Martians."

"Are you crazy?" Scowling darkly, Melvin turned toward Rupert and jerked an accusing thumb in my direction. "Dr. Onslo thinks my amplifier still works even though half the tubes are burned out."

"He's a psychiatrist," Rupert explained. "He knows nothing about engineering. How was your catatonic stupor?"

"Restful. You'll have to come along some time."

"I haven't got the courage," said Rupert.

Melvin was enchanted by the gift of the bananas, and even more enchanted to be reunited with his fellow paranoid. As the two middle-aged madmen headed east, swapping jokes and stories like old school chums, I could barely keep up with their frenetic pace. After passing Sixth Avenue they turned abruptly into Bryant Park, where they found an abandoned soccer ball on the grass. For twenty minutes they kicked it back and forth, then grew weary of the sport. They sat down on a bench. I joined them. Survivors streamed by holding handkerchiefs over their faces.

"The city's dying," I told Melvin. "We need your help."

"Rupert, have you still got the touch?" Melvin asked his friend.

"I believe I do," said Rupert.

"Rupert can fix burned-out vacuum tubes merely by laying his hands on them," Melvin informed me. "I call him the Cathode Christ."

Even before Melvin finished his sentence, Rupert had begun fondling the amplifier. He rubbed each tube as if the warmth of his hand might bring it to life.

"You've done it again!" cried Melvin, putting on his headphones. "I'm pulling in a signal from Ceres! I think it might be just the place for us to retire, Rupert! No capital gains tax!" He removed the phones and looked me in the eye. "Do you solicit me as head of the Epistemology Committee, or in my capacity as a paranoid schizophrenic?"

"The former," I said. "I'm hoping you've managed to define the Phobos-Deimos rift."

"You came to the right place." Melvin ate a banana, depositing the peel in the dish antenna atop his head. "It's the most basic of *Weltanschauung* dichotomies. Here on Earth many philosophers would trace the problem back to all that bad blood between the Platonists and the Aristotelians–you know, idealism versus realism–but it's actually the sort of controversy you can have only after a full-blown curiosity about nature has come on the scene."

"Do you speak of the classic schism between scientific materialists and those who champion presumed numinous realities?" I asked.

"Exactly," said Melvin.

"There–what did I tell you?" said Rupert merrily. "I *knew* old Melvin would set us straight."

"On the one hand, Deimos, moon of the logical positivists," said Melvin. "On the other hand, Phobos, bastion of revealed religion."

"Melvin, you're a genius," said Rupert, retrieving his telescope from my rucksack.

"Should we infer that the Phobosians are loath to evoke Darwinian mechanisms in explaining why they look so different from the Deimosians?" I asked.

"Quite so." Melvin unstrapped the dish antenna, scratched his head, and nodded. "The Phobes believe that God created them in his own image."

"They think God looks like a pencil sharpener?"

"That is one consequence of their religion, yes." Melvin donned his antenna and retrieved a bottle of red capsules from his bathrobe pocket. He fished one out and ate it. "Want to hear the really nutty part? The Phobes and the Deems are genetically wired to abandon any given philosophical position the moment it encounters an honest and coherent refutation. The Martians won't accept no for an answer, and they won't accept yes for an answer either–instead they want rational arguments."

"Rational arguments?" I said. "Then why the hell are they killing each other and bringing down New York with them?"

"If you were a dog, a dead possum would look like the Mona Lisa," said Rupert.

Melvin explained, "No one has ever presented them with a persuasive discourse favoring either the Phobosian or the Deimosian worldview."

"You mean we could end this nightmare by supplying the Martians with some crackerjack reasons why theistic revelation is the case?" I said.

"Either that, or some crackerjack reasons why scientific materialism is the case," said Melvin. "I realize it's fashionable these days to speak of an emergent compatibility between the two idioms, but you don't have to be a rocket scientist to realize that the concept of materialistic supernaturalism is oxymoronic if not plainly moronic, and nobody knows this better than the Martians." He pulled the headphones over his ears. "Ha! Just as I suspected. The civilization on Ceres divides neatly into those who have exact change and those who don't."

"The problem, as I see it, is twofold," said Rupert, pointing his telescope south toward the Empire State Building. "We must construct the rational arguments in question, and we must communicate them to the Martians."

"They don't speak English, do they?" I said.

"Of *course* they don't speak English," said Rupert, exasperated. "They're Martians. They don't even have language as we commonly understand the term." He poked Melvin on the shoulder. "This is clearly a job for Annie."

"What?" said Melvin, removing the headphones.

"It's a job for Annie," said Rupert.

"Agreed," said Melvin.

"Who?" I said.

"Annie Porlock," said Rupert. "She built her own harpsichord."

"Soul of an artist," said Melvin.

"Heart of an angel," said Rupert.

"Crazy as a bedbug," and Melvin.

"For our immediate purpose, the most relevant fact about Annie is that she chairs our Interplanetary Communications Committee, in which capacity she cracked the Martian tweets and twitters, or so she claimed right before the medics took her away."

"How do we find her?" I asked.

"For many years she was locked up in some wretched Long Island laughing academy, but then the family lawyer got into the act," said Melvin. "I'm pretty sure they transferred her to a more humane facility here in New York."

"What facility?" I said. "Where?"

"I can't remember," said Melvin.

"You've *got* to remember."

"Sorry."

"*Try.*"

Melvin picked up the soccer ball and set it in his lap. "Fresh from the guillotine, the head of Maximillien François Marie Isidore de Robespierre," he said, as if perhaps I'd forgotten he was a paranoid schizophrenic. "Oh, Robespierre, Robespierre, was the triumph of inadvertence over intention ever so total?"

I brought both lunatics home with me. Valerie greeted us with the sad news that the Winter Garden, the Walter Kerr, the Eugene O'Neill, and a half-dozen other White Way theaters had been lost in the Battle of Times Square. I told her there was hope for the Big Apple yet.

"It all depends on our ability to devise a set of robust arguments favoring either scientific materialism or theistic revelation and then communicating the salient points to the Martians in their nonlinguistic language, which was apparently deciphered several years ago by a paranoid schizophrenic named Annie Porlock," I told Valerie.

"That's not a sentence you hear every day," she replied.

It turns out that Melvin is even more devoted to board games than Rupert, so the evening went well. We played Scrabble, Clue, and Monopoly, after which Melvin introduced us to an amusement of his own invention, a variation on Trivial Pursuit called Teleological Ambition. Whereas the average Trivial Pursuit conundrum is frivolous, the challenges underlying Teleological Ambition are profound. Melvin remembered at least half of the original questions, writing them out on three-by-five cards. If God is infinite and self-sufficient, why would he care whether his creatures worshiped him or not? Which thought is the more overwhelming: the possibility that the Milky Way is teeming with sentient life, or the possibility that Earthlings and Martians occupy an otherwise empty galaxy? That sort of thing. Bobby hated every minute, and I can't say I blame him.

11

AUGUST 12

Shortly after breakfast this morning, while he was consuming what may have been the last fresh egg in SoHo, Melvin announced that he knew how to track down Annie Porlock.

"I was thinking of how she's a walking Rosetta Stone, our key to deciphering the Martian tongue," he explained, strapping on his dish antenna. "Rosetta made me think of Roosevelt, and then I remembered that she's living in a houseboat moored by Roosevelt Island in the middle of the East River."

I went to the pantry and filled my rucksack with a loaf of stale bread, a jar of instant coffee, a Kellogg's Variety Pack, and six cans of Campbell's soup. The can opener was nowhere to be found, so I tossed in my Swiss army knife. I guided my lunatics out the door.

There were probably only a handful of taxis still functioning in New York—most of them had run out of gas, and their owners couldn't refuel because the pumps worked on electricity—but somehow we managed to nab one at the corner of Houston and Forsyth. The driver, a Russian émigré named Vladimir, was not surprised to learn we had no cash, all the ATM's being dormant, and he agreed to claim his fare in groceries. He piloted us north along First Avenue, running straight through fifty-seven defunct traffic signals, and left us off at the Queensboro Bridge. I gave him two cans of chicken noodle soup and a single-serving box of Frosted Flakes.

The Martian force-field dome had divided Roosevelt Island right down the middle, but luckily Annie Porlock had moored her houseboat on the Manhattan side. "Houseboat" isn't the right word, for the thing was neither a house nor a boat but a decrepit two-room shack sitting atop a half-submerged barge called the *Folly to Be Wise*. Evidently the hull was leaking. If Annie's residence sunk any lower, I thought as we entered the shack, the East River would soon be lapping at her ankles.

A ruddy, zaftig, silver-haired woman in her mid-fifties lay dozing in a wicker chair, her lap occupied by a book about Buddhism and a large calico cat. Her harpsichord rose against the far wall, beside a lamp table holding a large bottle of orange capsules the size of jellybeans. Our footfalls woke her. Recognizing Rupert, Annie let loose a whoop of delight. The cat bailed out. She stood up.

"Melvin Haskin?" said Annie, sashaying across the room. "Is that really you? They let you out?"

Annie extended her right hand. Melvin kissed it.

"Taa-daa!" shouted Rupert, stepping out from behind Melvin's bulky frame. His pressed his mouth against Annie's cheek.

"Rupert Klieg–they sprang you too!" said Annie. "If I knew you were coming, I'd have baked a fruitcake."

"The First Annual Reunion of the Asaph Hall Society will now come to order," said Melvin, chuckling.

"Have you heard about the Martians?" said Rupert.

Annie's eyes widened grotesquely, offering a brief intimation of the derangement that lay behind. "They've landed? Really? You can't be serious!"

"Cross my heart," said Rupert. "Even as we speak, the Phobes and the Deems are thrashing out their differences in Times Square."

"Just as we predicted," said Annie. Turning from Rupert, she fixed her frowning gaze on me. "I guess that'll show you doubting Thomases ..."

Rupert introduced me as "Dr. Onslo, the first in a long line of distinguished psychiatrists who tried to help me before hyperlithium came on the market," and I didn't bother to contradict him. Instead I explained the situation to Annie, emphasizing Melvin's recent deductions concerning Martian dialectics. She was astonished to learn that the Deimosians and the Phobosians were occupying Manhattan in direct consequence of the old materialism-supernaturalism dispute, and equally astonished to learn that, in contrast to most human minds, the Martian psyche was hardwired to favor rational discourse over pleasurable opinion.

"That must be the strangest evolutionary adaptation ever," said Annie.

"Certainly the strangest we know about," said Melvin.

"Can you help us?" I asked.

Approaching her harpsichord, Annie sat on her swiveling stool and rested her hands on the keyboard. "This looks like a harpsichord, but it's really an interplanetary communication device. I've spent the last three years recalibrating the jacks, upgrading the plectrums, and adjusting the strings."

Her fingers glided across the keys. A jumble of notes leaped forth, so weird and discordant they made Schönberg sound melodic.

"There," said Annie proudly, pivoting toward her audience. "In the

Martian language I just said, 'Before enlightenment, chop wood, carry water. After enlightenment, chop wood, carry water.'"

"Wow," said Klieg.

"Terrific," said Melvin.

Annie turned back to the keyboard and called forth another unruly refrain.

"That meant, 'There are two kinds of naïveté, the naïveté of optimism and the naïveté of pessimism,'" she explained.

"Who would've guessed there could be so much meaning in cacophony?" I said.

"To a polar bear, the Arctic Ocean feels like a Jacuzzi," said Rupert.

Annie called forth a third strain–another grotesque non-melody.

"And the translation?" asked Rupert.

"It's an idiomatic expression," she replied.

"Can you give us a rough paraphrase?"

"'Hi there, baby. You have great tits. Would you like to fuck?'"

Melvin said, "The problem, of course, is that the Martians are likely to kill each other–along with the remaining population of New York–before we can decide conclusively which worldview enjoys the imprimatur of rationality."

"All is not lost," said Rupert.

"What do you mean?" I asked.

"We might, just might, have enough time to formulate strong arguments supporting a side of the controversy chosen ... arbitrarily," said Rupert.

"Arbitrarily?" echoed Annie, voice cracking.

"Arbitrarily," repeated Rupert. "It's the only way."

The four of us traded glances of reluctant consensus. I removed a quarter from my pants pocket.

"Heads: revelation, God, the Phobes," said Melvin.

"Tails: materialism, science, the Deems," said Rupert.

I flipped the quarter. It landed under Annie's piano stool, frightening the cat.

Tails.

And so we went at it, a melee of discourse and disputation that lasted through the long, hot afternoon and well into evening. We napped on the floor. We pissed in the river. We ate cold soup and dry Raisin Bran.

By eight o'clock we'd put the Deimosian worldview on solid

ground–or so we believed. The gist of our argument was that sentient species emerged in consequence of certain discoverable properties embedded in nature. Whether Earthling or Martian, aquatic or terrestrial, feathered or furred, scaled or smooth, all lifeforms were inextricably woven into a material biosphere, and it was this astonishing and demonstrable connection, not the agenda of some hypothetical supernatural agency, that made us one with the cosmos and the bearers of its meaning.

"And now, dear Annie, you must set it all to music," I told the Communications Chairperson, giving her a hug.

Rupert and Melvin decided to spend the night aboard the *Folly to Be Wise*, providing Annie with moral support and instant coffee while she labored over her translation. I knew that Valerie and Bobby would be worried about me, so I said my farewells and headed for home. So great was my exhilaration that I ran the whole three miles to Delancey Street without stopping–not bad for a weekend jogger.

I'm writing this entry in our bedroom. Bobby's asleep. Valerie wants to hear about my day, so I'd better sign off. The news from Clarence Morant is distressing. Defeated in the Battle of Times Square, the Deimosians have retreated to the New York Public Library and taken up positions on the steps between the stone lions. The Phobosians are encamped outside Grand Central Station, barely a block away.

There are over two million volumes in the New York Public Library, Morant tells us, including hundreds of irreplaceable first editions. When the fighting starts, the Martians will be firing their heat rays amidst a paper cache of incalculable value.

AUGUST 13

Phobos and Deimos. When Asaph Hall went to name his discoveries, he logically evoked the two sons and companions of Ares, the Greek god of war. Phobos, avatar of fear. Deimos, purveyor of panic.

Fear and panic. Is there a difference? I believe so. Beyond the obvious semantic distinction–fear the chronic condition, panic the acute–it seems to me that the Phobosians and the Deimosians, whether through meaningless coincidence or Jungian synchronicity, picked the right moons. Phobos, fear. Is fear not a principal engine behind the supernaturalist worldview? (The universe is manifestly full of terrifying forces controlled by powerful gods. If we worship them, maybe they won't destroy us.) Deimos, panic. At first blush, the scientific worldview has nothing to do with panic. But consider the etymology here. *Panic* from Pan, Greek god of forests, pastures, flocks, and shepherds. Pan affirms the physical world. Pan says yes to material reality. Pan might panic on occasion, but he does not live in fear.

When I returned to the *Folly to Be Wise* this morning, the lunatics were asleep, Rupert lying in the far corner, Annie curled up in her tiny bedroom, Melvin snoring beside her. He still wore his dish antenna. The pro-Deimosian argument lay on the harpsichord, twelve pages of sheet music. Annie had titled it "Materialist Prelude and Fugue in C-Sharp Minor."

I awoke my friends and told them about the imminent clash of arms at the New York Public Library. We agreed there was no time to hear the fugue right now—the world premiere would have to occur on the battlefield—but Annie could not resist pointing out some of its more compelling passages. "Look here," she said, indicating a staff in the middle of page three. "A celebration of the self-correcting ethos at the heart of the scientific enterprise." She turned to page seven and ran her finger on the topmost measures. "A brief history of postmodern academia's failure to relativize scientific knowledge." She drew my attention to a coda on page eleven. "Depending on the definitions you employ, the materialist worldview precludes neither a creator-god nor the possibility of transcendence through art, religion, or love."

I put the score in my rucksack, and then we took hold of the harpsichord, each of us lifting a corner. We proceeded with excruciating care, as if the instrument were made of glass, lest we misalign any of Annie's clever tinkerings and canny modifications. Slowly we carried the harpsichord across the deck, off the island, and over the bridge. At the intersection of Second Avenue and 57th Street, we paused to catch our breath.

"Fifteen blocks," said Rupert.

"Can we do it in fifteen minutes?" I asked.

"We're the Asaph Hall Society," said Annie. "We've never failed to thwart an extraterrestrial invasion."

And so our great mission began. 56th Street. 55th Street. 54th Street. 53rd Street. Traffic being minimal, we forsook the sidewalks with their frequent impediments—scaffolding, trash barrels, police barriers—and moved directly along the asphalt. Doubts tormented me. What if we'd picked the wrong side of the controversy? What if we'd picked the right side but our arguments sounded feeble to the Phobosians? What if panic seized Annie, raw Deimosian panic, and she choked up at the keyboard?

By the time we were in the Forties, we could hear the Martians' glissando chirpings. Our collective pace quickened. At last we reached 42nd Street. We turned right and bore the peace machine past the Chrysler Building and the Grand Hyatt Hotel. Arriving at Grand Central Station, we paused to behold the Phobosian infantry maneuvering for a frontal assault on the Deimosian army, still presumably holding the library steps. The air vibrated with extraterrestrial tweets and twitters, as if midtown Manhattan had become a vast pet store filled with demented parakeets.

We transported the harpsichord another block and set it down at the Madison Avenue intersection, from which vantage we could see both Grand Central Station and the library. The Phobosian army had indeed spent the night bivouacked between the stone lions. Inevitably I thought of Gettysburg—James Longstreet's suicidal sweep across the Pennsylvania farmlands, hurtling his divisions against George Meade's Army of the Potomac, which had numerical superiority, a nobler cause, and the high ground.

Rupert took the score from my sack, laid the twelve pages against the rack, and made ready to turn them. Melvin removed his dish antenna and got down on all fours before the instrument. Annie seated herself on his massive back. She laid her hands on the keyboard. A stiff breeze arose. If the score blew away, all would be lost.

Annie depressed a constellation of keys. Martian language came forth, filling the canyon between the skyscrapers.

A high bugling wail emerged from deep within the throats of the Deimosian officers, and the soldiers began their march. Annie played furiously. "Materialist Prelude and Fugue," page one ... page two ... page three ... page four. The soldiers kept on coming. Page five ... page six ... page seven ... page eight. The Deimosians continued their advance, parting around the harpsichord like an ocean current yielding to the prow of a ship. Page nine ... page ten ... page eleven ... page twelve. Among the irreplaceable volumes in the New York Public Library, I recalled, were first editions of Nicolaus Copernicus's *De Revolutionibus*, William Gilbert's *De Magnete*, and Isaac Newton's *Principia Mathematica*.

Once again the Deimosian officers let loose a high bugling wail.

The soldiers abruptly halted their advance.

They threw down their weapons and broke into a run.

"Good God, is it working?" asked Rupert.

"I think so," I replied.

"It worked!" insisted Annie.

"Really?" said Melvin, whose perspective on the scene was compromised by his function as a piano stool.

"We've done it!" I cried. "We've really done it!"

Within a matter of seconds the Deimosians accomplished a reciprocal disarmament. They rushed toward their former enemies. The two forces met on Fifth Avenue, Phobosians and Deimosians embracing passionately, so that the intersection seemed suddenly transformed into an immense railroad platform on which countless wayward lovers were meeting sweethearts from whom they'd been involuntarily separated for years.

Now the ovation came, two hundred thousand extraterrestrials cheering and applauding Annie as she climbed off Melvin's back and stood up straight. She took a bow, and then another.

A singularly appreciative chirp emerged from a Phobosian general, whereupon a dozen of his fellows produced the identical sound.

Annie got the message. She seated herself on Melvin's back, turned to page one, and played "Materialist Prelude and Fugue in C-Sharp Minor" all over again.

August 18

The Martians have been gone for only five days, but already Manhattan is healing. The lights are back on. Relief arrives from every state in the Union, plus Canada.

Valerie, Bobby, and I are now honorary members of the Asaph Hall Society. We all gathered this afternoon at Gracie Mansion in Carl Schurz Park, not far from Annie's houseboat. Mayor Margolis will let us use his parlor whenever we want. In fact, there's probably no favor he won't grant us. After all, we saved his city.

Annie called the meeting to order. Everything went smoothly. We discussed old business (our ongoing efforts to contact the Galilean satellites), new business (improving patient services at the Frye Institute and the Krauss Clinic), and criteria for admitting new participants. As long as they remember to take their medicine, my lunatics remain the soul of reason. Melvin and Annie plan to marry in October.

"I'll bet we're all having the same thought right now," said Rupert before we went out to dinner.

"What if Dr. Onslo's quarter had come up heads?" said Melvin, nodding. "What if we'd devised arguments favoring the Phobosians instead? What then?"

"That branch of the reality tree will remain forever hidden from us," said Annie.

"I think it's entirely possible the Deimosians would've thrown down their arms," said Valerie.

"So do I," said Melvin. "Assuming our arguments were plausible."

"Know what I think?" said Rupert. "I think we all just got very lucky."

Did we merely get lucky? Hard to say. But I do know one thing. In two weeks the New York Philharmonic will perform a fully orchestrated version of "Materialist Prelude and Fugue in C-Sharp Minor" at Lincoln Center, which miraculously survived the war, and I wouldn't miss it for the world.

The wisdom of the skin

Even as I hauled his shivering body from the river and dragged it onto the pier, examining his ancient face as a numismatist might scrutinize a rare coin, I did not recognize him. He was supposed to be dead, after all—killed along with his wife when their rental Citroën transmuted into a fireball following its collision with a concrete wall in Florence. Not until he'd stopped wheezing, lifted his head, and placed a kiss of gratitude on my cheek did I understand that the newspaper accounts of his incineration were false. This was surely Bruno Pearl. I'd been privileged to rescue the genius who'd given his audiences Sphinx Recumbent, Flowering Judas, and a dozen other masterpieces of copulation.

Just as musical comedy eclipsed operetta—just as silent movies killed vaudeville, talkies usurped the silents, and television reduced radio drama to a prolix mockery of itself—so did the coming of the Siemanns plasmajector spell the demise of the sex artists, whose achievements today survive largely in the memories of aging aficionados. I shall always regret that I never saw a live concert. How enthralling it must have been to enter a public park during the last century knowing that you might witness a pair of high-wire sensualists, avant-garde couplers, or Viennese orgasmeisters. It was an age of giants. Sara and Jaspar. Quentin and Alessandra. Roger and Dominic. The anonymous Phantoms of Delight. Teresa and Gaston, also known as the Portions of Eternity. Marge and Annette, who styled themselves Enchanted Equinox. You might even find yourself in the legendary presence of Bruno and Mina Pearl.

During my student days at the New England School of Art and Design, I was shrewd enough to take Aesthetics 101, "Metaphysics of the Physical," taught by the benignly fanatical Nikolai Vertankowski. Thanks to Vertankowski's extensive collection of pirate videos and bootleg DVD's, his students experienced tantalizing intimations of the medium that Bruno Pearl and his wife took to such dazzling heights. We learned of the couple's chance meeting at the audition for Trevor Paisley's defiant presentation of *Oedipus Rex* (it began with Antigone's conception), as well as their early struggles on the eros circuit and their eventual celebrity. At the height of the lovers' fame nobody came close to matching their carnal sorcery, their lubricious magic, that bewitchment for which there is no name. Vertankowski also taught us about Bruno and Mina's uncanny and unaccountable decline: the inexplicable fact that, when their Citroën exploded, they had not given a memorable performance in over two years.

Throughout the work week I cross the Hudson twice a day, riding the ferry back and forth between the unfocused city of Hoboken, where I live, and the cavernous reaches of lower Manhattan, where I work. A decade ago my independent film company, Kaleidoscope Productions, received an Oscar nomination for *The Rabble Capitalists*, a feature-length documentary about the unlicensed peddlers of Gotham, those dubious though ambitious folk you see selling fake Rolexes, remaindered books, and sweatshop toys on street corners and in subway stations. Alas, my success was fleeting, and I eventually resigned myself to a career in cranking out instructional videos (tedious and talky shorts intended to galvanize sales forces, inspire stockholders, and educate dentists' captive audiences). One of these days I'm going to sell the business and return to my former life as the SoHo bohemian who signed her oil paintings "Boadicea," though my name is really Susan Fiore.

The night I delivered Bruno Pearl from death, my mood was not far from the syndrome explicated in the Kaleidoscope video called *Coping with Clinical Depression.* At the beginning of the week I'd broken up with Anson, a narcissistic though singularly talented sculptor for whom I'd compliantly aborted a pregnancy one month earlier. As always occurs when I lose a lover, I'd assumed a disproportionate share of the blame, and I was now engaged in a kind of penance, pacing around on the ferry's frigid upper level as the wind cut through my fleece jacket and iced my bones. Despite my melancholy, I took note of the old man, the only other passenger on the weather deck. He was leaning over the stern rail, a skeletal septuagenarian in a tweed overcoat, his face as compacted as a hawk's, his nose supporting a pair of eyeglasses, one lens held in place by a ratty pink Band-Aid. He stared at the Statue of Liberty, an intense gaze, far-reaching, immune to the horizon. My forlorn companion, it seemed, could see all the way to Lisbon.

Glancing north, I fixed on the brightly lit George Washington Bridge, each great sagging cable gleaming like a rope of luminous pearls. Anson believed that our descendants will regard suspension bridges with the same admiration we ourselves accord cathedrals and clipper ships, and tonight I understood what he meant. I turned back to the Statue of Liberty. The gentleman with the broken glasses was gone. In his place—a void: negative space, to use one of Anson's favorite terms.

I peered over the rail. If suicide had been the old man's aim, he'd evidently thought better of the decision; he was thrashing about amid the ferry's widening wake with a desperation indistinguishable from panic. For a fleeting instant the incongruity transfixed me—the lower Hudson, an aquatic wasteland, a place for concrete quays and steel scows but not this fleshy jetsam—and then I tossed aside my rucksack, inhaled sharply, and jumped.

Anyone who has ever studied under Nikolai Vertankowski knows better than to equate performance intercourse with displays of more recent vintage. Today's amateur exhibitionists and open-air stunt fuckers, the professor repeatedly reminded us, are not carrying on a tradition—they are desecrating it. For the true sex artist, all was subtext, all was gesture and grace. In revealing their skin to the world, the classical copulationists achieved not pornographic nudity but pagan nakedness. When Bruno and Mina ruled the eros circuit, they shed each garment so lissomely, planted each kiss so sublimely, and applied each caress so generously that the spectators experienced this tactile cornucopia no less than the lovers themselves.

Then, of course, there was the conversation. Before and after any overt hydraulics, Bruno and Mina always talked to each other, trading astute observations and reciting stanzas of poetry they'd composed especially for the occasion. Sensitive women wept at this linguistic foreplay. Canny men took notes. But the connections themselves remained the *sine qua non* of each concert. By the time they were famous, Bruno and Mina had perfected over a dozen acts, including not only Sphinx Recumbent and Flowering Judas but also Fearful Symmetry, Sylph and Selkie, Chocolate Babylon, Holy Fools, Menses of Venus, Onan in Avalon, Beguiling Serpent, Pan and Syrinx, and Fleur de Lis. When their passions were spent, their skins sated, and their reservoirs of postcoital verse exhausted, Bruno and Mina simply got dressed and watched approvingly as the spectators dropped coins and folding money into their gold-hinged mahogany coffer.

Performance copulators lived by a code, a kind of theatric chivalry, its nuances known only to themselves. None had an agent or manager. They never published their touring schedules or distributed press kits. Souvenir mongering was forbidden. Videotaping by spectators was tolerated but frowned upon. The artists always arrived unexpectedly, without fanfare, like a goshawk swooping down on a rabbit or a fox materializing in a henhouse. Naturally they favored the major venues, appearing frequently in Golden Gate Park, Brussels Arboretum, Kensington Gardens, and Versailles, but sometimes they brought their brilliance to the humblest of small-town greens and commons. Quixotic tutelaries. Daemons of the flesh. Now you saw them, now you didn't.

Although I had never before attempted the maneuvers illustrated in the Kaleidoscope video called *Deep Water Rescue*, my relationship with that particular short was so intimate that, upon entering the Hudson, I spontaneously assumed a backstroke position, placed one hand under the drowning man's chin, bade him relax, and, kicking for motive power, towed him to New Jersey. The instant I levered him onto the derelict wharf, his teeth started chattering, but he nevertheless managed to explain how his eyeglasses had slipped from his face and how in grabbing for them he'd lost his balance and tumbled over the rail. He chastised himself for never learning to swim. Then came the kiss on the cheek–and then the flash of recognition.

"You're Bruno Pearl," I told him.

Instead of responding to my assertion, he patted his pants, front and back, soon determining that his wallet and keys had survived the misadventure.

"Such a wonderfully courageous, a *foolishly* courageous young woman." His teeth continued to vibrate, castanets in the hands of a lunatic. "Tell me your name, dear lady."

"Susan Fiore."

"Call me John."

24

"You're Bruno Pearl," I informed him again. When you've just saved a person's life, a certain impertinence comes naturally. "You're Bruno Pearl, and the world believes you're dead."

He made no response, but instead rubbed each arm with the opposite hand. "In my experience, lovely Susan," he said at last, "appearances are deceiving."

Whether this was Bruno Pearl or not, my obligation to him clearly had not ended. My beneficiary's most immediate problem was not his lost eyeglasses–though he said he was functionally blind without them–but the threat of hypothermia. When the gentleman revealed that he lived in north Hoboken, near the corner of Willow Avenue and 14th Street, I proposed that we proceed directly to my apartment, a mere two blocks from the wharf.

He readily assented, and so I took him by the hand and led him into the nocturnal city.

By the time we reached my apartment he'd stopped shivering. Supplying him with a dry wardrobe posed no challenge: although my ex-lovers are a heterogeneous bunch, they share a tendency to leave their clothes behind. That night Bruno received Warren's underwear, Jack's socks, Craig's dungarees, and Rich's red polo shirt. I actually had more difficulty replacing my own soggy attire, but eventually I found a clean blouse and presentable khakis.

While Bruno got dressed, I spread the contents of his wallet–money, credit cards, an ancient snapshot of Mina–across the kitchen counter to dry. Next I telephoned the ferry terminal: good news–not only had some admirable soul turned in my abandoned rucksack, the dispatcher was willing to hold it for me. Before Bruno emerged from the bedroom, I managed to feed my cat, Leni, an affectionate calico with a strong sense of protocol, and prepare hot tea for the artist and myself. The instant he appeared in the kitchen, I handed him a steaming mug of oolong, seeking thereby to elevate his spirits and raise his core temperature.

"I had a college professor once, Nikolai Vertankowski, your most devoted fan," I told him as, tea mugs in hand, we moved from my cramped kitchen to my correspondingly miniscule parlor. "We spent most of Aesthetics 101 watching Bruno and Mina tapes, especially the Boston Common concerts."

He settled into my wing chair, fluted his lips, and at long last drew a measure of liquid warmth into his body. He frowned. "Mina and I never authorized any recordings," he muttered, acknowledging his identity for the first time. "Your professor trafficked in contraband."

"He knew that," I replied. "The man was obsessed. Probably still is."

Leni jumped into Bruno's lap, tucked her forelegs beneath her chest, and purred. "Obsessed," he echoed, taking a second swallow of tea. He brushed Leni's spine, his palm smoothing her fur like a spatula spreading frosting on a cake. "Obsession is something I can understand–obsession with thanatos, obsession with the élan vital. Speaking of life, I owe you mine. In return, I shall grant you any favor within my capabilities."

"Talk to me."

"A great sex artist is celebrated for his conversation," he said, nodding.

"Talk to me, Bruno Pearl. Tell me the truth about yourself."

"There was a bullet," he said.

꿍 ▦ 꿍

There was a bullet. But before the bullet, there was a triumphant performance in Philadelphia. On only two previous occasions had Mina and Bruno succeeded in accomplishing both Fleur de Lis and Holy Fools in a single afternoon. The Fairmount Park concert had elicited raucous cheers, rapturous sighs, and thunderous applause.

To celebrate their success, the artists treated themselves to a lobster dinner in their hotel room, followed by a stroll along the Delaware. At some undefined moment they crossed an indeterminate boundary, moving beyond the rehabilitated sector of Front Street, with its well-lighted walkways and quaint restaurants, and entering the warehouse district, domain of illegal transactions in flesh and pharmaceuticals. Under normal conditions the artists might have noted their seedy surroundings, spun around in a flurry of self-preservation, and headed south, but they were too intoxicated by their recent success, too high on Aphrodite. Fleur de Lis and Holy Fools, both in the same concert.

The bullet came from above, flying through a window on the second floor of a gutted factory and subsequently following its evil and inexorable trajectory downward. Bruno would later remember that the shot was actually the first in a series. A heroin deal gone wrong, he later surmised, or possibly a violent altercation between a prostitute and her pimp.

Spiraling toward Mina, the bullet drilled through the left side of her head, drove bits of skull into her cerebral cortex, entered her midbrain, and lodged in her cerebellum.

"Oh my God," I said.

"Those were my exact words," Bruno said. "'Oh my God,' I screamed."

"Did she die?"

Bruno pleasured my cat with his long delicate fingers. "The odds were against her," he replied cryptically.

Mina, delirious, collapsed in Bruno's arms, blood geysering from the wound. He laid her on the asphalt. It was surprisingly warm. Somehow he remained sane enough to administer first-aid, tearing off his shirt and bandaging her leaking head. He carried her one block west and hailed a cab. The driver, a Mexican, ten years behind the wheel, had seen worse, much worse, and without a breath of hesitation he drove them to Thomas Jefferson Memorial Hospital. Twenty minutes after her arrival in the emergency room, Mina lay beneath two halogen lamps, hovering on the cusp of oblivion as a surgical team struggled to reassemble her shattered brain.

A soothing and attractive Pakistani nurse directed Bruno down the hall to an ecumenical chapel—a dark place, soft, small, stinking of lilies and candle wax. He was the only patron. Religious music of unknown origin and protean denomination wafted through the air. The artist believed in neither Jehovah, Jesus, Allah, nor Krishna. He beseeched them all. He solicited divine intervention more devoutly than when, at age ten, he still knew, absolutely knew, that God always came through for you in the end, that it was just a matter of waiting.

"After I finished praying, I held my hand over a candle flame." Bruno showed me his right palm. The pale, fibrous scar had pulled the skin into a shape resembling a Star of David. "To this day, I'm not sure why I did it. A kind of oblation, I suppose. I felt nothing at first. A tickle. I actually smelled my burning flesh before I apprehended the pain."

Near dawn a bulky man in a white smock waddled into the chapel and introduced himself as Gregor Croom, chief among the surgeons who'd operated on Mina. Dr. Croom was perhaps the most physically unappealing person Bruno had ever met. A great mass of superfluous tissue clung to his upper spine, forcing him into a stoop. Mounds of overlapping flab drooped from the sides of his face, so that his tiny black eyes suggested raisins embedded in a pudding.

The surgeon spoke clinically, phlegmatically. They'd stopped the bleeding, he said, internal and external, and her vital signs were stable–but she'd lost massive quantities of irreplaceable neural matter. It was doubtful that she would ever again move her limbs of her own volition. In all likelihood the bullet had excised her ability to speak.

"I wept," Bruno said, finishing his tea. Leni's errant tail slapped his knee. "I wept like a baby."

"Dear Lord," I said. "My poor Mr. Pearl."

Dr. Croom's demeanor underwent an abrupt transformation. His manner grew gentle, his voice mellifluous. Locking a gnarled hand around Bruno's wrist, he confessed that he was as steadfast an apostle as the sex artists would ever know, proud owner of ninety-eight Bruno and Mina tapes of dubious provenance. His failure to foresee and attend that afternoon's concert in Fairmount Park would haunt him for years to come.

"Please know I shall do all within my power to return Mina to the eros circuit," Dr. Croom told the despairing Bruno. "My expertise lies wholly at your disposal, free of charge."

"Are you saying ... there's hope?"

"More than hope, Mr. Pearl. A cure."

As the anemic light of dawn washed over Philadelphia, Dr. Croom told Bruno how he had recently perfected a new, audacious, auspicious–and untested–method for rehabilitating victims of neural trauma. He freely revealed that his colleagues had no faith in the technique, and he admitted that it lay outside the bounds of orthodox medical practice. The pioneering experiment would occur in Croom's private laboratory, which he maintained in the basement of his Chestnut Hill mansion.

"The doctor proposed to employ a unique genetic-engineering technology," Bruno told me, massaging Leni with extravagant strokes that began at her nose and continued to the end of her tail. "His desire was to create an embryo bearing Mina's precise genetic heritage. He would then accelerate the fetus's development through hormonal manipulation, so that it would become an infant within seven days, an adolescent within five weeks, and a woman of thirty-six years–Mina's age–in a matter of months. The result, he promised me, would be an exact biological duplicate of my wife."

"But it would *not* be a duplicate," I protested. "It would have none of her experiences, none of memories."

"You may be sure that I presented this objection to Dr. Croom. His answer astonished me."

The doctor told Bruno about a heuristic computer, the JCN-5000-X. Among the machine's several spectacular functions was an ability to scan a person's cerebrum, encode the totality of its electrochemical contents, and insert these byzantine files into the *tabula rasa* that is the nervous system of a genetically-engineered, hormonally-accelerated human replica. In Croom's view, a complete restoration of Mina was entirely feasible, for the bullet had damaged her brain's motor and autonomic areas only–the very motor and autonomic areas that the hypothetical duplicate would boast in full. With the exceptions of certain trivial skills and some useless bits of nostalgia, the facsimile Mina would enjoy a selfhood identical to that possessed by the original before the bullet arrived.

"Look at me, Mr. Pearl," Dr. Croom said. "Contemplate my ugliness. What woman would have this walrus for her lover? And yet, thanks to you and your wife, I have known many a sybaritic satisfaction."

Bruno grew suddenly aware of the pain throbbing in his palm. "This person you're proposing to create ... would it truly be Mina–Mina restored, Mina reborn–or would it be ... somebody else?"

"I'm not a philosopher," Dr. Croom replied. "Neither am I a theologian nor a sage. I'm a cyberneurologist with a mission. Sanction this procedure, I beg you. For the sake of art–for the sake of all the world's freaks and Quasimodos–allow me to resurrect your wife."

Bruno requested a second mug of tea. I retired to the kitchen, brewed the oolong, and, upon handing him his replenished mug, voiced my opinion that the duplicate Mina Pearl and the original Mina Pearl would be exactly the same person.

He scowled.

"You disagree?" I said.

JAMES MORROW

"Imagine, sweet Susan, that you have faithfully recorded your every memory, belief, dream, hope, and habit in some massive journal. Call it *The Book of Susan*. Each time you finish making the day's entry, you store the volume on a high shelf in your private library. After your death, the executor of your will–a cousin, let's say–decides to browse among your bookshelves. She spies *The Book of Susan*, stretches for it, dislodges it. Suddenly the volume falls heavily on her head, rendering her unconscious. Five hours later, the executor awakens–as a total amnesiac. She notices the open book in front of her and immediately starts to read it. Her empty mind is like a sponge, absorbing every one of your recorded experiences. Now, dear Susan. Here's the question. At the precise moment when your cousin finishes reading the book and rises from the library floor, have you been reborn?"

"Reborn?"

"Take all the time you want," he said.

"Of *course* I haven't been reborn," I said.

"Quod erat demonstrandum."

"And so you refused to let Dr. Croom carry out his experiment?"

"No," he said.

"No?"

Bruno scratched Leni behind the ears. "I told him he could proceed–proceed with my blessing ... provided he acceded to one extreme condition. He must also make a duplicate of me, someone to look after the original Mina, nourishing her, cleaning her, caressing her, while my real self again joined the circuit."

"And Croom agreed?"

Bruno nodded. "The man was a romantic."

Like most other Bruno and Mina enthusiasts, I had often wondered about the one-year hiatus in their career. Had they become ill? Grown weary of the circuit? Now the riddle was solved. Throughout his absence Bruno had occupied a motel on the outskirts of Philadelphia–the first time he had ever settled in one place for more than a week–caring for his frightened, aphasic, and largely paralyzed wife.

He fed her three meals a day, changed her diapers faithfully, and spent many hours reading poetry and fiction aloud in her presence.

Despite the lost neurons, Mina retained a modicum of control over her dominant hand, and she managed to compose, at least twice a week, a letter filled with ardor and appreciation. The effort depleted her, and her script bordered on the illegible, but it was obvious from these exchanges that the primal Mina was no zombie. She knew what had happened to her. She understood that her doppelgänger was growing in a Chestnut Hill basement. She realized that a duplicate Bruno would soon replace the loving husband who attended her, so that he might go forth and again practice his art.

"Did Mina approve?" I asked.

"She said she did," Bruno replied. "I was skeptical, naturally, but her letters evinced no feelings of betrayal. Whenever I suggested that she was telling me what I wanted to hear, she became angry and hurt."

Nine months after the bullet ruined Mina's brain, Dr. Croom summoned Bruno to his ramshackle laboratory and presented him not only with a facsimile of the artist's wife but also with his own artificial twin.

"I can't tell you which phenomenon amazed me more"–Bruno finished his second mug of tea–"seeing and speaking with Mina's replica, or interviewing my second self."

"Credible copies?" I asked.

"Perfect copies. And yet I kept wondering: if this was Mina, then who was that person back in my hotel room? I wholly admired the duplicate. You might even say I cherished her. Did I love her? Perhaps. I don't know. My mind was not on love that day."

And so Bruno hit the road once more, coupling with the forged Mina in forty-two parks–famous and obscure, metropolitan and suburban, Old World and New–over the course of a full year. It was one of their most successful tours ever, drawing unqualified accolades from the critics even as audiences presented the artists with vast quantities of applause, adulation, and cash.

"But the new Mina–the Mina duplicate–what did she make of all this?" I asked.

"She didn't like to talk about it. Whenever I broached the subject, she offered the same reply, 'My life is my art,' she said. 'My life is my art.'"

While Bruno and the new Mina pursued the eros circuit, their shadow halves–the doppelgänger Bruno and the damaged Mina–journeyed to the south of France, moving into a farmhouse outside of Nîmes. No member of this odd quartet took much joy in the arrangement, but neither did anyone despair. Never before in human history, Bruno speculated, had irreversible brain injury been so cleverly accommodated.

"But cleverness, of course, mere cleverness–it's an ambiguous virtue, no?" Bruno said to me. "After pursuing Dr. Croom's ingenious scheme a mere fourteen months, I felt an overwhelming urge to abandon it."

"Because it was clever?"

"Because it was clever and not beautiful. Everything I knew, everything I held dear, had become false, myself most especially. *The Book of Bruno* had lost its poetry, and instead there was only correct punctuation, and proper spelling, and subjects that agreed with their verbs."

Bruno Pearl, the falsest thing of all, the man with the glass eyes, wooden teeth, crepe hair, and putty nose. He could enact his passion for Mina, but he could not experience it. He could enter her body, but not inhabit it. The flawless creature in his arms, this hothouse orchid, this unblemished replica who wore his wife's former face and spoke in her previous voice–nowhere in her flesh did he sense the ten million subtle impressions that had accrued, year by year, decade by decade, to their collective ecstasy.

"The skin is wise," he told me. "Our tissues retain echoes of every kiss and caress, each embrace and climax. Blood is not deceived. Do you understand?"

"No," I said. "Yes," I added. "I'm not sure. Yes. Quite so. I understand, Mr. Pearl."

I did.

Shortly after a particularly stunning concert in Luxembourg Gardens, Bruno and the duplicate Mina drove down to Nîmes, so that the four of them might openly discuss their predicament.

The artists gathered in the farmhouse kitchen, the primal Mina resting in her wheelchair.

"Tell me who you are," the primal Bruno asked the counterfeit.

"Who am I?" the forged Bruno said.

"Yes."

"I ponder that question every day."

"Are you I?" the primal Bruno asked.

"Yes," the forged Bruno replied. "In theory, yes–I am you."

"I was not created to be myself," the facsimile Mina noted.

"True," the primal Bruno said.

"I was created to be someone else," the facsimile Mina said.

"Yes," the primal Bruno said.

"If I am in fact you," the forged Bruno asked, "why do I endure a meaningless and uneventful life while the world lays garlands at your feet?"

"I need to be myself," the facsimile Mina said.

"I hate you, Bruno," the forged Bruno said.

The primal Mina took up a red crayon and scrawled a tortured note. SET THEM FREE, she instructed her husband.

ह्ने ▦ ह्ने

"The right and proper course was obvious," Bruno told me. "My twin and I would trade places."

"Of course," I said, nodding.

"I told my doppelgänger and the duplicate Mina that if they wished to continue the tour, I would respect and support their decision. But I would never do Sphinx Recumbent or any other act in public again."

Bruno was not surprised when, an hour before their scheduled departure from Nîmes, the replicas came to him and said that they intended to pursue their careers. What *else* were they supposed to do? Performance intercourse was in their bones.

For nearly five years, the duplicates thrived on the circuit, giving pleasure to spectators and winning plaudits from critics. But then the unexpected occurred, mysterious to everyone except Mina and Bruno and their doubles–and perhaps Dr. Croom comprehended the disaster as well. The ersatz copulators lost their art. Their talent, their touch, their *raison d'être*–all of it disintegrated, and soon they suffered a precipitous and inevitable decline. Months before the automobile accident, audiences and aestheticians alike had consigned these former gods to history.

"Naturally one is tempted to theorize that the Citroën crash was not an accident," Bruno said.

"The despair of the fallen idol," I said.

"Or, if an accident, then an accident visited upon two individuals who no longer wished to live."

"I guess we'll never know," I said.

"But if they deliberately ran their car into that concrete wall, I suspect that the reason was not their waning reputation. You see, lovely Susan, they didn't know who they were."

ꝺ 🎛 ꝼ

A fat, sallow, October moon shone into my apartment. It was nearly ten o'clock. Bruno gently dislodged Leni from his lap, then rose from my wing chair and requested that I lead him home. Naturally I agreed. He shuffled into the kitchen, reassembled his wallet, and slid it into his back pocket.

Gathering up Bruno's clothes, still damp, I dumped them into a plastic garbage bag. I told him he was welcome to keep Craig's dungarees, everything else too. I gave him Anson's boiled wool coat as well, then escorted him to the door.

"How do you feel?" I asked.

"Warm," he said, slinging the plastic bag over his shoulder. Leni pushed against Bruno's left leg, wrapped herself around his calf. "Restored."

Retrieving my motorcycle jacket from the peg, I realized that I still felt protective toward my charge: more protective, even, then when I'd first pulled him from the Hudson. As we ventured through the city, I insisted on stopping before each red traffic light, even if no car was in sight. Noticing an unattended German shepherd on the sidewalk ahead, I led us judiciously across the street. Finally, after a half-hour of timid northward progress, we reached 105 Willow Avenue.

Removing his keys from Craig's dungarees, Bruno proceeded to enact a common ritual of modern urban life–a phenomenon fully documented in the Kaleidoscope video called *Safe City Living*. Guided by my fingertips, he ascended the stoop, opened the lock on the iron gate, unlatched the main door, climbed one flight of stairs, and, finally, let himself into his apartment.

"Darling, I want you to meet someone," Bruno said, crossing the living room.

Mina Pearl sat in a pool of moonlight. She wore nothing save a wristwatch and a jade pendant. Her bare, pale skin gleamed like polished marble. A fanback wicker chair held her twisted body as a bamboo cage might enclose a Chinese cricket.

"This is Susan Fiore," Bruno continued. "As unlikely as it sounds, I fell off the ferry tonight, and she rescued me. I lost my glasses."

Mina worked her face into the semblance of a smile. She issued a noise that seemed to amalgamate the screech of an owl with the bleating of a ewe.

"I'm pleased to meet you, Mrs. Pearl," I said.

"Tomorrow I'm going to sign up for swimming lessons," Bruno averred.

As I came toward Mina, she raised her tremulous right hand. I clasped it firmly. Her flesh was warmer than I'd expected, suppler, more robust.

She used this same hand to gesture emphatically toward Bruno–a private signal, I concluded. He opened a desk drawer, removing a sheet of cardboard and a felt-tip marker. He brought the implements to his wife.

THANK YOU, Mina wrote. She held the message before me.

"You're welcome," I replied.

Mina flipped the cardboard over. PAN AND SYRINX, she wrote.

For the second time that evening, Bruno shed all his clothes. Cautiously, reverently, he lifted his naked wife from the wicker chair. She jerked and twitched like a marionette operated by a tipsy puppeteer. As her limbs writhed around one another, I thought of Laocoön succumbing to the serpents. A series of thick, burbling, salivary sounds spilled from her lips.

Against all odds, Mina and Bruno connected. It took them well over an hour, but eventually they brought Pan and Syrinx to a credible conclusion. Next came a two-hour recital of Flowering Judas, followed by an equally protracted version of Sphinx Recumbent.

The lovers, sated, sank into the couch. My applause lasted three minutes. I said my good-byes, and before I was out the door I understood that no matter how long I lived or how far I traveled, I would never again see anything so beautiful as Bruno and Mina Pearl coupling in their grimy little Willow Avenue apartment, the pigeons gathering atop the window grating, the traffic stirring in the street below, the sun rising over Hoboken.

martyrs of the upshot knothole

I sit in the comfort of my easy chair, the cat on my lap, the world at my command. With my right index finger I press the button, and seconds later the hydrogen bomb explodes.

The videocassette in question is *Trinity and Beyond*, a documentary by Peter Kuran comprising two hours of restored footage shot in full color by the U.S. Air Force's 1352nd Motion Picture Squadron, "The Atomic Cinematographers." I am watching the detonation of February 28, 1954: Castle Bravo, fifteen megatons, in its day the largest atmospheric thermonuclear test ever conducted on planet Earth.

Red as the sun, the implacable dome of gas and debris expands outward from ground zero, suggesting at first an apocalyptic plum pudding, then an immense Santiago pilgrim's hat. The blast front flattens concrete buildings, tears palm trees out by the roots, and draws a tidal wave from the Pacific. Now the filmmakers give us a half-dozen shots of the inevitable mushroom cloud. I gaze into the roiling crimson mass, reading the entrails of human ingenuity.

→ ✸ ←

"You're free of cancer" and "You're the lover I've been looking for my whole life" are surely two of the most uplifting sentences a person will ever hear, and it so happened that both declarations came my way during the same week. An optimist at heart, I took each affirmation at face value, so naturally I was distressed when the speakers in question began backpedaling.

No sooner had Dr. Joshua Pryce told me that the latest lab report indicated no malignant cells in my body, not one, than he hastened to add, "Of course, this doesn't mean you're rid of it forever."

"You think it will come back?" I asked.

"Hard to say."

"Could you hazard a guess?"

Dr. Pryce drew a silk handkerchief from his bleached lab coat and removed his bifocals. "Let me emphasize the positive." In a fit of absentmindedness, the oncologist repocketed his glasses. "For the moment you're definitely cured. But cancer has a will of its own."

In the case of the man who called me his ideal lover–Stuart Randolph, the semi-retired NYU film historian with whom I've shared a bohemian loft overlooking Washington Square for the past eighteen years–I logically expected that his subsequent remarks would concern the institution of marriage. But instead Stuart followed his declaration by arguing that there were two kinds of commitment in the world: the contrived commitment entailed in the matrimonial contract, and the genuine commitment that flowed from the sort of "perfect rapport and flawless communication" that characterized our relationship.

"If we enjoyed perfect rapport and flawless communication, we wouldn't be having this discussion," I said. "I want to get married, Stu."

"Really?" He frowned as if confronting a particularly egregious instance of postmodern film criticism. Stuart's an auteurist, not a deconstructionist.

"Really."

"You truly want to become my fourth wife?"

"As much as I want you to become my fifth husband."

"Why, dear?" he said. "Do you think we're living in sin? Senior citizens can't live in sin."

"*Imitation of Life* is a lousy movie, but I like it anyway," I said. "Marriage is a bourgeois convention, but I like it anyway."

"Should the cancer ever return, dearest Angela, you'll be glad you've got a committed lover by your side, as opposed to some sap who happens technically to be your husband."

Stuart was not normally capable of bringing romance and reason into such perfect alignment, but he'd just done so, and I had to admire his achievement.

"I cannot argue with your logic," I told him. And I couldn't. All during my treatments, Stuart had been an absolute prince, driving me to the hospital a hundred times, holding my head as I threw up, praising the doctors when they did their jobs properly, yelling at them when they got haughty. "Checkmate."

"Love and marriage," he said. "They go together like a horse and aluminum siding."

Have no fear, reader. This is not a story about what I endured at the hands of Western medicine once its avatars learned I'd developed leukemia. It's not about radiation treatments, chemotherapy, violent nausea, suicidal depression, paralyzing fear, or nurses poking dozens of holes in my body. My subject, rather, is the last performance ever given by an old colleague of mine, the biggest box-office star of all time, John Wayne—a performance that was never committed to celluloid but that leaves his Oscar-winning Rooster Cogburn gagging in the dust.

→ ※ ←

It would be inaccurate to say that Duke and I hated each other. Yes, I detested the man—detested everything he stood for—but my loathing was incompletely requited, for at some perverse level Duke clearly relished my companionship. Our irreconcilable philosophies first emerged when we appeared together in the 1953 survival melodrama, *Island in the Sky*, and ever since then our political clashes, too uncivilized to be called conversations or even debates, provided Duke with a caliber of stimulation he could obtain from no other liberal of his acquaintance. Throughout his career he routinely convinced the front office to offer me a marginal role in whatever John Wayne vehicle was on the drawing board, thereby guaranteeing that the two of us would briefly share the same soundstage or location set, and he could spend his lunch hours and coffee breaks reveling in the pleasurable rush he got from our battles over what had gone wrong with America.

As I write these words, it occurs to me that any self-respecting actress would have spurned this peculiar arrangement—a kind of love affair animated by neither affection nor physical desire but rather by the male partner's passion for polemic. No public adulation or peer recognition could possibly accrue to the parts Duke picked for me. There is no Oscar for Best Performance by an Actress Portraying a Cipher. But while I am normally self-respecting, I have rarely achieved solvency, and thus over a span of nearly twenty years I periodically found myself abandoning my faltering Broadway career, flying to Hollywood, and accepting good money for reciting bad dialogue.

In 1954 I played a fading opera diva trapped aboard a crippled airliner in *The High and the Mighty*, which Bill Wellman directed with great flair. Next came my portrayal of Hunlun, mother of Genghis Khan, née Temujin, in *The Conqueror*, probably the least watchable of the films produced by that eccentric American aviator and storm trooper, Howard Hughes. Subsequent to *The Conqueror* I essayed a middle-aged Comanche squaw in *The Searchers*, the picture on which Duke started referring to me, unaffectionately, as "Egghead." Then came my blind wife of a noble Texan in *The Alamo*, my over-the-hill snake charmer in *Circus World*, and my pacifist Navy nurse in *The Green Berets*. Finally, in *Chisum* of 1970, I was once again cast as Duke's mother, although my entire performance ended up in the trim bin.

It was Stuart who first connected the dots linking John Wayne, myself, and nearly a hundred other cancer victims in a fantastic matrix of Sophoclean terror and Kierkegaardian trembling. Six weeks after Dr. Pryce had labeled me cancer-free, Stuart was scanning the *New York Times* for March 15, 1975, when he happened upon two ostensibly unrelated facts: the Atomic Energy Commission was about to open its old nuclear-weapons proving ground in Nevada to the general public, and former screen goddess Susan Hayward had died the previous day from brain cancer. She was only fifty-six. Something started Stuart's mind working on all cylinders, and within twenty-four hours he'd made a Sherlock Holmesian deduction.

"*The Conqueror*," he said. We were having morning tea in our breakfast nook, which is also our lunch nook and our dinner nook. "*The Conqueror*—that's *it*! You shot the thing in Yucca Flat, Nevada, right?"

"An experience I'd rather forget," I said.

"But you shot it in Yucca Flat, right?"

"No, we shot it in southwest Utah, the Escalante Desert and environs—Bryce Canyon, Snow Canyon, Zion National Park ..."

"Southwest Utah, close enough," said Stuart, shifting into lecture mode. "*The Conqueror*, 1956, Cinemascope, Technicolor, the second of Dick Powell's five lackluster attempts to become a major Hollywood director. In the early sixties, Powell dies of cancer. A decade or so later, you're diagnosed with leukemia. Somewhere in between, John Wayne has a cancerous lung removed, telling the press, 'I licked the Big C.' And now the female lead of *The Conqueror* is dead of a brain tumor."

The epic in question had Susan playing a fictitious Tartar princess named Bortai (loosely based on Genghis Khan's wife of the same name), daughter of the fictitious Tartar chief Kumlek (though the screenwriter was perhaps alluding to the real-life Naiman chief Kushlek), who slays Temujin's nonfictitious father, Yesukai, offscreen about fifteen years before the movie begins. "The curse of *The Conqueror*," I muttered.

"Hell, there's no curse going on here, Angela." Stuart used a grapefruit spoon to retrieve his ginseng tea bag from the steaming water. "This is entirely rational. This is about gamma radiation."

According to the *Times*, he explained, the military had conducted eleven nuclear tests on the Nevada Proving Ground in the spring of 1953, an operation that bore the wonderfully surrealistic name Upshot Knothole. The gamma rays were gone now, and civilians would soon be permitted to visit the site, but during the Upshot Knothole era anyone straying into the vicinity would have received four hundred times the acceptable dose of radiation. The last detonation, "Climax," had occurred on the fourth of June.

"And one year later, almost to the day, the *Conqueror* company arrives in the Escalante Desert and starts to work," I said, at once impressed by Stuart's detective work and frightened by its implications.

My lover exited the breakfast nook, removed the cat from our coffee-table atlas, and opened to a spread that displayed Utah and Nevada simultaneously. "You were maybe only a hundred and thirty miles from the epicenter. Eleven A-bombs, Angela. If the winds were blowing the wrong way ..."

"Obviously they were," I said. "And the Atomic Energy Commission now expects *tourists* to show up?"

"Never underestimate the power of morbid curiosity."

A quick trip through the back issues of *Film Fan Almanac* was all Stuart needed to reinforce his theory with two additional Upshot Knothole casualties. Unable to cope with his cancer any longer, Pedro Armendariz, who played Temujin's "blood brother" Jamuga, had shot himself in the heart on June 18, 1963. Exactly eight years later–on June 18, 1971–cancer deprived the world of Thomas Gomez, who portrayed Wang Khan, the Mongol ruler whom Temujin seeks to usurp (thereby bestowing a throne on himself and a plot on the movie). Like Susan, Tom was only fifty-six.

"We are the new *hibakusha*," I mused bitterly. The *hibakusha*, the "explosion-affected persons," as the Hiroshima survivors called themselves. "Me, Duke, Dick, Susan, Pedro, and Tom. The American *hibakusha.* The Howard Hughes *hibakusha.* I'd never tell Duke, of course. Irony makes him mad."

Our obligation was manifest. We must contact the entire *Conqueror* company–stars, supporting players, camera operators, sound men, lighting crew, costume fitters, art director, special effects technician, hair stylist, makeup artist, assistant director–and advise them to seek out their doctors posthaste. For five months Stuart and I functioned as angels of death, fetches of the Nuclear Age, banshees bearing ill tidings of lymphoma and leukemia, and by the autumn of 1976 our phone calls and telegrams had generated two catalogues, one listing eighty *Conqueror* alumni who were already dead (most of them from cancer), the other identifying one hundred forty survivors. Of this latter group, one hundred sixteen received our warning with graciousness and gratitude, three told us we had no business disrupting their lives this way and we should go to hell, and twenty-one already knew they had the disease, though they were astonished that we'd gleaned the fact from mere circumstantial evidence.

John Wayne himself was the last person I wanted to talk to, but Stuart argued that we had no other choice. We'd been unable to locate Linwood Dunn, who did the on-location special effects, and Duke might very well have a clue.

I hadn't spoken with the old buzzard in nine years, but our conversation was barely a minute underway before we were trading verbal barrages. True to form, this was not a fond sparring-match between mutually admiring colleagues but a full-blown war of the *Weltanschauungen,* the West Coast patriot versus the East Coast pinko, the brave-heart conservative versus the bleeding-heart liberal. According to Duke's inside sources, President Jimmy Carter was about to issue a plenary pardon to the Vietnam War draft evaders. Naturally I thought this was a marvelous idea, and I told Duke as much. John Wayne–the same John Wayne who'd declined to don a military uniform during World War II, fearing that a prolonged stint in the armed forces would decelerate his burgeoning career–responded by asserting that once again Mr. Peanut Head was skirting the bounds of treason.

Changing the subject, I told Duke about my leukemia ordeal, and how this had ultimately led Stuart to connect the Nevada A-bomb tests with the *Conqueror* company's astonishingly high cancer rate. Predictably enough, Duke did not warm to the theory, with its implicit indictment of nuclear weapons, the Cold War, and other institutions dear to his heart, and when I used the phrase "Howard Hughes *hibakusha*," he threatened to hang up.

"We need to find Linwood Dunn," I said. "We think he's at risk."

In a matter of seconds Duke located his Rolodex and looked up Linwood's unlisted phone number. I wrote the digits on the back of a stray *New Republic.*

"Well, Egghead, I suppose it can't hurt for Lin to see the medics, but this doesn't mean I buy your nutty idea," said Duke. "Howard Hughes is a true American."

He should have said Howard Hughes *was* a true American, because even as we spoke the seventy-year-old codeine addict was dying of kidney failure in Houston.

"You may have just saved Lin's life," I said.

"Possibly," said Duke. "Interesting you should get in touch, Egghead. I was about to give you a call. I'm thinking of shooting a picture in your neck of the woods next year, and there's a real sweet part in it for you."

I drew the receiver away from my ear, cupped the mouthpiece, and caught Stuart's attention with my glance. "He wants me in his next movie," I said in a coherent whisper.

"Go for it," said Stuart. "We need the money."

I lifted my hand from the mouthpiece and told Duke, "I'll take any role except your mother."

"Good," he said. "You'll be playing my grandmother." He chuckled. "That's a joke, Egghead. I have you down for my mentor, a retired school teacher. We finish principal photography on *The Shootist* in two weeks, and then I'm off to New York, scouting locations. We'll have dinner at the Waldorf, okay?"

"Sure, Duke."

Later that day, Stuart and I telephoned Linwood Dunn.

"You folks may have saved my life," he said.

→ ✹ ←

I'm probably being unfair to Duke. Yes, his primitive politics infuriated me, but unlike most of his hidebound friends he was not a thoughtless man. He enjoyed a certain salutary distance from himself. Of his magnum opus, *The Alamo*, he once told a reporter, "There's more to that movie than my damn conservative attitude," and I have to agree. Beneath its superficial jingoist coating, and beneath the layer of genuine jingoism under that, *The Alamo* exudes an offbeat and rather touching generosity of spirit. The freedom-loving frontiersmen holding down the fort do not demonize Santa Ana's army, and at one point they praise their enemy's courage. I think also of Duke's willingness to appear in a 1974 public forum organized by the editors of the *Harvard Lampoon*. When a student asked him where he got the "phony toupee," he replied, "It's not phony. It's real hair. Of course, it's not mine, but it's real." Another student wanted to know whether Mr. Wayne's horse had recovered from his hernia now that the superstar was dieting. "No, he died," Duke answered, "and we canned him, which is what you're eating at the Harvard Club."

This refreshing streak of self-deprecation surfaced again when we met in New York at the Waldorf-Astoria. As we dug into our steaks and baked potatoes, Duke told me his idea for an urban cop picture, which he wanted to call *Lock and Load.* He'd seen Clint Eastwood's first two Harry Callahan movies, *Dirty Harry* and *Magnum Force,* and he was beguiled by both their vigilante ethos and their hefty profits. "If a liberal like Eastwood can make a fascist film," said Duke with a sly smile, "imagine what a fascist like me could do with that kind of material."

I laughed and patted him on the arm. "You'll make Harry Callahan look like Adlai Stevenson."

It was obvious to both of us that there would probably never be a John Wayne picture called *Lock and Load.* We were eating not in the hotel restaurant but in his room, so that the general public wouldn't see what a wreck he'd become. Maybe Duke had licked the Big C in 1964, but thirteen years later it was back for a rematch. He breathed only with the help of a sinister looking portable inhaler, and he had a male nurse in permanent attendance, a swarthy Texan named Sweeney Foote, forever fidgeting in the background like a Doberman pinscher on guard.

"You look terrific, Egghead," he said. He was wearing his famous toupee, as well as a lush Turkish bathrobe and leather slippers. "I'm sure you gave the Big C a knockout punch."

"The doctors aren't that optimistic."

Duke worked his face into a sneer. "Doctors," he said.

I glanced around the suite, appointed with tasteful opulence. Sweeney Foote sat hunched on the mattress, playing solitaire. I'd never been in the Waldorf-Astoria before, and I wondered if Duke had selected it for its symbolic value. When the Hollywood Ten's highly publicized appearance before the House Un-American Activities Committee started going badly (not only were the Ten actual by-God former Communists, they didn't seem particularly ashamed of it), the heads of the major studios called an emergency meeting at the Waldorf. Before the day was over, the money men had agreed that unemployment and ostracism would befall any Hollywood actor, writer, or director who defied a Congressional committee or refused to come forward with his or her non-Communist credentials.

"Tell me about *Lock and Load*," I said.

"Hell of a script," said Duke. "Jimmy's best work since *The Alamo*. I'm Stonewall McBride, this maverick police captain who likes to do things his own way."

"Novel concept," I said dryly.

"Stonewall has stayed in touch with his fifth-grade teacher, kind of a mother-figure to him, regularly advising him on how to get along in a dog-eat-dog world."

"I've always enjoyed Maria Ouspenskaya."

Duke nodded, smiled, and gestured as if tipping an invisible Stetson, but then his expression became a wince. "I'll be honest, Egghead." He popped an analgesic pill and washed it down with beer. "I'm not here just to scout locations. Fact is, the Big C has me on the ropes. The medics say it's in my stomach now, as if I didn't know."

"I'm sorry, Duke."

"Back in L.A. I kept meeting folks who're into herbal medicines and psychic cures and such, and they advised me to go see this swami fella, Kieran Morella of the Greater Manhattan Heuristic Healing Center."

"Southern California at your fingertips, and you had to come to *New York* to find a hippie guru flake?"

"You can laugh if you want to, Egghead, but I hoofed it over to Kieran's office the instant I stepped off the plane, and what he said made sense to me. Sure, it's an unconventional treatment, but he's had lots of success. He uses a kind of hypnotism to send the patient back to the exact moment when some little part of him turned cancerous, and then the patient imagines his immune system rounding up those primal malignant cells the way a cowboy rounds up steers."

"Steers? Hey, this is the cure for you, Duke."

"Next the patient tries to tune in these things called quantum vibrations, and before long the space-time continuum has folded back on itself, and it's as if he'd never developed cancer in the first place."

"'Unconventional' is a good word here, Duke."

45

He swallowed another analgesic. "To help the patient get the proper pictures flowing through his mind—you know, images of his lymphocytes corralling the original cancer cells—Kieran shows him clips from *Red River*. Kinetotherapy, he calls it."

"Jesus, he must have been thrilled to meet you," I said. *Red River* is one of the few John Wayne westerns that Stuart and I can watch without snickering.

"He almost creamed himself. Now listen tight, Egghead. You might think I'm just talking about me, but I'm also talking about you. All during my flight east, I kept thinking about that American *hibakusha* business, and eventually I decided maybe your theory's not so crazy after all."

"Howard Hughes has nuked us, Duke. Your fellow Bircher has pumped us full of gamma rays."

"Let's leave Howard out of this, Robert Welch too. Here's the crux. The minute I told Kieran about this possible connection between *The Conqueror* and the Big C, and how the Cinemascope lenses may have captured the very moment when the radiation started seeping into me—how it's all up there on the silver screen—well, he got pretty damn excited."

"I can imagine."

"He kept saying, 'Mr. Wayne, we must get a print of this film. Get me a print, Mr. Wayne, and I'll cure you.'"

Duke snapped his fingers. Taking care not to disturb his matrix of playing cards, Sweeney Foote rolled off the bed. He went to the closet, reached into a valise, and drew out an object that looked like a Revell plastic model of the cryptic black monolith from *2001: A Space Odyssey*, a movie that Duke had refused to see on general principles.

"*The Conqueror* arrived this morning, special courier, along with the necessary hardware," said Duke. He took the little monolith from Sweeney, then passed it to me. "Brand-new technology, Jap thing called Betamax, a spool of half-inch videotape in a plastic cassette. Sony thinks it'll be the biggest thing since the Crock-Pot."

The Betamax cassette featured a plastic window offering a partial view of both the feed core and the take-up spindle. Somebody had written "The Conqueror" on a piece of masking tape and stuck it across the top edge. "Ingenious," I said.

"It's all very well to wring your hands over Hiroshima, but if you ask me the Japs have done pretty well for themselves since then, especially the Sony people. My first kinetotherapy treatment occurs in two days and–you know what, Angela?–I'd like you to come along. You could help me concentrate, and you might even get a healing effect yourself."

"I couldn't afford it."

"I'll pay for everything. You're not out of the woods yet."

"I'm not out of the woods," I admitted ruefully.

"Monday afternoon, two o'clock, the Heuristic Healing Center, 1190 West 41st Street near Tenth Avenue. There's a goddamn mandala on the door."

"Let me talk it over with Stuart."

"With the Big C, you're never out of the woods."

→ ✹ ←

I pour myself a glass of sherry, rewind *Trinity and Beyond*, and press *Play*. As before, the fiery mushroom cloud from the Castle Bravo explosion fills my television screen, shot after shot of billowing radioactive dust, and for a fleeting instant I experience an urge to bow down before it.

How beautiful art thou, O Mighty Fireball. How fair thy countenance and frame. Give me coffers of gold, O Great One, and I shall heap sacrifices upon thy altar. Give me silken raiment and shining cities, and I shall wash thy graven feet with rare libations.

→ ✹ ←

Stuart and I decided that as long as Duke was picking up the tab I should indeed give kinetotherapy a try, and so on Monday afternoon I took the N Train to Times Square. Ten minutes later I marched into the foyer of the Heuristic Healing Center, its walls hung with Hindu tapestries, its air laden with patchouli incense, and announced myself to the receptionist, a stately black woman wearing a beige Nehru jacket. The nameplate on her desk read "Jonquil." Duke was waiting for me, outfitted in blue denims, a checked cotton shirt, a red bandana, and tooled-leather cowboy boots. He looked like a supporting player in a bad science fiction movie about time travel. Sweeney Foote lurked near the coatrack, Duke's inhaler slung over his shoulder, a large crushproof envelope tucked under his arm like a private eye's holster.

Duke and I had barely said hello when Kieran Morella, a pale slender man dressed in a flowing white caftan and sporting a salt-

and-pepper-goatee, orange beads, and a silver-gray ponytail–a counterculture point guard–sashayed out of his office, all smiles and winks. He gave us each a hug, which did not go down well with Duke, then took the envelope from Sweeney and ushered us into Treatment Salon Number Three, a velvet-draped chamber suggesting an old-style Hollywood screening room. At the far end two brown, tufted, vinyl recliner chairs faced a television set connected to a squat device that I took to be a Betamax videocassette recorder.

As Sweeney slunk into the shadows, Kieran produced a coffee tin crammed with neatly rolled joints, presenting the stash to us as a hostess might offer her bridge club a box of chocolates. Getting stoned was optional, the therapist explained, but it would help us reach a "a peak of relaxed concentration."

"Hey, Doc, I've never smoked that Timothy Leary stuff in my life, and I'm not about to start now," said Duke. "Don't you have any drinking whiskey around here?"

"I could send Jonquil out for something," said Kieran.

"Jack Daniels, okay?"

"Tennessee's finest"–Kieran issued a nervous laugh–"endorsed by Davy Crockett himself."

Duke and Kieran spent the next twenty minutes talking about their favorite John Wayne movies. They were both keen on the so-called Cavalry Trilogy that Duke made under John Ford's direction: *Fort Apache, She Wore a Yellow Ribbon, Rio Grande*–three pictures that leave me cold. (I much prefer Duke and Ford in Irish mode: *The Quiet Man, The Long Voyage Home.*) At last Jonquil appeared with a quart of Jack Daniels and a shot glass. Kieran guided us into the recliner chairs and removed *The Conqueror* from Sweeney's envelope. He fed the cassette into the Betamax, flipped on the TV, and bustled about the room lighting incense and chanting under his breath.

"Your job is simple, Mr. Wayne." Kieran seized a remote control connected to the Betamax by a coaxial cable. "Each time you appear out there in the Escalante Desert, I want you to imagine a kind of psychic armor surrounding your body, filtering out the gamma rays. Ms. Rappaport, you have exactly the same task. During every shot you're in"–he handed me a box of wooden matches–"you must imagine a translucent shield standing between yourself and the radioactivity. If you folks can get the right quantum vibrations going, your screen images will acquire visible protective auras."

"We'll really see *auras?*" said Duke, impressed.

"There's a good chance of it," said Kieran.

Duke poured himself a slug of whiskey. I took a joint from the coffee tin, struck a match, and lit up. Kieran positioned himself behind our chairs, laying a soothing hand on each of our heads.

"This is going to be fun," I said, drawing in a puff of magic smoke.

"Concentrate," said Kieran.

I held my breath, slid the joint from my lips, and passed it to Kieran. He took a toke. The credits came on, a roll call of the dead, the doomed, and the fortunate few, this last category consisting mainly of people who didn't have to sweat under the Utah sun to get their names on the picture: the associate producer, the writer, the film editor, the sound editor.

As the movie unspooled in all its pan-and-scan glory–the film-chain operator had astutely decided that the original anamorphic images would not prosper on the average TV screen–it occurred to me that my running feud with Duke encapsulated the history of the Cold War. During the making of *The High and the Mighty*, we fought about the imminent electrocution of the "atomic spies," Julius and Ethel Rosenberg. While shooting *The Searchers*, we nearly came to blows concerning the Senate's recent decision to censure Joseph McCarthy. ("Old Joe will have the last laugh," Duke kept saying.) *The Alamo* found us at odds over the upcoming presidential election, Duke insisting that there would be jubilation in the Kremlin if Jack Kennedy, the likely Democratic contender, beat Richard Nixon, the shoo-in for the Republican nomination. Between takes on *Circus World*, we nearly drew blood over whether the Cuban Missile Crisis obliged the superpowers to start taking disarmament seriously or whether, conversely, it meant that America should ratchet up her arsenal to a higher level of overkill. On the sets of both *The Green Berets* and *Chisum*, the Vietnam War inevitably got us going at each other tooth and nail.

And what about *The Conqueror* itself? What issue fueled our hostility during that benighted project? Believe it or not, our bone of contention was atomic testing, even though we knew nothing of Upshot Knothole and the radioactive toxins seething all around us. Fear of Strontium-90–like Strontium-90 itself–was in the air that year. *Fallout* had become a household word. Each night after we were back at the Grand Marquis Hotel in St. George, our base of operations during the *Conqueror* shoot, most of the cast and crew would stand around in the lobby watching Walter Cronkite, and occasionally there'd be a news story about a politician who believed that unlimited on-continent testing of nuclear devices would eventually make lots of Americans sick, children especially. (Strontium-90 was ending up in the milk of dairy cows.) One such report included the latest figures on leukemia cases attributable to Hiroshima and Nagasaki.

"Poor old Genghis Khan," I said to Al D'Agostino, the art director. "He had to spend *weeks*, sometimes *months*, bringing down a city."

"Whereas Paul Tibbets and his B-52 managed it in the twinkling of an eye," said Al, who in those days was almost as far to the left as I.

"Poor old Genghis Khan," echoed the assistant director, Ed Killy. Ed was likewise a leftist, although he usually kept it under wraps, thereby maintaining his friendship with Duke.

"You people seem to forget that Hiroshima and Nagasaki kept our boys from having to invade Japan," said Duke. "Those bombs saved thousands of American lives."

"Well, Temujin," I said, sarcasm dripping from every syllable, "I guess that settles the matter."

The Conqueror had been on Kieran's TV barely ten minutes when I decided that it wasn't a costume drama after all. It was really yet another John Wayne western, with Tartars instead of Comanches and the Mongol city of Urga instead of Fort Apache. But even the feeblest of Duke's horse operas—*The Lawless Range*, say, or *Randy Rides Alone*—wasn't nearly this enervated. None of those early Republic or Monogram westerns had Duke saying, before the first scene was over, "There are moments for wisdom, Jamuga, and then I listen to you. And there are moments for action, and then I listen to my heart. I feel this Tartar woman is for me. My blood says, 'Take her!'"

"Concentrate," Kieran exhorted us, returning the joint to my eager fingers. "Repulse those gamma rays. Bend the fabric of space-time."

"I'm trying, Doc," said Duke, downing a second slug of Jack Daniels.

"Why would anybody want to make a movie celebrating a demented brute like Temujin?" I asked rhetorically. I'd read the *Encyclopedia Britannica*'s account of Genghis Khan the night before, baiting my hook. "Bukhara was one of medieval Asia's greatest cities, a center of science and culture. At Temujin's urging, his army burned it to the ground, all the while raping and torturing everybody in sight."

"Ms. Rappaport, I must ask you not to disrupt the healing process," said Kieran.

"When the citizens of Herat deposed the governor appointed

by one of Temujin's sons, the retaliatory massacre lasted a week," I continued. "Death toll, one million, six hundred thousand. Genghis Khan was a walking A-bomb."

"Let's not get too high and mighty, Egghead," said Duke. "Hunlun wasn't exactly Florence Nightingale, but as I recall you didn't run screaming from the part. You picked up your paycheck along with the rest of us."

Duke had me on both counts, historical and ethical. Shortly after Temujin became the titular Mongol ruler at age thirteen, Hunlun emerged as the power behind the throne, and she governed with an iron hand. When a group of local tribes turned rebellious, Hunlun led an expeditionary force against the obstreperous chiefs, and eventually she brought over half of them back into the fold.

"Please, people, let's focus," said Kieran. "This won't work unless we focus."

Screenwriter Oscar Millard had given my character three major scenes. In the first, Hunlun sternly reprimands her son for abducting the nubile Bortai from her fiancé, a Merkit chief named Targatai–not because it's wrong to treat women as booty, but because Bortai's father murdered Hunlun's husband. "Will you take pleasure with the offspring of your father's slayer?!" Hunlun asks Temujin. "She will bring woe to you, my son, and to your people!" In Hunlun's second major scene, she bemoans the Mongol casualties that attended both Temujin's initial seizure of Bortai and Targatai's attempt to reclaim her. "And what of your dead, those who died needlessly for this cursed child of Kumlek's?!" Hunlun's final sequence is her longest. While applying healing leaves and ointments to Temujin's arrow wound, Hunlun takes the opportunity to tell him that, thanks to his obsession with Bortai, he is losing track of his destiny. "Did I not hold our tribe together and raise you with but one thought–to regain your father's power and avenge his death?!"

I hadn't seen my work in *The Conqueror* since the world premiere, and I hated every frame of it. It took a full measure of willpower to ignore this embarrassing one-note performance and concentrate instead on conjuring an anti-radiation aura around my pan-and-scan form.

Despite all the encouragement from Kieran and the marijuana, I failed to build the necessary shield, and Duke didn't have any luck either. From the first shot of Temujin (our hero leading a cavalry charge) to the last (the Mongol emperor standing beside his bride

51

as they proudly survey their marching hordes), Duke's Betamax simulacrum never once acquired anything resembling psychic armor. He made no effort to hide his disappointment.

"Doc, I think we're pissing in the wind."

"Kinetotherapy takes time," said Kieran. "Can you both come back tomorrow at two o'clock?"

"For grass of such quality, I'd watch this piece of crap every day for a year," I said.

"Make sure you've got plenty of Jack Daniels on the premises," said Duke.

→ ✳ ←

The instant Kieran activated his television on Tuesday afternoon, the picture tube burned out, the image imploding like a reverse-motion shot of an A-bomb detonation. Of course, it's not difficult to purchase a new TV set in New York City, and Jonquil accomplished the task with great efficiency. Our second kinetotherapy session started only forty minutes late.

As Kieran got the cassette rolling, Sweeney assumed his place in the shadows, Duke poured himself a shot of Jack Daniels, and I inhaled a lungful of pot. Today's weed was even better than yesterday's. Kieran might be a lunatic and a charlatan, but he knew his hallucinogens.

"Want to know the really scary thing about the Upshot Knothole tests?" I said. I'd spent my evening reading *The Tenth Circle of Hell*, Judith Markson's concise narrative of the Nevada Proving Ground. "By this point in history such devices were considered *tactical*–not strategic, *tactical*."

"Take it easy, Egghead," said Duke.

"Time to watch the movie," said Kieran.

"The monster that killed seventy thousand Hiroshima civilians is suddenly a fucking *battlefield weapon!*" I passed the joint to Kieran. "Isn't that *sick?* They even fired a Knothole bomb out of an *artillery cannon!* They called it 'Grable'–from Betty Grable, no doubt–fifteen kilotons, same as the Hiroshima blast. A goddamn artillery cannon."

As the screen displayed the opening logo, Kieran drew some illegal vapor into his body, then gave me back the joint. AN RKO RADIO PICTURE FILMED IN CINEMASCOPE.

"Focus, my friends," said Kieran. "Tune in the quantum vibrations."

HOWARD HUGHES PRESENTS ... THE CONQUEROR ... STARRING JOHN WAYNE ...

"Then there was 'Encore,' dropped from a plane." I sucked on the joint, inhaled deeply, and, pursing my lips, let the smoke find its way to my brain. "They suspended another payload from a balloon, dropped another from a steel tower."

SUSAN HAYWARD ... CO-STARRING PEDRO ARMENDARIZ ... WITH ANGELA RAPPAPORT–THOMAS GOMEZ–JOHN HOYT–WILLIAM CONRAD ...

"Battlefield atomic bombs." I gave the joint to Kieran. He took a toke and handed it back. "What barbarous insanity."

WRITTEN BY OSCAR MILLARD ... ASSOCIATE PRODUCER RICHARD SOKOLOVE ... MUSIC BY VICTOR YOUNG ...

"Your opinion's been noted, Egghead," said Duke.

PRINT BY TECHNICOLOR ... DIRECTOR OF PHOTOGRAPHY JOSEPH LA SHELLE ... PRODUCED AND DIRECTED BY DICK POWELL.

And then the movie came on: Temujin abducting Bortai from the Merkit caravan (a kind of medieval wagon train) ... Hunlun criticizing her son's choice in sex objects ... Targatai attempting to steal Bortai back ... Hunlun denouncing the bloodshed that has accrued to Temujin's infatuation ... Temujin traveling to Urga and allying with Wang Khan ... our hero falling to the Mongol arrow and hiding in a cave ... Bortai returning to her depraved Tartar father ... Jamuga inadvertently leading Kumlek's henchmen to his blood brother ... Temujin struggling beneath the weight of an ox-yoke as his captors march him toward Kumlek's camp (an image that inspired one of Stuart's students, in a paper that received a B-minus, to call Wayne's character a Christ figure) ... our hero standing humbled before the Tartar chief ... Bortai becoming conscious of her love for Temujin and forthwith aiding his escape ... Temujin arriving half-dead in the Mongol camp ...

At no point in this cavalcade of nonsense did either Temujin or his mother acquire a perceptible shield against the omnipresent radiation. But then, as my third major scene hit the screen–Hunlun treating her son's wound–something utterly amazing occurred. A rainbow aura, glowing and pulsing like Joseph's Coat of Many Colors, materialized on Hunlun's head and torso as she uttered the line, "Would that I could cure the madness that possesses you!"

It's the pot, I told myself. I'm high on hemp, and I'm seeing things.

"Good God!" I gasped.

"You've done it, Ms. Rappaport!" shouted Kieran.

"I see it too!" cried Duke. "She's got a damn rainbow around her!"

"Wang Khan–he will betray you into disaster," insisted Hunlun, "or rob you of your spoils in victory."

53

But then, to my dismay, the crone's anti-radiation suit started to dissolve.

"Concentrate!" cried Kieran

My cloak continued to fade.

"Focus, Egghead!" demanded Duke.

I stared at the screen, concentrating, concentrating.

Hunlun insisted, "Were you not blinded by lust for this woman?"

"Lust?!" echoed Temujin. "You, too, are blind, my mother–blinded by your hatred for her."

"Shields at maximum, Ms. Rappaport!" shouted Kieran. "We're going to make you well!"

In a full-spectrum flash, red to orange to yellow to green to blue to indigo to violet, Hunlun's aura returned. "Daughter of Kumlek!" she sneered.

"Way to go, Ms. Rappaport!" exclaimed Kieran.

"Congratulations!" cried Duke.

"Even if you were right about Wang Khan, yet I would venture this unaided," said Temujin. Sealed head to toe in her luminous armor, Hunlun glowered at her son. "For I will have Bortai," he continued, "though I and all of us go down to destruction."

The scene ended with a dissolve to Jamuga riding through the gates of Urga, whereupon Kieran picked up the remote control and stopped the tape. It would be best, he explained, to quit while my triumph was at its zenith and the quantum vibrations were still folding back into the space-time continuum.

"Sounds reasonable to me," said Duke.

"Soon it will come to pass that the gamma rays never even penetrated your body." Kieran ejected the cassette. "Ms. Rappaport, I must applaud you. By reweaving the cosmic tapestry, you have conquered your past and reshaped your future."

"That aura wasn't real," I said, wondering whether I believed myself. "It was an illusion born of Jack Daniels and marijuana."

"That aura was more real than the bricks in this building or the teeth in my jaw," said Kieran.

Duke caught my eye, then waved his shot glass in Kieran's direction. "Told you this guy's a pro. Most swamis don't know their higher planes from a hole in the ground, but you're in good hands with Doc Morella."

"I hope you're not jealous, Duke," I said. "There was no aura. It was just the booze and the dope."

"I've had a full life, Egghead."

→ ✳ ←

For the third time in a week I contemplate the Castle Bravo explosion while drinking a glass of sherry.

The mushroom cloud, I realize, is in fact a Nuclear Age inkblot test, a radioactive Rorschach smear. In the swirling vapors I briefly glimpse my has-been diva from *The High and the Mighty* as she speculates that nobody will miss her if the airliner goes into the drink. Next I see my *Alamo* character, the insufferably selfless Blind Nell, giving her husband permission to enter into a suicide pact with the boys instead of wasting his life taking care of her. And now I perceive the school teacher in *Lock and Load*, telling Duke to be the best obsessive-compulsive loose-cannon police captain he can be.

Slowly the quotidian seeps into my consciousness: my TV set, my VCR, my sherry, the cat on my lap–each given form and substance by my dawning awareness that the film called *Lock and Load* does not exist.

→ ✳ ←

Was it just the booze and the dope? I simply couldn't decide, and Stuart had no theories either. Despite his unhappiness with postmodern scorched-earth relativism, despite his general enthusiasm for the rationalistic worldview, he has always fancied himself an intellectually vulnerable person, open to all sorts of possibilities.

"Including the possibility of a mind-body cure," he said.

"A mind-body cure is one thing, and Kieran Morella's deranged quantum physics is another," I replied. "The man's a goofball."

"So you're not going back?" asked Stuart.

"Of course I'm going back. Duke's paying for the weed. I have nothing to lose."

Kieran normally spent his Wednesdays downtown, teaching a course at the New School for Social Research, *Psychoimmunology 101: Curing with Quarks*, and Thursdays he always stayed home and meditated, so Duke and I had to wait a full seventy-two hours before entering Treatment Salon Number Three again. In a matter of minutes we were all primed for transcendence, Duke afloat on a cloud of Jack Daniels, Kieran and me frolicking through a sea of grass. Our therapist announced that, before we tried generating any more quantum vibrations, we should take a second look at Tuesday's breakthrough.

"Whatever you say, Doc," said Duke.

"It was all a mirage," I said.

"Seeing is believing," said Kieran.

I retorted with that favorite slogan of skeptics, "And believing is seeing."

Kieran fastforwarded the *Conqueror* cassette to Hunlun treating Temujin's wound. He pressed *Stop*, then *Play*.

Against my expectations, Hunlun's aura was still there, covering her like a gown made of sunflowers and rubies.

"Thundering Christ!" I said.

This time around, I had to admit that the aura was too damn intricate and splendid–too existentially *real*–to be a mere pothead chimera.

"It's a goddamn miracle!" shouted Duke.

"I would join Mr. Wayne in calling your gamma-ray shield a miracle, but I don't think that's the right word," said Kieran, grinning at me as he pressed the rewind button. "'Miracle' implies divine intervention, and you accomplished this feat through your own natural healing powers. How do you feel?"

"Exhilarated," I said. Indeed. "Frightened." Quite so. "Grateful. Awestruck."

"Me too," said Duke.

"And angry," I added.

"Angry?" said Duke.

"Mad as hell."

"I don't understand."

"Anger has no place in your cure, Ms. Rappaport," said Kieran. "Anger will kill you sooner than leukemia."

As with our first two sessions, Duke's third attempt at kinetotherapy got him nowhere. Temujin went through the motions of the plot–he seized Bortai, speared Targatai, met with Wang Khan, suffered the Tartar arrow, endured imprisonment by Kumlek, won Bortai's heart, fled Kumlek's camp, conspired with Wang Khan's soothsayer, captured the city of Urga, appropriated Wang Khan's forces, led the expanded Mongol army to victory against the Tartars, and slew Kumlek with a knife–but at no point did Duke's celluloid self acquire any luminous armor.

My character, on the other hand, was evidently leading a charmed life. No sooner did Hunlun admonish Temujin for courting his father's murderer than, by Kieran's account at least, I once again molded reality to my will, sheathing the crone's body against gamma rays. When next Hunlun entered the film, lamenting the pointless slaughter Temujin's lust has caused, she wore the same vibrant attire. Her final moments on screen–treating her son's wound while criticizing his life-style–likewise found her arrayed in an anti-radiation ensemble.

"Duke, I'm really sorry this hasn't gone better for you," I said.

The late Jamuga, now transformed into Temujin's spiritual guide, spoke the final narration, the one piece of decent writing in the film. "And the great Khan made such conquests as were undreamed of by mortal men. Tribes of the Gobi flocked to his standard, and the farthest reaches of the desert trembled to the hoofs of his hordes ..."

Saying nothing, Duke set down his whiskey bottle, rose from his recliner, and shuffled toward the Betamax.

"At the feet of the Tartar woman he laid all the riches of Cathay," said Jamuga. "For a hundred years, the children of their loins ruled half the world."

Duke depressed the Eject lever. The cassette carriage rose from the recorder console and presented *The Conqueror* to the dying actor.

"Maybe you'll get your aura next week," I said. I took a toke, approached Duke, and squeezed his arm. "Never say die, sir. Let's come back on Monday."

"We lost in Vietnam." Duke pulled the cassette free of the machine. He removed his bandana, mushed it together, and coughed into the folds. "Nixon signed a SALT agreement with the Russians." Again he coughed. "The Air Force Academy is admitting women. The phone company is hiring flits. Peanut Head"–he gasped–"is bringing the draft dodgers"–and gasped–"home."

Duke lurched toward me, tipped his invisible Stetson, and, still gripping the cassette, collapsed on the carpet.

Inhaler at the ready, Sweeney bounded across the room. Falling to his knees, he wrapped his arms around the supine superstar and told Kieran to apply the plastic mask to Duke's nose and mouth. It was a familiar tableau–we had just seen it on the screen: Bortai cradling the wounded Temujin as she comes to understand that this particular egomaniacal sociopathic warlord is a real catch. ("He has suffered much," says Bortai to her servant. And the servant, who knows subtext when she hears it, responds, "Deny not the heart.") Kieran handled the oxygen rig with supreme competence, and in a matter of seconds the mask was in place and Duke had stopped gasping.

"You want another shot of whiskey?" I asked, kneeling beside Duke.

"No thanks." He pressed the cassette into my hands and forced himself into a sitting position. "I know when I'm licked, Egghead," he rasped. "It's not my America any more."

"You aren't licked," I said.

"You must have faith," said Kieran.

Sweeney proffered an analgesic pill. Duke swallowed it dry. "I've got plenty of faith," he said. "I've got faith running out my ears. It's strength I'm lacking, raw animal strength, so I figured I should hoard it for Egghead."

"For me?" I said.

"I projected all my quantum vibrations onto Hunlun," he said.

"You mean ... you augmented Ms. Rappaport's shield?" Kieran bent low, joining our pietà.

"Augmented?" said Duke. "Let's talk plain, Doc–I made it *happen.* I threw that bubble around old Hunlun like Grant took Richmond. I blocked that radiation till Hell wouldn't have it again." He set a large, sweating hand on my shoulder. "The Big C conquered John Wayne a long time ago, but you've still got a fighting chance, Egghead."

"Duke, I'm speechless," I said.

"I've never bent the space-time continuum for anybody before, but I'm glad I did it in your case," said Duke.

"I'm touched to the core," I said.

"Why does the aura make you angry?" he asked.

It took me several seconds to formulate an answer in my head, and as I started to speak the words, Duke coughed again, closed his eyes, and fainted dead away.

→ ※ ←

Before the day was over Sweeney got Duke admitted to the Sloan-Kettering Memorial Cancer Center, where they gave the old cowboy all the morphine and Jack Daniels he wanted. A week later Duke received open-heart surgery, and by the end of the month he was back home in L.A., attended around the clock by his wife, his children, and, of course, his faithful nurse.

The Big C accomplished its final assault on June 11, 1979, stealing the last breath from John Wayne as he lay abed in the UCLA Medical

Center.

Duke always wanted his epitaph to read FEO, FUERTE Y FORMAL, but I've never visited his grave, so I don't know what's on the stone. *Feo, Fuerte y Formal*: "Ugly, Strong, and Dignified"–a fair summary of that box-office giant, but I would have preferred either the characteristic self-knowledge of *There's More to That Movie Than My Damn Conservative Attitude* or else the intentional sexual innuendo of the eulogy he wrote for himself while drinking scotch during the *Chisum* wrap party: *He Saw, He Conquered, He Came.*

Hunlun's aura still angers me. Kinetotherapy still makes me see red. "If Kieran Morella is on to something," I told Stuart, "then the universe is far more absurd than I could possibly have imagined."

A Japanese city has been reduced to radioactive embers? No problem. We can fix that with happy thoughts. The Castle Bravo H-bomb test has condemned a dozen Asian fisherman to death by leukemia? Don't worry. Just pluck the quantum strings, tune in the cosmos, and the pennies will trickle down from heaven.

"The miracle is the cruelest trick in God's repertoire," I told Stuart. "God should be ashamed of himself for inventing the miracle."

Next Tuesday I'm going to the polls and casting my vote for Bill Clinton: not exactly a liberal but probably electable. (Anything to deprive that airhead plutocrat George Bush of a second term.) The day after that, my eighty-first birthday will be upon me. Evidently I'm going to live forever.

"Don't count on it," Stuart warned me.

"I won't," I said.

According to today's *Times*, the Nevada Test Site, formerly the Nevada Proving Ground, is still open to visitors. They have a webpage now, www.nv.doe.gov. The tour features numerous artifacts from the military's attempts to determine what kinds of structures might withstand nuclear blast pressures. You'll see crushed walls of brick and cinder block, pulverized domes fashioned from experimental concrete, a railroad bridge whose I-beams have become strands of steel spaghetti, a bank vault that looks like a sand castle after high tide, and a soaring steel drop-tower intended to cradle an H-bomb that, owing to the 1992 Nuclear Testing Moratorium, was never exploded.

Disney World for Armageddon buffs.

Kieran let me keep the kinetotherapy cassette, but I've never looked at it, even though there's a Betamax somewhere in our closet. I'm afraid those goddamn psychedelic shields will still be there, enswathing my on-screen incarnation. Tomorrow I plan to finally rid myself of the thing. I shall solemnly bear the cassette to the basement and toss it into the furnace, immolating it like the Xanadu work crew burning Charles Foster Kane's sled. Stuart has promised to go with me. He'll make sure I don't lose my nerve.

I simply can't permit the universe to be that absurd. There are certain kinds of cruelty I won't allow God to perform. In the ringing words of Hunlun, "My son, this you cannot do."

→ ✻ ←

Once again I import the Castle Bravo explosion into my living room. I drink my glass of sherry and study the Rorschachian obscenities.

This time I'm especially struck by the second shot in the mushroom-cloud montage, for within the nodes and curls of this burning Satanic cabbage I perceive a human face. The mouth is wide open. The features are contorted in physical agony and metaphysical dread.

Try this at home. You'll see the face too, I promise you. It's not the face of John Wayne–or Genghis Khan or Davy Crockett or Paul Tibbets or the Virgin Mary or any other person of consequence. The victim you'll see is just another nobody, just another bit-player, another *hibakusha*, eternally trapped on a ribbon of acetate and praying–fervently, oh so fervently–that this will be the last replay.

come Back, Dr. sarcophagus

Encircled by a spotlight, two figures huddle together stage left, each perched on a stepladder. The younger of the pair, TOM MOODY, a diffident but likeable fellow whose appeal lies partly in his awareness of being a nerd, nervously grips the microphone of an unseen tape recorder. He is interviewing EDGAR WEST, alias Dr. Sarcophagus, former host of Frisson Theater *on a Philadelphia UHF station. Now in his eighties, Edgar has retained the energetic eccentricities that once made him a celebrity.*

The interview is occurring in Edgar's frigid apartment. Both men wear gloves, scarves, and knitted watch caps, and throughout the play they periodically blow on their hands and kick their feet against the ladders. At rise, in response to a request from Tom, Edgar launches into his famous Frisson Theater *sign-off.*

> EDGAR: Farewell, fans of fiends! Adios, toasters of ghosts! Au revoir, mavens of noir! And remember this, my friends! Life is full of peasants with torches, but the sequel belongs to *you!*
>
> TOM: Oooo, Mr. West, that was perfect!
>
> EDGAR: I did it better in the old days.

Tom: No, really–I felt a *chill* go up and down my spine.

Edgar: Of course you felt a chill–it's thirty degrees in here. This morning they finally got around to fixing the furnace, but it'll be an hour before the heat reaches my apartment.

Tom: Oh, I don't mind. I'll pretend I'm in that frigid cavern beneath the castle in *Frankenstein Meets the Wolf Man.*

Edgar: I remember when we revived that one. I showed the fans how they could build astonishing new insects out of the dead flies and dried crickets they found behind their hot-water heaters.

Tom: Then there was the time you revived *Werewolf of London* and gave away packets of *marifasa lumina lupina* seeds to the first thousand viewers who sent in postcards. *(nostalgic)* I planted mine in Mom's rose garden. What came up looked suspiciously like dandelions, so she ripped 'em all out.

Edgar: Your mother is obviously not a botanist, Tom. *(beat)* And the *name* of your august journal is...?

Tom: *Macabre Monsters of the Movies.*

Edgar: Once there were three different fanzines devoted entirely to Dr. Sarcophagus. The *Mortuary Monitor*, the *Pall Bearer*, and ... I forget.

Tom: The *Carrion Clarion*. I'd like to begin with–

Edgar: With the astonishing events of February the 23rd, 1975.

Tom: *(taken aback)* How'd you know?

EDGAR: Yesterday I entertained a reporter from *Frightening Freaks of Filmdom*, and last week I spoke with *Abominable Aberrations of the Silver Screen*. You *all* want to know about February the 23rd. *(entering a reverie)* My ex-wife was the first to arrive in the studio that afternoon, and then came the station manager ...

As Edgar reminisces, the spotlight fades, and an eerie luminescence suffuses the stage, revealing the set of Frisson Theater, the sort of low-budget horror-host program that flourished on UHF television during the pre-cable 1970s. The one impressive appointment is a gaudy casket resting on saw-horses. Otherwise, we see only the standard spiderwebs, rubber bats, human skulls, ornate candelabrum, and fake dungeon masonry, plus ERIK THE ORANGUTAN, a tattered stuffed ape reclining on a Victorian couch.

Just out of camera range, a bar stool holds an elaborate make-up kit, jammed with an assortment of fright wigs, putty noses, latex scars, horned brows, grotesque dentures, and tubes of grease paint. A mirror dangles from a nearby coat rack.

Edgar's ex-wife, RUTH HENDRICKS, thirty-five, bustles about the dungeon set, arranging the tacky props. She is an attractive and generous woman who suffers fools too gladly for her own good. Enter ALBERT MEINSTER, the station manager, early forties, cradling an exquisite porcelain vase. Though fiercely devoted to the bottom line, Albert is someone for whom a diagnosis of boorishness normally suffices to counter any suspicions of corruption.

Ruth acknowledges Albert's presence by picking up Erik the Orangutan and caressing the ape fondly.

RUTH: Remember when we ran *Return of the Ape Man*?

ALBERT: *(nodding, disgusted)* Edgar spent twenty minutes expounding on the metaphysical implications of transplanting a man's brain into an ape's body. Our lowest ratings ever.

63

RUTH: But we received a dozen letters from philosophy students who said they understood Descartes for the first time.

Albert draws close to Ruth.

ALBERT: Might I have a word with you?

RUTH: *(annoyed)* I have to dress the set.

ALBERT: It's about your future.

RUTH: *(impatient)* My future is that we go on the air in ten minutes.

ALBERT: I've thought about it long and hard, and I've decided you'd be the ideal producer for our new cooking show.

RUTH: I don't know anything about food.

ALBERT: Before I convinced you to produce *Frisson Theater*, you didn't know anything about monster movies either.

RUTH: *(cynical)* And in a mere ten years my understanding has become positively ... pathological. "Even a man who's pure in heart, and says his prayers at night, may become a wolf when the wolfsbane blooms, and the autumn moon is bright."

ALBERT: Here's the idea, Ruth—we're going to combine cooking with dancing. *Crockery Rock.* Catchy, eh? It'll probably make Channel 56 the biggest UHF station in Philadelphia.

RUTH: I once dated a man who wanted to create the largest hog wallow in Tuscaloosa. *(indicates vase)* What's this? Are you also launching an antiques show?

ALBERT: A very strange episode. I bought it from a sidewalk vendor on Market Street. Distinguished looking fellow. Well-dressed. Down on his luck, I guess. Mostly he was selling the usual junk–flimsy umbrellas, phony watches, wind-up toys–but then my eye caught what I'm pretty sure, knock on wood, kiss my shamrock, is a genuine *Ming vase*!

RUTH: I know even less about antiques than I do about cooking.

ALBERT: He charged me ten dollars, but I'll bet it's worth a *thousand*. Naturally I hoofed it over to Chinatown right away. Two different restaurant owners told me it's quite possibly authentic.

RUTH: Authentic? Then forget about your thousand dollars, Albert. We're talking maybe a quarter of a million!

ALBERT: *(astonished)* Golly.

Ruth animates Erik the Orangutan, working his arms and dubbing his voice.

RUTH: Can I hold it, Mr. Meinster? Can I play with it?

Albert panics, hiding the porcelain vase behind his back.

ALBERT: I've got a second proposition for you, Ruth. An exquisite little Italian place just opened in Chestnut Hill. How about you and me twirl some linguini tonight?

RUTH: *(unenthused)* Sure, Albert. Sounds like fun. But remember ... *(Lugosi imitation)* "I never drink ... wine."

ALBERT: We won't talk about Bela Lugosi, only

65

interesting things. The Phillies. *Crockery Rock.* Jeez, Ruth, how did you *stand* being married all those years to a man who was obsessed with *horror films?*

RUTH: *(corroborating)* He brought a Bell and Howell Autoload projector along on our honeymoon, plus his 16mm prints of *Dracula's Daughter* and *The Mummy's Ghost.*

ALBERT: You should've bailed out then and there.

RUTH: *(defensive) The Mummy's Ghost* is actually a very romantic movie. *(wistful)* There's more to Edgar than you imagine.

ALBERT: So ... how did he take the news?

RUTH: *(aghast)* I thought *you* were supposed to tell him.

ALBERT: No, *you* were supposed to tell him.

RUTH: No, *you* were.

ALBERT: No, *you* were.

RUTH: *You* were.

ALBERT: *You* were.

Suddenly the casket lid flies back, and an athletic man vaults from the chamber and lands on the floor, dressed in evening clothes and an Edwardian greatcoat. The new arrival is the same Edgar West we met earlier, only now he's on the spry side of forty. Albert is so startled he nearly drops the porcelain vase.

RUTH: Yikes!

ALBERT: Eeeggaahh!

RUTH: Shame on you, Edgar!

EDGAR: *(closing casket)* What's this big news you're both so eager to tell me?

ALBERT: I'm in dire need of a cup of coffee.

Albert exits, holding the vase firmly against his chest.

EDGAR: Is it *good* big news or *bad* big news?

RUTH: *(temporizing)* Sooo ... what movie are we running this afternoon? I forget.

EDGAR: *The Mummy's Curse.* Stick around, okay, darling? You won't be disappointed. I've got a great bit worked out.

Edgar approaches the make-up kit. During the following exchange, he stares into the dangling mirror and transforms himself into Dr. Sarcophagus—puffy cheeks, protuberant teeth, billowing fright wig: Dr. Caligari's campy cousin.

RUTH: *(a kind of catechism)* *The Mummy's Hand ... The Mummy's Tomb ... The Mummy's Curse ... The Mummy's Ghost.* Ah, so you're showing sequel number *three*.

EDGAR: *(mock distress)* No, no, no, it's *Hand, Tomb, Ghost, Curse*—don't you know *anything*? *Hand, Tomb, Ghost, Curse.*

Ruth winces, picks up Erik the Orangutan, and hugs the ape fiercely.

RUTH: Get ready for a kick in the teeth, Edgar. Ever since August our ratings have been slipping, and the advertisers are going through a lot of pain. So Albert decided—

EDGAR: *(launching into routine)* Three tana leaves, brewed into a reanimating fluid during the cycle of the full moon, will keep the Mummy's heart beating. Nine tana leaves will endow Kharis with mobility, dexterity, and libidinous impulses toward the Princess Ananka. Fifteen tana leaves will make him functional enough to run for Congress.

RUTH: So Albert decided to cancel *Frisson Theater*. Today's broadcast is our last. Next week–

EDGAR: Twenty-one tana leaves enable Kharis to sire his own dynasty and dance like Fred Astaire.

RUTH: *(to Erik the Orangutan)* He's not listening to me. *(ape voice)* He's not listening to you.

EDGAR: Twenty-seven tana leaves, and they'll let him teach Egyptian Studies at Princeton.

RUTH: Next week Albert is replacing us with NCAA basketball.

EDGAR: Thirty-three tana leaves– *(double take)* Basketball?

RUTH: Villanova versus Northeastern.

Having transmuted into Dr. Sarcophagus, Edgar releases a howl of animal anguish and throws himself across the casket. As if responding to a cue, the floor manager, CINDY SMITH, a pert young Temple graduate, strides onto the set wearing headsets and holding a clipboard.

CINDY: You're on in six minutes, Mr. West.

EDGAR: Basketball? Basketball? *Anything* but basketball!

CINDY: *(to Ruth)* Sometimes I think he's better in

rehearsals than during the broadcast.

Cindy executes an about-face and marches away. Edgar pushes off from the casket and stands up straight.

> EDGAR: *(devastated)* Oh, Ruth, what are we going to *do?*

Ruth approaches Edgar and gives him a succinct but heartfelt hug.

> RUTH: *I'm* going to produce a stupid cooking show, and *you're* ... *(beat)* I feel completely rotten about this.

> EDGAR: Nobody remembers a basketball game two weeks or even two *days* after the broadcast.

> RUTH: True.

> EDGAR: Whereas *The Bride of Frankenstein* stays with you a lifetime. I could deal with getting blindsided by *Gilligan's Island* reruns, but *basketball* ...

> RUTH: Maybe you could become a special guest host. Tell everybody the point guard is really dribbling a human brain.

> EDGAR: *(intrigued)* Do you think they'd go for it?

Ruth scowls and rolls her eyes.

> RUTH: There's a good chance Albert can find you a job in marketing.

> EDGAR: *(sarcastic)* You two can talk about it during your big dinner date tonight.

Ruth takes Edgar's arm and strokes it affectionately.

RUTH: I'll never be able say "Frisson Theater" again without choking up.

EDGAR: *(attempting stoicism)* It was fun while it lasted.

RUTH: Remember when you needed a vat of epidermis to make a vulture stew for Granny Maleficium's arthritis, and you told the fans to send you some?

EDGAR: By the end of the week, the mail room was jammed with three thousand pounds of toenail clippings.

RUTH: And then we made our big discovery ...

EDGAR: There is nothing, absolutely nothing, you can do with toenail clippings!

RUTH: Well, we did get *one* idea ...

Edgar and Ruth point at each other and giggle.

EDGAR: Beanbags for bad children!

Giddy with rapport and nostalgia, Edgar and Ruth start laughing. Albert strides into the studio holding a Styrofoam cup of coffee, the porcelain vase secured under the opposite arm.

ALBERT: You're taking this setback awfully well, Edgar. I'm impressed.

EDGAR: *(pointing)* I'd never want a Ming vase in *my* house. Those things are such *clichés*. Like Stradivarius violins.

ALBERT: My intention is to *sell* it.

EDGAR: Or Dom Perignon champagne.

ALBERT: *(sarcastic, to Ruth)* The man has his own print of *Revenge of the Zombies*, and suddenly he's snooty about *clichés?*

Edgar feigns a look of horror and abruptly gestures toward the empty space behind Albert.

EDGAR: Albert, look out! Behind you!

Albert drops his coffee and spins around to face the nonexistent menace. Taking advantage of Albert's confusion, Edgar wrests the vase from his grasp, then retreats behind the casket. When Albert rushes toward Edgar, he raises the vase high above his head.

EDGAR: *(cont'd)* Don't move! I can be merciless with Ming!

ALBERT: You creeping piece of crud!

EDGAR: One more step, and all the king's horses and all the king's men ...

Cindy strides into the studio and plants herself near the front edge of the set, presumably between camera one and camera two.

CINDY: Twenty seconds, Mr. West. We're bringing you up on camera one.

EDGAR: *(to Albert)* Here's the deal. Go to the control room and tell Arthur that for the next two hours he has to broadcast *everything* I say! Each time camera one goes dark, I want to see the tally on two start glowing like Boris Karloff in *The Invisible Ray*! The minute anybody cuts me off, your precious little cuspidor gets shattered in front of a million loyal Sarcophiles!

ALBERT: This is blackmail.

EDGAR: This is live television.

CINDY: Five seconds, Mr. West. Four, three, two...

Albert, defeated, throws up his hands and stalks off, headed for the control room. Ruth steps out of camera range but remains on the studio floor. As the discordant THEME MUSIC for Frisson Theater pours from the speakers, Edgar places the porcelain vase in the embrace of Erik the Orangutan. Edgar assumes a dignified posture and stares into camera one.

> NARRATOR: *(off-stage)* Chilling tales of the supernatural and the paranormal! Horrifying yarns drawn from the archives of the Frankenstein family and the annals of the Dracula clan! Channel 56 is proud to present *Frisson Theater*–with your host, Dr. Sarcophagus!

Cindy points to Edgar, cueing him to begin his shtick.

> EDGAR: *(to camera)* Welcome, Sarcophiles! This afternoon we bring you the fourth and final entry in the Kharis quartet from Universal Pictures–yes, you guessed it, *The Mummy's Curse*!

He pulls out a sealed envelope from his pocket.

> EDGAR: *(cont'd)* But right now I want to tell you the results of our First Annual *Frisson Theater* Scenery Chewing Contest. Over two thousand viewers mailed in ballots, up five hundred from last year's Name Dr. Sarcophagus's Pet Armadillo Competition. *(reads back of envelope)* The nominees for Scenery Chewer of the Century are Charles Laughton in *The Island of Lost Souls*, George Zucco in *Dead Men Walk*, Peter Lorre in *The Beast With Five Fingers*, and Bela Lugosi in *The Raven*. And the winner is ... *(opens envelope, draws out paper)* Bela Lugosi in *The Raven*! "Poe, you are avenged!"

Leaning into the casket, Edgar retrieves a bottle of catsup and a plastic potted fern.

EDGAR: *(cont'd)* And here's Bela's prize—a genuine piece of edible scenery, equally delicious with catsup or mustard.

He slops catsup on the fern, then takes a bite, chewing with hammy delight.

EDGAR: *(cont'd)* Hmmm, hmmm, good! The next time I see that hungry Hungarian, I'll be sure to give him his trophy.

Returning the fern and the catsup to the casket, Edgar retrieves the vase from Erik the Orangutan.

EDGAR: *(cont'd)* And now it's time to play Guess the Title of Next Week's Movie. Your clue is this porcelain vase from seventeenth century China. Go ahead, shout out your ideas, I can hear 'em all, my fearing-aid is turned up full. (cups left ear) What's that, Tony Cochantropolis of Mount Airy? You think it might be *Charlie Chan in Transylvania?* Nope, sorry. *(cups right ear)* Ah-hah! Right you are, Lucy Wintergreen of Manayunk—next week's movie is *The Mask of Fu Manchu. (tosses the vase, catches it)* And now I have an important issue to discuss with Sarcophiles everywhere. It seems that the High Priests of Karnak no longer believe in *Frisson Theater*. Starting next week, they intend to fill this slot with NCAA basketball. Can you *imagine?* NCAA—No Creatures At All. So here's my idea. During the next twenty minutes, instead of watching *The Mummy's Curse*, let the powers-that-be know that monster movies aren't simply escapist trash—they're escapist trash that *matters.* Send telegrams, call the station, or visit us here at 1600 City Line Avenue. But you must act immediately, or there'll be the Devil to pay! (glances off-stage) Okay, Ivan—roll the flick!

As the famous 1940's Universal fanfare fills the air, the Frisson Theater *set goes dark, and the spotlight again falls stage left. Tom*

Moody continues to interview the aging Edgar.

> TOM: The fans really rose to the occasion, didn't they?

> EDGAR: Six hundred telegrams. Three hundred phone calls–and heaven knows how many viewers couldn't get through. But the big surprise was the legions of Sarcophiles who showed up at the station, even though it was the dead of winter. During act two of *The Mummy's Curse*, Albert Meinster agreed to meet with them.

The spotlight fades, and once again a high-key glow illuminates the Frisson Theater *set. Cindy stands at her post between camera one and camera two. Still gripping the porcelain vase, Edgar paces behind the casket, waiting for the next break in the broadcast of* The Mummy's Curse. *Ruth fidgets near Erik the Orangutan.*

Having descended from the control booth, Albert stands just out of camera range, facing three of Edgar's most devoted fans. The first to speak is MARGE TURNER, a plump middle-aged mother. She marches up to Albert and looks him in the eye.

> MARGE: I would've brought my boy Willy along, but he's away at college. What you have to understand, Mr. Meinster, is that Willy was just about the most pathetic case that ever went to Glenside Junior High School. No friends. Didn't fit in. Other kids always picking on him.

She turns and faces the audience, so that she seems to be speaking to the whole world.

> MARGE: *(cont'd)* But then Willy got interested in *Frisson Theater*, and sometimes I watched it with him, which is how I became hooked, and we really liked the way Dr. Sarcophagus would talk about the Frankenstein Monster. *(points toward dungeon set)* That man you got over there, Edgar West, he

has a *gift*. He explained to the fans that the Monster never *asked* to be the way he is, all clumsy and ugly, it wasn't his *fault*, and the *real* problem is narrow-minded villagers who think they have to reject anybody who doesn't wear lederhosen and carry a shillelagh. Well, that took a big load off Willy's shoulders, and eventually he started to relax, and by the time he got to high school he wasn't totally miserable anymore, just unhappy like most kids.

Marge backs away. Next to approach Albert is JAKE GINSBERG, age twenty-three, poised, confident, amiable.

JAKE: (points to Marge) I guess I was a lot like that woman's kid, you know, an outcast, and to top it off all these *changes* were happening to me. I was starting to notice girls, and my complexion was worse than a pineapple's, and I had so many braces my smile looked like the grille of a '59 Chevy Impala.

He turns and faces the audience.

JAKE: *(cont'd)* But every Saturday afternoon I'd watch *Frisson Theater*. It was kind of my duty, since I was president of the Sarcophiles, Germantown Chapter. Mr. West really understood what we were going through. He told us how teenagers often feel like the Wolf Man—you know, our bodies out of control, spouting hair and everything, but he said we just had to *hang in there*, the way Larry Talbot does in *House of Dracula*, and if you remember that movie, Mr. Meinster, you know that the werewolf gets *cured* in the end.

ALBERT: *(to Jake)* If it's about a werewolf, why is it called *House of Dracula*?

Jake, exasperated, rolls his eyes and steps away. LOU SPINELLI, a bewildered fifty-year-old with a Tor Johnson physique, marches up to Albert.

LOU: My wife is working down at the truck stop now, or she would've come along too, 'cause this is about her as well as me. You see, Mr. Meinster, when I decided to marry Alice I knew she had a couple of pretty serious addictions—rather like poor old Bela Lugosi—but I thought everything would turn out all right if I just loved her enough. Pretty stupid, huh?

He turns and faces the audience.

LOU: *(cont'd)* Anyway, one day the police show up, and they take Alice away, and they tell the judge she's a *dealer*, which is a lousy lie, so after Alice goes through rehab she has to spend seven years in Wyncote Penitentiary, *seven years*, and I take to relieving my stress by watching *Frisson Theater*. Half of me wants to back out of the marriage and start playing the field, but old Doc Sarcophagus, he's always showing his Mummy movies, and he keeps reminding the fans how Kharis really knew the meaning of faithfulness. That loyalty idea, well, it kinda struck a chord with me, and I said to myself, "Heck, Lou, if Kharis can stay true to the Princess Ananka for something like three thousand years, you can certainly stand by Alice for seven."

Lou backs away from Albert. Cindy gestures Ruth off the set, then signals for Edgar to face camera one.

CINDY: Mr. West, we're up on camera one. Ten, nine, eight ...

To amuse himself, Edgar starts tossing the vase in the air and catching it. Albert nearly has a heart attack. He takes two steps toward the set.

EDGAR: Humpty-Dumpty sat on the wall ...

Albert stops abruptly, groans.

CINDY: Three, two ...

She cues Edgar to begin.

> EDGAR: *(to camera)* Hello again, boys and ghouls, crazies and gentlemen. We've had a *very* eventful afternoon here at Channel 56, and I want to thank all of you who sent telegrams, made phone calls, and darkened our door. Unfortunately, it's too early to tell whether our hidebound station manager has seen the light. *(flourishes vase)* You know, this Ming vase reminds me of an exciting offer available exclusively to all Sarcophiles. Just last week the station acquired a limited quantity of *authentic Egyptian entrail containers*. For only ten dollars you can get a canopic jar big enough to hold a large intestine, or colon, and for five dollars we'll send you one that's perfect for a small intestine, or semicolon. *(beat)* And now–the exciting climax of *The Mummy's Curse!* *(glances off-stage)* Roll it, Ivan!

As before, the Frisson Theater *set goes dark, and the spotlight falls stage left on Tom Moody and the elderly Edgar.*

> TOM: *(awestruck)* You saved that man's marriage. You helped all those kids cope with adolescence.

> EDGAR: And I gave the Sarcophiles two hours of pleasure every Saturday afternoon–that's what I'm *really* proud of.

> TOM: And yet Albert Meinster still wanted to cancel the show.

> EDGAR: Those endorsements went right over his head. But you know, Tom, I *did* get through to the person who mattered most ...

As the spotlight fades, the familiar glow bathes the Frisson Theater *set. The three witnesses are gone. Cindy stands at her post. Albert stalks around the studio.*

Ruth rushes toward Edgar, arms outstretched. Edgar balances the vase on the casket lid and receives Ruth's embrace.

> RUTH: Oh, Edgar, I had no idea anybody was actually *listening* to all that Mister Rogers stuff you've been doling out.

> ALBERT: *(singing sarcastically)* It's a beautiful day in the netherworld ...

> CINDY: Mr. West, when the show's over, could I have one of those autographed photos you like to give your fans?

> EDGAR: *(to Cindy)* Sure thing.

Edgar and Ruth relax their embrace.

> ALBERT: *(indicating Edgar)* The Role Model from the Black Lagoon.

Suddenly Albert springs onto the set and swoops the vase off the casket lid.

> ALBERT: *(cont'd)* Ah-hah!

Albert turns, lurches forward, and presses the vase into Cindy's grasp.

> ALBERT: *(cont'd)* Hide it some place where a washed-up horror host would never think to look. Do the job right, and I'll give you a raise.

Vase in hand, Cindy rips off her headset, drops it on the floor, and makes an abrupt exit.

RUTH: *(to Edgar)* Surely you were moved by all those testimonials.

ALBERT: Beat the bushes hard enough, you'll find somebody who'll say the Three Stooges saved him from a life of crime.

RUTH: The Three Stooges maybe. Basketball never.

ALBERT: I just did the math. The NCAA broadcasts will double our revenue.

RUTH: I just did the math too. The chances of my having dinner with you tonight are one in seven hundred and thirty-eight thousand. *(to Edgar)* Even if you didn't save *Frisson Theater*, today's efforts were not in vain.

EDGAR: My canopic jar runneth over.

RUTH: Kharis and Ananka—now and forever!

EDGAR: Now and forever!

ALBERT: *(to Ruth)* Piffle. Leaving this lunatic was the smartest thing you ever did.

Suddenly, unexpectedly, the air vibrates with an unearthly WHIRRING, and an incandescent figure materializes stage right.

RUTH: Jeez!

EDGAR: Whoa!

We have just witnessed the arrival of PYTER PERIPHRASTIC, a judgmental but enlightened alien. Pyter wears a luminous silver jumpsuit featuring a high art-deco collar and, wrapped around his brow, a Ninja headband. He carries a Flash Gordon-style ray gun.

ALBERT: *(to Edgar)* I don't care *how* many of your

fans show up here. You're *not* getting your show back.

EDGAR: Er, Ruth, Albert, I'd like you to meet Pyter Periphrastic, my supervisor in the Pangalactic Public Service Corps.

Pyter strides into the studio.

PYTER: *(to Edgar)* I'd forgotten how *weird* this planet is. Only two genders. No haiku in the gas-station bathrooms. *(to Ruth and Albert)* He's telling the truth. Incredible as it sounds, Edgar West, alias Dr. Sarcophagus, was not born on Earth.

ALBERT: Nonsense.

RUTH: *(to Edgar)* Does this explain why we never had children?

Edgar nods and grins sheepishly.

RUTH: *(cont'd)* And that thing we used to do in bed with the eggbeater and the Saran Wrap and the yogurt?

EDGAR: It *also* explains why I simply *have* to keep playing Dr. Sarcophagus.

PYTER: On Sirius Prime, every person must spend the first ten years after puberty doing good in some underprivileged sector of the galaxy.

EDGAR: Running a soup kitchen, teaching first-graders to read, visiting the sick, hosting a horror show.

Pyter removes his headband. A third eye sits prominently in the middle of his brow.

PYTER: If Edgar successfully completes a full decade

of *Frisson Theater*, he'll receive his third eye and become a full-fledged citizen.

EDGAR: And if I lose my job, I'll be exiled to the phlogiston mines of Borgazia Eleven.

RUTH: *(to Albert)* So now you *have* to give *Frisson Theater* another year.

ALBERT: *(shakes head)* Broadcasting is a business, Ruth.

Pyter strides up to Albert.

PYTER: You should get around more. On Epsilon Eridani Prime, television producers are expected to lose money on at least half their programs. It's the only way to keep the poetry slams from driving the wrestling matches off the air.

Cindy returns, minus the porcelain vase. She picks up her headset, slips it over her ears.

CINDY: *(pointing upward)* What's going on? In the control room they've all fainted dead away.

PYTER: *(indicating gun)* I used my catatonia ray.

EDGAR: Cindy, this is Pyter Periphrastic. He's from another planet.

CINDY: Cool.

ALBERT: *(to Pyter)* You look familiar. Have we met before?

PYTER: This morning. I was the sidewalk vendor who sold you that hunk of porcelain you covet so much–a good way for me to intervene in Edgar's case without anybody noticing.

ALBERT: Is it a *real* Ming vase?

PYTER: Phony as a rubber chicken.

ALBERT: Faugh.

PYTER: At this point, Mr. Meinster, I have no choice but to subject you to some shameless transdimensional manipulation. When I took your ten dollars for the vase, I simultaneously scanned your brain. Evidently you harbor a deep desire to become a Hollywood producer.

ALBERT: True enough.

Pyter draws a phosphorescent packet from his tunic.

PYTER: I have here detailed descriptions of twelve feature film concepts that, according to Laplacian prognosticatory dynamics, are likely to find huge audiences in the decades to come. They're yours to keep ... under one condition.

ALBERT: Huge audiences? How huge?

PYTER: You can't imagine. Bigger than the audiences for the Sophocles revivals on Cygni Beta Nine.

For a protracted beat, Albert ponders his options.

ALBERT: *(to Edgar)* All right, Doc. You win. I'll give you another season.

EDGAR: You won't regret this.

RUTH: *(to Albert)* You might recall that next Saturday Edgar promised to show *The Mask of Fu Manchu*. Any idea where I can get a decent print?

ALBERT: That's your problem, Ruth! I'm off to Hollywood!

Pyter delivers the glowing packet into Albert's eager hands.

PYTER: Find the humans with talent, convince them to make these movies, and you'll become a mogul in no time.

Albert tears open the packet, retrieves the dozen pages, and begins to study them. Edgar and Ruth renew their embrace. Cindy steps up to Pyter.

CINDY: Excuse me, sir, but we're going live in one minute. Could you please unfreeze our director?

Pyter backs into the darkness from which he came. Albert starts out of the studio, leafing through the film concepts.

ALBERT: *(incredulous)* A man-eating shark off the coast of Massachusetts? Spaceships over the White House? Yet another movie about the *Titanic*? A comic-book adaptation featuring martial arts and philosophical drivel?

Exit Albert. Edgar and Ruth embrace more tightly than ever.

RUTH: So you're really willing to give our marriage a second chance?

EDGAR: A third chance, a fourth chance, a fifth chance.

RUTH: Even though we can't have children?

CINDY: *(consulting watch)* Ten seconds, Mr. West.

EDGAR: Actually we *can* have children, but it's complicated.

RUTH: You can bring any movie you want along

on our second honeymoon. Even the one where Karloff straps Lugosi to the torture rack.

EDGAR: Actually, Lugosi strapped Karloff to the rack.

RUTH: *(playful)* Can this marriage be saved?

Edgar and Ruth disengage. Cindy positions herself between camera one and camera two.

CINDY: Coming up on camera one.

As Ruth sidles off the set, Edgar faces the camera.

CINDY: *(cont'd)* Five, four, three, two ...

Cindy points to Edgar.

EDGAR: *(to camera)* Well, I guess that about wraps it up for our friend Kharis, and the Princess Ananka too. But here's some news to brighten your day–it looks like *Frisson Theater* is good for at least one more year! Alas, I'm afraid that next week we *won't* be showing *The Mask of Fu Manchu*. Instead you'll get to see ...

He glances off-camera, toward Ruth.

RUTH: *The Bride of Dr. Sarcophagus!*

EDGAR: *(without thinking) The Bride of Dr. Sarcophagus!* *(double take)* No, seriously, folks, next week's flick is, er ...

RUTH: *House of Frankenstein!*

EDGAR: *House of Frankenstein!* Did you know that in order to get this job, I had to explain the *plot* of *House of Frankenstein* to the station owners? You see, the unscrupulous Dr. Niemann has decided to transplant the Monster's brain into the Wolf Man's body, even though he promised that sturdy frame to his hunchbacked assistant. The Monster's worn-out body, meanwhile, is earmarked for Niemann's old enemy, Ullman, and the Wolf Man's brain will go to Niemann's *other* enemy, Strauss ...

As Dr. Sarcophagus babbles the plot of House of Frankenstein, *the dungeon set dissolves into darkness, and the spotlight returns to Tom Moody and the elderly Edgar, seated on their stepladders.*

> TOM: Wow, what a story! My readers will be thrilled!

> EDGAR: I'm sorry you didn't get to meet Ruth, but she's visiting our granddaughter on Altair Four. *(beat)* Hey, I think the heat's finally on!

Edgar and Tom remove their gloves and watch caps. A third eye sits prominently in the middle of Edgar's forehead. Tom pulls a copy of Macabre Monsters of the Movies *from his coat and hands it to Edgar.*

> TOM: This is for you. Hot off the presses.

Edgar takes out his three-lens spectacles, puts them on, and scans the magazine cover.

> EDGAR: *(reading)* "In this issue: Lon Chaney Junior filmography ... the making of *Dracula's Daughter* ... figuring out the plot of *House of Frankenstein*." *(fixes on Tom)* So, when do you begin your own horror-hosting career?

> TOM: They're beaming me down to Pittsburgh next month.

> EDGAR: Looking forward?

TOM: Actually, I'm pretty scared. I don't really have much confidence in myself.

EDGAR: That will come, Tom.

TOM: You really think so?

EDGAR: Is the Mummy old enough to get a driver's license?

Tom hops off the stool.

TOM: So long, Dr. Sarcophagus ... Mr. West.

EDGAR: Edgar.

TOM: Edgar. *(starts away)* I'll remember this hour for the rest of my life.

EDGAR: Have a safe trip home.

Tom backs into the darkness. After a beat, Edgar calls after him.

EDGAR: Farewell, you fan of fiends! Adios, you toaster of ghosts! Au revoir, you maven of noir! And remember this, Tom Moody! Life is full of peasants with torches, but the sequel belongs to *you!*

The curtain falls.

The fate of Nations

Pushing aside the knotted pairs of running socks, I lift the journal from my dresser drawer. I unfasten the delicate lock, turn to a fresh page, and ready my ballpoint pen. Click.

Dear Diary, let me say at the outset that I once counted myself among the luckiest of women. Dennis had a lucrative job as a software engineer at Micromega. Our daughter, Angela, loved school and always brought home top grades. Thanks to the saltwater fish fad, my little pet shop–Carlotta's Critturs in Copley Square–was turning a tidy profit.

The first signs of trouble were subtle. I'm thinking especially of Dennis's decision to become a Boston Bruins fan and a Philadelphia Flyers fan simultaneously, an allegiance that served no evident purpose beyond allowing him to watch twice as much hockey as before. I also recall his insistence on replacing our coffee cups and drink tumblers with ceramic mugs bearing the New England Patriots logo. Then there was Dennis's baseball-card collection, featuring the 1986 Red Sox starting lineup. Wasn't that a hobby more suited to a ten-year-old?

It soon became clear that Dennis was battling a full-blown addiction. The instant he got home from work, he plunked himself in front of the tube and start watching ESPN, ESPN2, or ESPN3. Dozens of teams enlisted his loyalty, not merely the Boston franchises. He followed the NFL, the NHL, the NBA, and Major League Baseball. Our erotic encounters were short and perfunctory, bounded by the seventh inning stretch. Whenever we went on vacation, Dennis brought his portable Sony along. Our trips to Martha's Vineyard were keyed to the All-Star Game. Our winter sojourns in Florida centered around the Stanley Cup.

"What do you get out of it?" I asked. The edge in my voice could nick a hockey puck.

"A great deal," he replied.

"What does it *matter?*" I wailed.

"I can't explain."

After much pleading, hectoring, and finagling, I convinced Dennis that we needed a marriage counselor. He insisted that we employ Dr. Robert Lezzer in Framingham. I acquiesced. A male therapist was better than none.

The instant I entered Dr. Lezzer's presence, I began feeling better. He was a small, perky, beaming gnome in a white cotton shirt and a red bowtie. He said to call him Bob.

It took me half an hour to make my case. The lonely dinners. The one-way conversations. The chronic vacancy in our bed. As far as I was concerned, ESPN stood for Expect Sex Probably Never.

No sooner had I offered my story than Dennis and Bob traded significant glances, exchanged semantically freighted winks, and favored each other with identical nods.

"Should I tell her?" asked Dennis.

"Depends on whether you trust her," Bob replied.

"I do."

"Then let her in. It's the only way to save your marriage."

Dennis bent back his left ear to reveal a miniscule radio receiver, no bigger than a pinhead, embedded in the fleshy lobe. The implantation had occurred on his eighteenth birthday, he explained, as part of an arcane initiation rite. Every adult male in North America had one.

"Throughout the long history of Western civilization," said Dennis, "no secret has been better kept."

"But what is it *for?*" I asked.

"If he gave you the short answer, you wouldn't believe him," said Bob, bending close so I could see his transceiver.

"Luckily, we're only four hours from New York City," said Dennis, stroking me affectionately on the knee.

Bob recommended that we leave as soon as possible. We arranged for Angela to spend the night at a friend's house, then took off at two o'clock. By dinner time we were zooming south down the West Side Highway, heading toward the heart of Manhattan.

We left our Volvo in the Park & Lock on 42nd Street near Tenth

Avenue, hiked four blocks east, and entered the MTA system. Although I'd often walked through the Times Square subway station during my undergraduate days at NYU, this was the first time I'd noticed a narrow steel door beside the stairwell leading to the N and R trains. Dennis retrieved his wallet, pulled out a black plastic card, and swiped it though a nearby magnetic reader, thereby causing the portal to open. An elevator car awaited us. We entered. The car descended for a full five minutes, carrying us a thousand feet into the bedrock.

Disembarking, we entered a small foyer decorated with two dozen full-figure portraits of men dressed in baseball uniforms. I recognized Ty Cobb and Pete Rose. Dennis guided me into an immense steel cavern dominated by a sparkling three-dimensional map that, according to the caption, depicted our spiral arm of the Milky Way. Five thousand tiny red lights pulsed amid the flashing white stars. Five thousand planets boasting intelligent life, Dennis explained. Five thousand advanced civilizations.

So: we were not alone in the galaxy–nor were we alone in the cavern. A dozen men wearing lime-green jumpsuits and walkie-talkie headsets paced in nervous circles before the great map, evidently receiving information from distant locales and relaying it to a hidden but eager audience.

I must admit, dear Diary, I'd never been more confused in my life.

Four other couples occupied the cavern. Each wife wore an expression identical to my own: exasperation leavened by perplexity. The husbands' faces all betrayed a peculiar mixture of fearfulness and relief.

"The Milky Way is a strange place," said Dennis. "Stranger than any of us can imagine. Some of its underlying laws may remain forevermore obscure."

"It's chilly down here," I said, rubbing each shoulder with the opposite hand.

"For reasons that scientists are just beginning to fathom," Dennis continued, "political events on these five thousand worlds are intimately connected to particular athletic contests on Earth. Before each such game, these dispatchers in the jumpsuits switch on their mikes and inform us exactly what's at stake."

"I don't understand."

"Women have difficulty with this. Bear with me. Here's how the universe works. Because the Dallas Cowboys won Super Bowl XII, the slave trade on 16 Cygni Beta ended after ten centuries of misery and oppression. By contrast, it's unfortunate that the Saint Louis Cardinals took home the National League Pennant in 1987, for this sparked the revocation of the Homosexual Toleration Act on 70 Virginis Kappa. Physicists call it PROSPOCAP–the Professional Sports Causality Principle. With me, darling?"

"I guess." I was so flabbergasted that my breath came only with great effort, although the cavern's poor ventilation was also to blame.

"Thanks to PROSPOCAP, we know that the advent of women's suffrage on 14 Herculis Gamma traced directly to the Oakland Raiders' emergence as the AFC Wild Card Team in 1980. We also realize that the end of theocratic dictatorship throughout 79 Ceti Delta followed directly upon the New York Yankees' trouncing of the Atlanta Braves in the 1999 World Series. On a darker note, the most devastating nuclear war ever to occur on Gliese 86 Omicron had its roots in the Boston Celtics' domination of the 1963 NBA Playoffs, Eastern Conference."

I decided to ask the obvious question. "How could a sports fan possibly cheer for his home team knowing that victory means nuclear war on another planet?"

"A fan learns the implication of any given win or loss only *ex post facto*. Until the moment of revelation, it makes sense to assume that your team is on the side of the angels. After all, even the most morally reprehensible outcome is preferable to oblivion."

"Oblivion?"

"The instant any team's supporters stop caring sufficiently, all the creatures on the affected planet become comatose."

I looked into Dennis's eyes. For the first time in our marriage, I understood my husband. "You care, don't you, darling? You really care."

"I really care."

"If only I'd *known*–I never would've harassed you for watching the Pro Bowl on my birthday. Do you forgive me?"

"Yes, Carlotta, I forgive you."

"Comatose? All of them?"

"Comatose. All of them. Death by dehydration follows in a matter of days."

Dennis went on to disclose an equally well established fact. When it came to awareness of PROSPOCAP, a radical numerical disparity between males and females was an ontological necessity. Should the ratio ever exceed one knowledgeable woman for every two hundred knowledgeable men, the entire galaxy would implode, sucking all sentient lifeforms into the resultant maelstrom.

So you see why I picked up my pen today, dear Diary. I simply had to tell *someone* about this vast, astonishing, and apparently benign conspiracy.

Earlier tonight Dennis and I watched the Denver Broncos face the San Diego Chargers on *Monday Night Football*. The Broncos won, 21 to 14. As a result, an airplane manufacturer on Epsilon Eridani Prime managed to recall four hundred defective jetliners before any fatal crashes occurred.

"I'm curious about something," I told Dennis as we trod the stairs to our bedroom. "Do they have athletic events on other planets?"

"Ball sports are a constant throughout the galaxy."

"And do these sports also have ... consequences?"

"In Terran Year 1863 CE, the Pegasi Secundus Juggernauts beat the Tau Bootes Berserkers in the Pangalactic Plasmacock Playoffs. A few hours later, three generals named Heth, Pender, and Pickett led the disastrous Confederate charge at Gettysburg."

"I see."

"In the subsequent century, the Iota Horologii Leviathans scored an upset over the Rho Cancri Demons in the Third Annual Ursa Majoris Lava Hockey Tournament, whereupon Communism began its rapid collapse in eastern Europe. Need I go on?"

"No, my sweet. You needn't."

As Dennis said when he first showed me the great map beneath Manhattan, the Milky Way is a strange place–stranger than any of us can imagine. But I am obligated to keep my awareness of PROSPOCAP a secret, lest the galaxy evaporate.

Next Monday evening the Patriots will play the Pittsburgh Steelers. I'll be there, oh yes, cheering my team on. You see, dear Diary, I've finally learned to care.

The Eye That Never Blinks

Unblinking, the disembodied eye stared at Pothinos from within its glimmering pyramid of ice.

"What kind of fish?" he asked defensively, rising from his desk. Even a prince among molecular biologists, as Pothinos surely was, could not be expected to identify a species on the evidence of a single organ.

"Hunt it in every zoology text ever written, and you will not find it," said his youthful visitor, a collection of nervous gestures in expensive clothing. He had given his name as Sebastian W. Stragon, though considering his aristocratic demeanor, Pothinos decided, there should have been either a Lord at the beginning or a Roman numeral at the end.

Issuing a quick little *brrrup*, Maxie the cat jumped on the desk and pranced toward the frozen eye. "Why bring it here?" Pothinos asked.

"You must work your cleverness on it." Stragon's sweeping arm seemed to encompass the entire Quantum Biology Institute. "If the rumors are true, you can fashion an adult cimberfish from one tiny particle of this eye."

Maxie's tongue stroked the ice pyramid. The creature had the persistence of Thomas Edison; left alone, Pothinos knew, she would eventually lick her way in. "There are easier ways to obtain a fish, Mr. Stragon." Crossing the lab, Pothinos absently tossed some mummified ants into the turtles' terrarium. "Try a trout stream. Or a pet store."

"There are no easier ways to get *this* fish," Stragon lamented, tugging at his thick golden hair as if to dislodge a toupee. He shooed the cat away. "Naturally I intend to reward you." From his silk vest he produced a check, waving it before Pothinos like a hypnotist's pendulum. He had already filled it out and added his signature; adjacent to Pothinos's name, an astonishing quantity of zeros trailed from the numeral *five* like spots on a python.

"Cimberfish?" said Pothinos, stifling a gasp. The hell with grant applications when half a million dollars lay right there in the lab, waiting to be claimed. "Never heard of a cimberfish."

The ice pyramid was melting now, puddling onto the gold salver. "Some fish live in the sea"–a lurid ellipsis–"and others live in Satan's blood." Stragon moved his lips oddly, as if he'd forgotten how a smile went. "Yes, doctor, beyond the veil lie truths of which reason can only dream."

Pothinos winced internally, grinned on the surface. For a cool half-million he was willing to endure almost anything, even Stragon's pieties.

The intruder repocketed the check and extended a sprightly index finger toward the vacuum footlocker from which the eye had come. He's testing me, Pothinos thought. Daring me to make him pack up his bizarre trophy and leave.

"Bring it here." After walking past heaps of cryule vials and titer boxes, Pothinos opened the main freezer, pushed aside the tissue cultures, and cleared a space for the unblinking eye.

"Your reputation circles the earth," said Stragon, starting forward, salver in hand. "When I heard how you violated that rabbit"–he set the ice pyramid in the freezer–"unraveling its life-strands, making rabbit after rabbit as would God himself, I knew that my search had ended." He closed the door and pressed the check into Pothinos's palm. "Regard the present sum as a down payment. You'll receive an identical amount when the cloning is accomplished. Do we have a bargain?"

The check's design, as elegant as Stragon himself, suggested an illuminated medieval manuscript. Was this aesthete deranged, or merely eccentric?

"A saltwater fish?" Pothinos asked.

"Fresh," his patron said.

A week later the thing was born. Strange, the ways of parthenogenesis. Who, looking at that mundane and bloated eye, would have predicted anything this delicate, this decorous, this weird? The cimberfish's red scales flashed like embedded rubies. Its fins put Pothinos in mind of oriental kites.

"Beautiful," Stragon gasped when he first beheld the completed clone navigating its circular universe. "Simply beautiful."

Pothinos's patron had been adamant. The moment the procedure bore fruit, Pothinos must contact Stragon, day or night, which is why the men now stood before a glass fishbowl shortly after three on a Sunday morning.

"You can't imagine how long I've waited." Stragon caressed the glass bowl as he might a lover's thigh. "Don't worry–the balance of your fee resides in my purse. But indulge me for a moment, will you?"

At present rates of pay, Pothinos was prepared to indulge Stragon for a month. "Yes...?"

"Where in this vicinity might a man go fishing?"

"Fishing? It's not my sport."

"Nor mine." Stragon hugged himself, as if to defeat a chill.

"What do you hope to catch? Another cimberfish?"

"No ... something else. Any old fishing hole will do." Pothinos told Stragon of Lake Rosamond, where his colleagues often hooked morose sharp-whiskered catfish during lunch hour. "A ten-minute walk through the woods," Pothinos explained.

"Are you up for some nocturnal angling?" Stragon asked.

"Me?"

"I would prize your company."

"You mean ... now?"

"Now. A fishing trip." Stragon's large, glossy eyes widened. "I want you to see that a magical realm is evermore at hand."

"Aren't they more likely to bite at dawn?"

"I cannot wait that long."

Like an antineutrino, Maxie appeared out of nowhere, dipping her paw in the fishbowl and eliciting from Stragon a scream so loud that Pothinos thought the glass might shatter. Instantly he snatched up the cat, tossing her into the hall.

"A fishing trip." Emphatically Pothinos shut the lab door. Why not? What did Stragon's madness matter, so long as his money remained such a deep and luxurious green? "It's been years since I went on a fishing trip."

⋖ ⧉ ⋗

In the moonlight a vast automobile gleamed blackly, a low mist lapping at its tires. A chauffeur stood by the rear door, his beatific smile and steady posture striking Pothinos as odd in a man employed by one so odd as Stragon.

"Tonight I shall travel by foot, George," Stragon explained, showing the chauffeur the glass bowl. Drifting placidly amid the perturbations, the cimberfish had evidently come to terms with its newfound existence.

"It's marvelous, sir," said George. Fog crawled up his body like ivy ascending a trellis. "I'm very happy for you."

The chauffeur opened the trunk, removing a fishing rod of manifestly recent and costly design. A gold filament joined the hook to a large gleaming reel whose housing proclaimed, in capital letters, that seven ball bearings lay within. If Stragon failed to hook a fish that night, it would not be for reasons of technology.

"Good fishing, sir," said George.

"A single catch will do," the young man noted, securing a tackle box from the front seat. He handed Pothinos the cimberfish. "One more miracle is all I need."

The fog lifted as Pothinos's patron led him away from the Quantum Biology Institute. Silver shafts of moonlight poured into the warm woods. Cradled in Pothinos's arms, the glass bowl glistened as the cimberfish circled.

"In my adolescence," Stragon began his story, shifting the fishing rod from one shoulder to the other, "I pursued a life of travel and adventure, and one bleak, gnarled autumn I found myself in a woods reminiscent of the one in which we now walk. Europe boasted a plenary cosmopolitanism in those days, so that it was not unusual to come upon a French priest in a Spanish garden or, as in the instance I am about to relate, an Italian scholar in a German forest. The scholar's predicament—that was unusual. Such a vicious way to die, being sucked into a swamp like that, the quicksand filling him up like seed forced into a goose. I was never particularly agile, but somehow I pulled him out."

Fat birds brooded in the trees. Pothinos half expected some winged predator to swoop down and snatch the cimberfish away.

"Immediately the scholar proposed to reward me," Stragon continued. "Reaching into his knapsack, he drew forth a jar containing three beautiful crimson fish, swimming round and round. Joy surged through me. Exotic pets fetched a high price then. Callow youth that I was, I failed to read the scholar's face correctly, failed to note the gleam in his eye as he explained that these three cimberfish, as he called them, were the only ones in the universe. I would be foolish to sell them, he insisted. No, instead I must acquire a fishing rod, and I must bait the hook with a cimberfish, and upon casting out my line I must make a wish over the water."

Glazed with moonlight, Lake Rosamond came into view. Curls of fog drifted across its surface like vapor rising from a crock of soup.

Make a wish? mused Pothinos. Had Stragon ordered up the cimberfish merely to illustrate a fairy tale?

Opening his tackle box, Stragon took out several sinkers and a phosphorescent bobber, which he promptly attached to his line.

"I did as the scholar instructed," he went on, "borrowing a rod from my uncle and setting off for the sea. A day's walk brought me to Lubeck Bay. What does a young man wish for? Love, you guess? Wrong, for love embraces only the possibility of itself, whereas wealth can purchase many things, including–let us not be sentimental, doctor–love. I baited my hook, threw out my line ... and wished for a fortune."

"Did you have to wait long?" Pothinos asked, curious in spite of himself.

"Barely a minute."

Stragon plunged his hand into the glass bowl, gripping the cimberfish and lifting it free. Mercilessly he impaled it on his hook. A crude way to treat such a rare and valuable creature, but evidently this step was essential.

"I caught a manta ray," Stragon said, "its great flaps covered with fabulous designs. Upon gaffing it, I dragged it on shore and slit it open."

"*Slit* it?"

"As my instincts bade. The ray contained the shredded corpse of my cimberfish ... and something else."

"Let me guess." Pothinos coughed on his cynicism. "Money."

"A leather sack. Inside, a fortune in precious gems. The descendents of those gems–the profits on the investments they bought–have enabled me to pay you so royally for your talents."

After casting out his tethered cimberfish, Stragon climbed onto a large rock that jutted into Rosamond like a pier and sat down.

"Knowing of my success with the first cimberfish," he resumed, "you will not be surprised to learn that barely a month went by before I was at it again. This time I tried the river that cut through my grandfather's farm in Bavaria. What good are riches if the Reaper comes? Hence, my second wish was, simply, to live forever. When I opened my catch–a wondrous eel with skin like wet silk–a glass phial rolled onto the ground. For several days I struggled with myself, eventually resolving to drink what the phial contained, a warm sour liquid that indeed proved to be the elixir of life."

Mosquitoes fidgeted around Stragon's bobber like a hundred satellites orbiting a planet.

"How old are you?" Pothinos inquired cautiously, stepping away from the rock as if his patron's warped imagination might be infectious.

"When did the Wars of the Roses begin?"

"The what?"

"Wars of the Roses."

"I don't know. Five centuries ago."

"I was twelve at the time."

Pothinos thought of his sister Lucinda–how she had walked into his bedroom on his seventeenth birthday and informed him that the Split Pea with Ham People had just arrived from Betelgeuse to make her Secretary General of Disneyland. This was somehow different. Stragon's tale had a coherence that bespoke sanity if not truth. He did not wander, as the mad do; his arguments contained no abrupt shifting of gears, as Lucinda's always did. But why all this pointless fantasy?

A sharp breeze moved across the lake, etching twists and zags in the water. Pothinos fixed on the bobber, the cynosure of his patron's scheme. Occasionally Stragon pulled back on the rod, moving the bright sphere and animating the half-dead bait.

"One whole cimberfish left," Stragon continued his story, "yet I could not settle on a third wish. Wealth and eternal youth: what more does a man need? I nurtured the remaining bait as best I could, keeping it alive as a kind of insurance policy. Even after the fish died, I sought to retard its putrefaction by soaking it in alcohol. Years passed. Decades. By the time I realized what my third wish might be–*must* be–it was too late. Nothing remained but an eye. I packed the organ in ice and set off on my quest."

The bobber, still afloat, sent tendrils of light across the lake. Against his better judgment, Pothinos wondered what his own third wish might have been. The mending of his sister's mind? A Nobel Prize? Or was he darker than that–the ruin of a colleague?

"I took to haunting fishing wharfs," Stragon said. "Zoos. Circus side shows. Any place where a cimberfish might turn up. Useless. I went fishing often, dissecting whatever I caught. Empty. To catch your fondest desire, you need the right bait." He slid his wallet from his vest, removed the promised payment from his vest, and thrust it toward Pothinos. "And then, just when I had abandoned hope, your cleverness came into the world."

"I suppose that my goal," said Pothinos, taking the check, "after wealth and long life, would be for my sister to–"

"Look!" Ecstasy seized Stragon. "There!" Rising, he jammed the handle tight against his abdomen. "I've got him!" He cranked the reel backward, filling the night with the stately buzz of its bearings. "Good God, I've got him!"

Pothinos studied Rosamond. The bobber had vanished.

"Here I am!" Stragon screamed. "Right here!"

Sinewy blackness crashed out of the lake, shattering its surface like a panther diving through a mirror. A fish, but one whose anatomy–slimy body, hatchet fins–seemed merely its mouth's way of getting from one place to another.

Pothinos's intestines writhed around themselves. His brain shivered in his skull.

"I wish for it to end!" screamed Stragon. His hand moved frantically, reeling in the fetid, organic abyss, its pulpy lips, gums like rotten logs, fangs thrusting downward like stalactites. "Hear me, fish? I want it to be over!"

Through the haze of his astonishment, Pothinos apprehended his patron's pain. Over. Yes, of course, the poor bastard wanted out, no more curse of immortality, no more standing by as his loved ones marched down the cold stone road to the tomb, leaving him behind.

Relentlessly Stragon's catch cruised toward shore, its eyes stroking the darkness like beacons marking the coast of hell. Even as Pothinos drew back–what an extraordinary event! what a dazzling datum!–his patron hurled down the fishing rod and jumped into the shallows.

"Over!"

A snap, a fat spasm of movement, and the wish was complete. Bait gone. Mouth gone. Stragon gone.

⋅⋅⋅ ✤ ⋅⋅⋅

Rosamond grew still, as if a blast of winter had sealed it with ice. Pothinos stood on the silent shore, vibrating with shock, gulping down air to feed his racing heart.

Slowly he picked up Stragon's abandoned fishing rod. He turned and staggered from the scene of the ... the what? *Miracle.* The word sounded eerily correct.

Or was it just a trick? In a few seconds Stragon would be at his side, pointing at him, sniggering?

No: the Rosamond beast was truly *outré*, something that present paradigms could not accommodate; tonight Pothinos had glimpsed the universe's secret smirk, row upon row of strange teeth flashing somewhere beyond the knowable. A miracle: then he must move with deliberation. Exactly how many cimberfish cells lay back at the Institute? A hundred million? Easily. A hundred million potential wishes, each a glint in its parent's unblinking eye. No: more. He could clone the clones, clone the clones of the clones! Endless wishes, spiraling to the edge of reality like interstellar dust!

An owl's hoot blasted through the gloomy woods like a landlocked foghorn. Careful, Pothinos told himself. Take it easy. Beware the rub.

Wish-makers, he saw, traditionally committed the same error. Each used the gift to improve his own situation, and, succumbing to greed, quickly came to ruin. Ah, but suppose the wish-maker never benefited himself? Suppose all his desires went toward fashioning some separate, distant dominion? What a fine, flawless world Pothinos might make: blue skies, green continents, a marvelously complex biosphere. Yes, it could be done, the fallacy outflanked, the rub circumvented, power both absolute and uncorrupting, yes, yes, yes ...

Pothinos ran. Dawn washed across the dark sky, conjuring fir trees and brick buildings from the gloom.

Defrosting the eye was the simplest of procedures. A moment to prepare the hot plate, a moment to thaw the surrounding ice. When Pothinos reached into the puddle to remove the cimberfish's remains, Maxie strutted over and wove amid his legs as if decorating a maypole.

Pothinos pulled away, leaving the animal startled and miffed. Was this truly the right course?

Arching her back, Maxie meowed.

Yes, this was right. The age of miracles, thank God, was over. A biologist, anyone, must live in his own time.

"Make a wish, Maxie!" Pothinos shouted, and he rolled the eye across the floor toward the waiting, hungry cat.

Director's Cut

The curtain rises on the prophet MOSES, caught in the glow of a spotlight and sitting atop a mound of Dead Sea sand. The famous Tablets of the Law stick out of the dune like ears on a Mickey Mouse cap. A large rear-projection video screen hangs over Moses's head. An off-stage INTERVIEWER addresses the patriarch.

INTERVIEWER: So there we are, me and Dad and my little sister, sitting in the old Ziegfeld Theatre on 54th Street. The lights go down, the Paramount logo flashes across the screen, and then the movie comes on, Cecil B. DeMille's *The Ten Commandments*.

MOSES: What a terrific picture.

INTERVIEWER: It sure impressed me as a kid. Today I find it a bit hokey.

MOSES: Hokey? Hokey? Hell, no, Mr. DeMille was a certifiable genius.

INTERVIEWER: Is it really true the original cut ran over seven hours?

MOSES: *(grunt of assent)* No theater was willing to book the thing. The management would've had to serve dinner in the middle, like on a transcontinental flight from New York to Paris.

INTERVIEWER: I heard a rumor that some of the original rushes still exist.

MOSES: No way, Marty. You pull papyrus out by the roots and–bang–it disintegrates in a few weeks.

Moses laughs boorishly.

INTERVIEWER: In fact, I understand that those very rushes are in your possession.

MOSES: Over the past forty years, I've managed to collect bits and pieces from nearly every missing scene.

INTERVIEWER: For example?

MOSES: The Plagues of Egypt. The release prints included blood, darkness, and hail ...

An excerpt from The Ten Commandments *appears on the video screen: fiery hail clattering across the balcony of Pharaoh's palace.*

MOSES: But they were lacking some of the really interesting ones. You should've seen what Mr. DeMille did with frogs.

The screen displays two elderly, working-class Egyptian women, BAKETAMON and NELLIFER, potters by trade, sitting on the banks of the Nile River. As they speak, BAKETAMON fashions a canopic jar, NELLIFER a soup tureen.

BAKETAMON: *(addressing interviewer)* The frogs? How could I ever forget the frogs?

NELLIFER: You'd open your dresser drawer, hoping to find some clean socks and–pop–one of those little fuckers would jump in your face.

INTERVIEWER: Which plague was the worst?

BAKETAMON: The boils, I think. My skin looked like the back of the moon.

NELLIFER: The boils, are you kidding? The locusts were far worse than the boils.

BAKETAMON: The mosquitoes were pretty nasty too.

NELLIFER: And the gadflies.

BAKETAMON: And the cattle getting murrain.

NELLIFER: And the death of the firstborn. A lot of people hated that one.

BAKETAMON: Of course, it didn't touch Nelli and me.

NELLIFER: We were lucky. Our firstborns were already dead.

BAKETAMON: Mine froze solid in the hail.

NELLIFER: Mine had been suffering from chronic diarrhea since he was a month old, so when the waters became blood—zap, kid got dehydrated.

BAKETAMON: Nelli, your mind's going. It was your secondborn who died when the waters became blood. Your firstborn died in the darkness, when he accidentally drank all that turpentine.

NELLIFER: No, my secondborn got run over by a horse. It had nothing to do with religion. My third born drank the turpentine. A mother remembers these things.

INTERVIEWER: I was certain you'd be more bitter about your ordeals.

NELLIFER: Initially we thought the plagues were a bit much. We even wrote a book about it.

BAKETAMON: *When Bad Things Happen to Good Pagans.*

NELLIFER: Then we came to understand our innate depravity.

BAKETAMON: There's only one really good person in the whole universe, and that's the Lord God Jehovah.

NELLIFER: Next to Him, we're a couple of slime molds.

INTERVIEWER: Sounds as if you've converted to monotheism.

BAKETAMON: *(nodding)* We love the Lord our God with all our heart.

NELLIFER: And all our soul.

BAKETAMON: And all our might.

NELLIFER: And besides, there's no telling what He might do to us next.

BAKETAMON: Fire ants, possibly.

NELLIFER: Killer bees.

BAKETAMON: Smallpox.

NELLIFER: I got two sons left.

BAKETAMON: I'm still up a daughter.

NELLIFER: The Lord giveth.

BAKETAMON: And the Lord taketh away.

NELLIFER: Blessed be the name of the Lord.

The screen goes blank.

INTERVIEWER: When you went up on Mount Sinai, Jehovah offered you a lot more than the Decalogue.

MOSES: *(displays excised footage)* Mr. DeMille shot everything, all six hundred and twelve laws. First to go were the prescriptions concerning slavery–the protocols for selling your daughter and so on. Unfortunately, those cuts reduced the running time a mere eight minutes.

An excerpt from The Ten Commandments *appears on the screen: God's animated forefinger etching the Decalogue onto the face of Sinai, while Charlton Heston watches with a mixture of awe, fascination, and incredulity. As the last rule is carved—THOU SHALT NOT COVET—the frame suddenly freezes.*

GOD: *(voice-over)* Now for the details. *(beat)* When you go to war against your enemies and the Lord your God delivers them into your power, if you see a beautiful woman among the prisoners and find her desirable, you may make her your wife.

INTERVIEWER: I have to admire Mr. DeMille for using something like that. Deuteronomy 21:10, right?

MOSES: He was a gutsier filmmaker than his

detractors imagine.

GOD: *(voice-over)* When two men are fighting together, if the wife of one intervenes to protect her husband by putting out her hand and seizing the other by the private parts, you shall cut off her hand and show no pity.

INTERVIEWER: Private parts?

MOSES: The original Hebrew is less euphemistic. Deuteronomy 25:11.

GOD: *(voice-over)* If a man has a stubborn and rebellious son, his father and mother shall bring him out to the elders of the town, and all his fellow citizens shall stone the son to death.

MOSES: Deuteronomy 21:18-21.

INTERVIEWER: And here I'd always thought DeMille was afraid of controversy.

MOSES: One ballsy mogul, Marty.

The screen goes blank.

INTERVIEWER: After the giving of the Law, *The Ten Commandments* jumps rather abruptly to the Children of Israel entering the Promised Land.

MOSES: Forty years of wandering in the wilderness, and poor Mr. DeMille had to edit out thirty-nine of them. The Book of Numbers ended up on the cutting room floor.

INTERVIEWER: He actually filmed those episodes?

MOSES: *(nodding)* The Lord giving my sister leprosy, causing the earth to swallow up Dathan, striking down the Israelites who disparaged Canaan, firebombing the ones who complained at Hormah, sending serpents against those who grumbled on the road from Mount Hor, visiting a plague on everybody who backslid at Peor ...

INTERVIEWER: Damn theater chains. They think they own the world.

MOSES: I especially hated to lose that stirring speech I made to my generals following the subjugation of the Midianites.

INTERVIEWER: Would you like to deliver it now, for the record?

MOSES: Sure would, Marty. Ready? Here goes. Numbers 31:15-18. *(clears throat)* Why have you spared the life of all the women? These were the very ones who perverted the sons of Israel! Kill all the male children! Kill also all the women who have slept with a man! Spare the lives only of the young girls who have not slept with a man, and take them for yourselves!

INTERVIEWER: Do you suppose we'll ever see the version of *The Ten Commandments* that Mr. DeMille intended?

MOSES: Only yesterday I was talking to some nice folks down at the National Endowment for the Arts. They're willing to kick in three million for a restoration.

INTERVIEWER: A worthy cause.

MOSES: The worthiest, Marty. Believe me, there's justice in this old world. You simply have to wait for it.

Curtain.

Auspicious Eggs

Father Cornelius Dennis Monaghan of Charlestown Parish, Connie to his friends, sets down the Styrofoam chalice, turns from the corrugated cardboard altar, and approaches the two young women standing by the resin baptismal font. The font is six-sided and encrusted with saints, like a gigantic hex nut forged for some obscure yet holy purpose, but its most impressive feature is its portability. Hardly a month passes in which Connie doesn't drive the vessel across town, bear it into some wretched hovel, and confer immortality on a newborn whose parents have grown too feeble to leave home.

"Merribell, right?" asks Connie, pointing to the baby on his left.

Wedged in the crook of her mother's arm, the infant wriggles and howls. "No—Madeleine," Angela mumbles. Connie has known Angela Dunfey all her life, and he still remembers the seraphic glow that beamed from her face when she first received the Sacrament of Holy Communion. Today she boasts no such glow. Her cheeks and brow appear tarnished, like iron corroded by the Greenhouse Deluge, and her spine curls with a torsion more commonly seen in women three times her age. "Merribell's over here." Angela raises her free hand and gestures toward her cousin Lorna, who is balancing Madeleine's twin sister atop her gravid belly. Will Lorna Dunfey, Connie wonders, also give birth to twins? The phenomenon, he has heard, runs in families.

Touching the sleeve of Angela's frayed blue sweater, the priest addresses her in a voice that travels clear across the nave. "Have these children received the Sacrament of Reproductive Potential Assessment?"

The parishioner shifts a nugget of chewing gum from her left cheek to her right. "Y-yes," she says at last.

Henry Shaw, the pale altar boy, his face abloom with acne, hands the priest a parchment sheet stamped with the Seal of the Boston Isle Archdiocese. A pair of signatures adorns the margin, verifying that two ecclesiastical representatives have legitimized the birth. Connie instantly recognizes the illegible hand of Archbishop Xallibos. Below lie the bold loops and assured serifs of a Friar James Wolfe, M.D., doubtless the man who drew the blood.

Madeleine Dunfey, Connie reads. *Left ovary: 315 primordial follicles. Right ovary: 340 primordial follicles.* A spasm of despair passes through the priest. The egg-cell count for each organ should be 180,000 at least. It's a verdict of infertility, no possible appeal, no imaginable reprieve.

With an efficiency bordering on effrontery, Henry Shaw offers Connie a second parchment sheet.

Merribell Dunfey. Left ovary: 290 primordial follicles. Right ovary: 310 primordial follicles. The priest is not surprised. What sense would there be in God's withholding the power of procreation from one twin but not the other? Connie now needs only to receive these barren sisters, apply the sacred rites, and furtively pray that the Eighth Lateran Council was indeed guided by the Holy Spirit when it undertook to bring the baptismal process into the age of testable destinies and ovarian surveillance.

He holds out his hands, withered palms up, a posture he maintains as Angela surrenders Madeleine, reaches under the baby's christening gown, and unhooks both diaper pins. The mossy odor of fresh urine wafts into the Church of the Immediate Conception. Sighing profoundly, Angela hands the sopping diaper to her cousin.

"Bless these waters, O Lord," says Connie, spotting his ancient face in the consecrated fluid, "that they might grant these sinners the gift of life everlasting." Turning from the vessel, he presents Madeleine to his ragged flock, over three hundred natural-born Catholics–sixth-generation Irish, mostly, plus a smattering of Portuguese, Italians, and Croats–interspersed with two dozen recent converts of Korean and Vietnamese extraction: a congregation bound together, he'll admit, not so much by religious conviction as by shared destitution. "Dearly beloved, forasmuch as all humans enter the world in a state of depravity, and forasmuch as they cannot know the grace of our Lord except they be born anew of water, I beseech you to call upon God the

Father that, through these baptisms, Madeleine and Merribell Dunfey may gain the divine kingdom." Connie faces his trembling parishioner. "Angela Dunfey, do you believe, by God's word, that children who are baptized, dying before they commit any actual evil, will be saved?"

Her "Yes" is begrudging and clipped.

Like a scrivener replenishing his pen at an inkwell, Connie dips his thumb into the font. "Angela Dunfey, name this child of yours."

"M-M-Madeleine Eileen Dunfey."

"We welcome this sinner, Madeleine Eileen Dunfey, into the mystical body of Christ"–with his wet thumb Connie traces a plus sign on the infant's forehead–"and do mark her with the Sign of the Cross."

Unraveling Madeleine from her christening gown, Connie fixes on the waters. They are preternaturally still–as calm and quiet as the Sea of Galilee after the Savior rebuked the winds. For many years the priest wondered why Christ hadn't returned on the eve of the Greenhouse Deluge, dispersing the hydrocarbon vapors with a wave of his hand, ending global warming with a heavenward wink, but recently Connie has come to feel that divine intervention entails protocols past human ken.

He contemplates his reflected countenance. Nothing about it–not the tiny eyes, thin lips, hawk's beak of a nose–pleases him. Now he begins the immersion, sinking Madeleine Dunfey to her skullcap ... her ears ... cheeks ... mouth ... eyes.

"No!" screams Angela.

As the baby's nose goes under, mute cries spurt from her lips: bubbles inflated with bewilderment and pain. "Madeleine Dunfey," Connie intones, holding the infant down, "I baptize you in the name of the Father, and of the Son, and of the Holy Ghost." The bubbles break the surface. The fluid pours into the infant's lungs. Her silent screams cease, but she still puts up a fight.

"No! Please! No!"

A full minute passes, marked by the rhythmic shuffling of the congregation and the choked sobs of the mother. A second minute–a third–and finally the body stops moving, a mere husk, no longer home to Madeleine Dunfey's indestructible soul.

"No!"

The Sacrament of Terminal Baptism, Connie knows, is rooted in both logic and history. Even today, he can recite verbatim the preamble to the Eighth Lateran Council's *Pastoral Letter on the*

113

Rights of the Unconceived. ("Throughout her early years, Holy Mother Church tirelessly defended the Rights of the Born. Then, as the iniquitous institution of abortion spread across Western Europe and North America, she undertook to secure the Rights of the Unborn. Now, as a new era dawns for the Church and her servants, she must make even greater efforts to propagate the gift of life everlasting, championing the Rights of the Unconceived through a Doctrine of Affirmative Fertility.") The subsequent sentence has always given Connie pause. It stopped him when he was a seminarian. It stops him today. ("This Council therefore avers that, during a period such as that in which we find ourselves, when God has elected to discipline our species through a Greenhouse Deluge and its concomitant privations, a society can commit no greater crime against the future than to squander provender on individuals congenitally incapable of procreation.") Quite so. Indeed. And yet Connie has never performed a terminal baptism without misgivings.

He scans the faithful. Valerie Gallogher, his nephews' zaftig kindergarten teacher, seems on the verge of tears. Keye Sung frowns. Teresa Curtoni shudders. Michael Hines moans softly. Stephen O'Rourke and his wife both wince.

"We give thanks, most merciful Father"–Connie lifts the corpse from the water–"that it pleases you to regenerate this infant and take her unto your bosom." Placing the dripping flesh on the altar, he leans toward Lorna Dunfey and lays his palm on Merribell's brow. "Angela Dunfey, name this child of yours."

"M-M-Merribell S-Siobhan ..." With a sharp reptilian hiss, Angela wrests Merribell from her cousin and pulls the infant to her breast. "Merribell Siobhan Dunfey!"

The priest steps forward, caressing the wisp of tawny hair sprouting from Merribell's cranium. "We welcome this sinner–"

Angela whirls around and, still sheltering her baby, leaps from the podium to the aisle–the very aisle down which Connie hopes one day to see her parade in prelude to receiving the Sacrament of Qualified Monogamy.

"Stop!" cries Connie.

"Angela!" shouts Lorna.

"No!" yells the altar boy.

For someone who has recently given birth to twins, Angela is amazingly spry, rushing pell-mell past the stupefied congregation and straight through the narthex.

"Please!" screams Connie.

But already she is out the door, bearing her unsaved daughter into the teeming streets of Boston Isle.

→ ⊕ ←

At 8:17 P.M., Eastern Standard Time, Stephen O'Rourke's fertility reaches its weekly peak. The dial on his wrist tells him so, buzzing like a tortured hornet as he scrubs his teeth with baking soda. *Skreee*, says the sperm counter, reminding Stephen of his ineluctable duty. *Skreee, skreee*: go find us an egg.

He pauses in the middle of a brush stroke and, without bothering to rinse his mouth, strides into the bedroom.

Kate lies on the sagging mattress, smoking an unfiltered cigarette as she balances her nightly dose of iced Arbutus rum on her stomach. Baby Malcolm cuddles against his mother, gums fastened onto her left nipple. She stares at the far wall, where the cracked and scabrous plaster frames the video monitor, its screen displaying the regular Sunday night broadcast of *Keep Those Kiddies Coming*. Archbishop Xallibos, seated, dominates a TV studio appointed like a day-care center: stuffed animals, changing table, brightly colored alphabet letters. Preschoolers crawl across the prelate's Falstaffian body, sliding down his thighs and swinging from his arms as if he is a piece of playground equipment.

"Did you know that a single act of onanism kills up to four hundred million babies in a matter of seconds?" asks Xallibos from the monitor. "As Jesus remarks in the Gospel According to Saint Andrew, 'Masturbation is murder.'"

Stephen coughs. "I don't suppose you're ..."

His wife thrusts her index finger against her pursed lips. Even when engaged in shutting him out, she still looks beautiful to Stephen. Her huge eyes and high cheekbones, her elegant swanlike neck. "Shhh–"

"Please check," says Stephen, swallowing baking soda.

Kate raises her bony wrist and glances at her ovulation gauge. "Not for three days. Maybe four."

"Damn."

He loves her so dearly. He wants her so much–no less now than when they received the Sacrament of Qualified Monogamy. It's fine to have a connubial conversation, but when you utterly adore your wife, when you crave to comprehend her beyond all others, you need to speak in flesh as well.

115

"Will anyone deny that Hell's hottest quadrant is reserved for those who violate the rights of the unconceived?" asks Xallibos, playing peekaboo with a cherubic toddler. "Who will dispute that contraception, casual sex, and nocturnal emissions place their perpetrators on a one-way cruise to Perdition?"

"Honey, I have to ask you something," says Stephen.

"Shhh–"

"That young woman at Mass this morning, the one who ran away ..."

"She went crazy because it was twins." Kate slurps down her remaining rum. The ice fragments clink against each other. "If it'd been just the one, she probably could've coped."

"Well, yes, of course," says Stephen, gesturing toward Baby Malcolm. "But suppose one of *your* newborns ..."

"Heaven is forever, Stephen," says Kate, filling her mouth with ice, "and Hell is just as long." She chews, her molars grinding the ice. Dribbles of rum-tinted water spill from her lips. "You'd better get to church."

"Farewell, friends," says Xallibos as the theme music swells. He dandles a Korean three-year-old on his knee. "And keep those kiddies coming!"

The path to the front door takes Stephen through the cramped and fetid living room–functionally the nursery. All is quiet, all is well. The fourteen children, one for every other year of Kate's post-pubescence, sleep soundly. Nine-year-old Roger is quite likely his, product of the time Stephen and Kate got their cycles in synch; the boy boasts Stephen's curly blond hair and riveting green eyes. Difficult as it is, Stephen refuses to accord Roger any special treatment–no private trips to the frog pond, no second candy cane at Christmas. A good stepfather didn't indulge in favoritism.

Stephen pulls on his mended galoshes, fingerless gloves, and torn pea jacket. Ambling out of the apartment, he joins the knot of morose pedestrians as they shuffle along Winthrop Street. A fog descends, a steady rain falls: reverberations from the Deluge. Pushed by expectant mothers, dozens of shabby, black-hooded baby buggies squeak mournfully down the asphalt. The sidewalks belong to adolescent girls, gang after gang, gossiping among themselves and stomping on puddles as they show off their pregnancies like Olympic medals.

Besmirched by two decades of wind and drizzle, a limestone Madonna stands outside the Church of the Immediate Conception.

Her expression lies somewhere between a smile and a smirk. Stephen climbs the steps, enters the narthex, removes his gloves, and, dipping his fingertips into the nearest font, decorates the air with the Sign of the Cross.

Every city, Stephen teaches his students at Cardinal Dougherty High School, boasts its own personality. Extroverted Rio, pessimistic Prague, paranoid New York. And Boston Isle? What sort of psyche inhabits the Hub and its surrounding reefs? Schizoid, Stephen tells them. Split. The Boston that battled slavery and stoked the fires beneath the American melting pot was the same Boston that massacred the Pequots and sent witchfinders to Salem. But here, now, which side of the city is emergent? The bright one, Stephen decides, picturing the hundreds of heaven-bound souls who each day exit Boston's innumerable wombs, flowing forth like the bubbles that so recently streamed from Madeleine Dunfey's lips.

Blessing the Virgin's name, he descends the concrete stairs to the copulatorium. A hundred votive candles pierce the darkness. The briny scent of incipient immortality suffuses the air. In the far corner, a CD player screeches out the Apostolic Succession doing their famous rendition of "Ave Maria."

The Sacrament of Extramarital Intercourse has always reminded Stephen of a junior high prom. Girls strung along one side of the room, boys along the other, gyrating couples in the center. He takes his place in the line of males, removes his jacket, shirt, trousers, and underclothes, and hangs them on the nearest pegs. He stares through the gloom, locking eyes with Roger's old kindergarten teacher, Valerie Gallogher, a robust thirtyish woman whose incandescent red hair spills all the way to her hips. Grimly they saunter toward each other, following the pathway formed by the mattresses, until they meet amid the morass of writhing soulmakers.

"You're Roger Mulcanny's stepfather, aren't you?" asks the ovulating teacher.

"Father, quite possibly. Stephen O'Rourke. And you're Miss Gallogher, right?"

"Call me Valerie."

"Stephen."

He glances around, noting to his infinite relief that he recognizes no one. Sooner or later, he knows, a familiar young face will appear at the copulatorium, a notion that never fails to make him wince. How could he possibly explicate the Boston Massacre to a boy who'd recently beheld him in the procreative act? How could he render the Battle of Lexington lucid to a girl whose egg he'd attempted to quicken on the previous night?

For ten minutes he and Valerie make small talk, most of it issuing from Stephen, as was proper. Should the coming sacrament prove fruitful, the resultant child will want to know about the handful of men with whom his mother connected during the relevant ovulation. (Beatrice, Claude, Tommy, Laura, Yolanda, Willy, and the others were forever grilling Kate for facts about their possible progenitors.) Stephen tells Valerie about the time his students gave him a surprise birthday party. He describes his rock collection. He mentions his skill at trapping the singularly elusive species of rat that inhabits Charlestown Parish.

"I have a talent too," says Valerie, inserting a coppery braid into her mouth. Her areolas seem to be staring at him.

"Roger thought you were a terrific teacher."

"No—something else." Valerie tugs absently on her ovulation gauge. "A person twitches his lips a certain way, and I know what he's feeling. He darts his eyes in an odd manner—I sense the drift of his thoughts." She lowers her voice. "I watched you during the baptism this morning. Your reaction would've angered the archbishop—am I right?"

Stephen looks at his bare toes. Odd that a copulatorium partner should be demanding such intimacy of him.

"Am I?" Valerie persists, sliding her index finger along her large, concave belly-button.

Fear rushes through Stephen. Does this woman work for the Immortality Corps? If his answer smacks of heresy, will she arrest him on the spot?

"Well, Stephen? Would the archbishop have been angry?"

"Perhaps," he confesses. In his mind he sees Madeleine Dunfey's submerged mouth, bubble following bubble like beads strung along a rosary.

"There's no microphone in my navel," Valerie asserts, alluding to a common Immortality Corps ploy. "I'm not a spy."

"Never said you were."

"You were thinking it. I could tell by the cant of your eyebrows." She kisses him on the mouth, deeply, wetly. "Did Roger ever learn to hold his pencil correctly?"

"'Fraid not."

"Too bad."

At last the mattress to Stephen's left becomes free, and they climb on top and begin reifying the Doctrine of Affirmative Fertility. The candle flames look like spear points. Stephen closes his eyes, but the effect is merely to intensify the fact that he's here. The liquid squeal of flesh against flesh grows louder, the odor of hot paraffin and warm semen more pungent. For a few seconds he manages to convince himself that the woman beneath him is Kate, but the illusion proves as tenuous as the surrounding wax.

When the sacrament is accomplished, Valerie says, "I have something for you. A gift."

"What's the occasion?"

"Saint Patrick's Day is less than a week away."

"Since when is that a time for gifts?"

Instead of answering, she strolls to her side of the room, rummages through her tangled garments, and returns holding a pressed flower sealed in plastic.

"Think of it as a ticket," she whispers, lifting Stephen's shirt from its peg and slipping the blossom inside the pocket.

"To where?"

Valerie holds an erect index finger to her lips. "We'll know when we get there."

Stephen gulps audibly. Sweat collects beneath his sperm counter. Only fools considered fleeing Boston Isle. Only lunatics risked the retributions meted out by the Corps. Displayed every Sunday night on *Keep Those Kiddies Coming*, the classic images–men submitting to sperm siphons, women locked in the rapacious embrace of artificial inseminators–haunt every parishioner's imagination, instilling the same levels of dread as Spinelli's sculpture of the archangel Chamuel strangling David Hume. There are rumors, of course, unconfirmable accounts of parishioners who'd outmaneuvered the patrol boats and escaped to Québec Cay, Seattle Reef, or the Texas Archipelago. But to credit such tales was itself a kind of sin, jeopardizing your slot in Paradise as surely as if you'd denied the unconceived their rights.

"Tell me something, Stephen." Valerie straps herself into her bra. "You're a history teacher. Did Saint Patrick really drive the snakes out of Ireland, or is that just a legend?"

"I'm sure it never happened literally," says Stephen. "I suppose it could be true in some mythic sense."

"It's about penises, isn't it?" says Valerie, dissolving into the darkness. "It's about how our saints have always been hostile to cocks."

119

JAMES MORROW

→ ⊕ ←

Although Harbor Authority Tower was designed to house the merchant-shipping aristocracy on whose ambitions the decrepit Boston economy still depended, the building's form, Connie now realizes, perfectly fits its new, supplemental function: sheltering the offices, courts, and archives of the archdiocese. As he lifts his gaze along the soaring facade, Connie thinks of sacred shapes–of steeples and vaulted windows, of Sinai and Zion, of Jacob's Ladder and hands pressed together in prayer. Perhaps it's all as God wants, he muses, flashing his ecclesiastical pass to the guard. Perhaps there's nothing wrong with commerce and grace being transacted within the same walls.

Connie has seen Archbishop Xallibos in person only once before, five years earlier, when the stately prelate appeared as an "honorary Irishman" in Charlestown Parish's annual Saint Patrick's Day Parade. Standing on the sidewalk, Connie observed Xallibos gliding down Lynde Street atop a huge motorized shamrock. The archbishop looked impressive then, and he looks impressive now–six-foot-four at least, Connie calculates, and not an ounce under three hundred pounds. His eyes are as red as a lab rat's.

"Father Cornelius Dennis Monaghan," the priest begins, following the custom whereby a visitor to an archbishop's chambers initiates the interview by naming himself.

"Come forward, Father Cornelius Dennis Monaghan."

Connie starts into the office, boots clacking on the polished bronze floor. Xallibos steps out from behind his desk, a glistery cube hewn from black marble.

"Charlestown Parish holds a special place in my affections," says the archbishop. "What brings you to this part of town?"

Connie fidgets, shifting first left, then right, until his face lies mirrored in the hubcap-size Saint Cyril medallion adorning Xallibos's chest. "My soul is in torment, Your Grace."

"'Torment.' Weighty word."

"I can find no other. Last Tuesday I laid a two-week-old infant to rest."

"Terminal baptism?"

Connie ponders his reflection. It is wrinkled and deflated, like a helium balloon purchased at a carnival long gone. "My eighth."

"I know how you feel. After I dispatched my first infertile–no left

120

testicle, right one shriveled beyond repair–I got no sleep for a week." Eyes glowing like molten rubies, Xallibos gazes directly at Connie. "Where did you attend seminary?"

"Isle of Denver."

"And on the Isle of Denver did they teach you that there are in fact two Churches, one invisible and eternal, the other–"

"Temporal and finite."

"Then they also taught you that the latter Church is empowered to revise its rites according to the imperatives of the age." The archbishop's stare grows brighter, hotter, purer. "Do you doubt that present privations compel us to arrange early immortality for those who cannot secure the rights of the unconceived?"

"The problem is that the infant I immortalized has a twin." Connie swallows nervously. "Her mother stole her away before I could perform the second baptism."

"Stole her away?"

"She fled in the middle of the sacrament."

"And the second child is likewise arid?"

"Left ovary, two hundred ninety primordials. Right ovary, three hundred ten."

"Lord ..." A high whistle issues from the archbishop, like water vapor escaping a tea kettle. "Does she intend to quit the island?"

"I certainly hope not, Your Grace," says the priest, wincing at the thought. "She probably has no immediate plans beyond protecting her baby and trying to–"

Connie cuts himself off, intimidated by the sudden arrival of a roly-poly man in a white hooded robe.

"Friar James Wolfe, M.D.," says the monk.

"Come forward, Friar Doctor James Wolfe," says Xallibos.

"It would be well if you validated this posthaste." James Wolfe draws a parchment sheet from his robe and lays it on the archbishop's desk. Connie steals a glance at the report, hoping to learn the baby's fertility quotient, but the relevant statistics are too faint. "The priest in question, he's celebrating Mass in"–sliding a loose sleeve upward, James Wolfe consults his wristwatch–"less than an hour. He's all the way over in Brookline."

Striding back to his desk, the archbishop yanks a silver fountain pen from its holder and decorates the parchment with his famous spidery signature.

"*Dominus vobiscum*, Friar Doctor Wolfe," he says, handing over

121

JAMES MORROW

the document.

As Wolfe rushes out of the office, Xallibos steps so close to Connie that his nostrils fill with the archbishop's lemon-scented aftershave lotion.

"That man never has any fun," says Xallibos, pointing toward the vanishing friar. "What fun do you have, Father Monaghan?"

"Fun, Your Grace?"

"Do you eat ice cream? Follow the fortunes of the Celtics?" He pronounces "Celtics" with the hard *C* mandated by the Seventh Lateran Council.

Connie inhales a hearty quantity of citrus fumes. "I bake."

"Bake? Bake what? Bread?"

"Cookies, Your Grace. Brownies, cheesecake, pies. For the Feast of the Nativity, I make gingerbread magi."

"Wonderful. I like my priests to have fun. Listen, no matter what, the rite must be performed. If Angela Dunfey won't come to you, then you must go to her."

"She'll simply run away again."

"Perhaps so, perhaps not. I have great faith in you, Father Cornelius Dennis Monaghan."

"More than I have in myself," says the priest, biting his inner cheeks so hard that his eyes fill with tears.

→ ⊕ ←

"No," says Kate for the third time that night.

"Yes," insists Stephen, savoring the dual satisfactions of Kate's thigh beneath his palm and Arbutus rum washing through his brain.

Pinching her cigarette in one hand, Kate strokes Baby Malcolm's forehead with the other, lulling him to sleep. "It's wicked," she protests, placing Malcolm on the rug beside the bed. "A crime against the future."

Stephen grabs the Arbutus bottle, pours himself another glass, and, adding a measure of Dr. Pepper, takes a greedy gulp. He sets the bottle back on the nightstand, next to Valerie Gallogher's enigmatic flower.

"Screw the unconceived," he says, throwing himself atop his wife.

On Friday he'd shown the blossom to Gail Whittington, Dougherty High School's smartest science teacher, but her verdict had proved unenlightening. *Epigaea repens*, "trailing arbutus," a species with at least two claims to fame: it is the state flower of the Massachusetts

122

Archipelago, and it has lent its name to the very brand of alcohol Stephen now consumes.

"No," says Kate once again. She drops her cigarette on the floor, crushes it with her shoe, and wraps her arms around him. "I'm not ovulating," she avers, forcing her stiff and slippery tongue into the depths of his mouth. "Your sperm aren't ..."

"Last night, the Holy Father received a vision," Xallibos announces from the video monitor. "Pictures straight from Satan's flaming domain. Hell is a fact, friends. It's as real as a stubbed toe."

Stephen whips off Kate's chemise with all the dexterity of Father Monaghan removing a christening gown. The rum, of course, has much to do with their mutual willingness (four glasses each, only mildly diluted with Dr. Pepper), but beyond the Arbutus the two of them have truly earned this moment. Neither has ever skipped Mass. Neither has ever missed a Sacrament of Extramarital Intercourse. And while any act of nonconceptual love technically lay beyond the Church's powers of absolution, surely Christ would forgive them a solitary lapse. And so they go at it, this sterile union, this forbidden fruitlessness, this coupling from which no soul can come.

"Hedonists dissolving in vats of molten sulfur," says Xallibos.

The bedroom door squeals open. One of Kate's middle children, Beatrice, a gaunt six-year-old with flaking skin, enters holding a rude toy boat whittled from a hunk of bark.

"Look what I made in school yesterday!"

"We're busy," says Kate, pulling the tattered muslin sheet over her nakedness.

"Do you like my boat, Stephen?" asks Beatrice.

He slams a pillow atop his groin. "Lovely, dear."

"Go back to bed," Kate commands her daughter.

"Onanists drowning in lakes of boiling semen," says Xallibos.

Beatrice fixes Stephen with her receding eyes. "Can we sail it tomorrow on Parson's Pond?"

"Certainly. Of course. Please go away."

"Just you and me, right, Stephen? Not Claude or Tommy or Yolanda or *anybody*."

"Flaying machines," says Xallibos, "peeling the damned like ripe bananas."

"Do you want a spanking?" seethes Kate. "That's exactly what you're going to get, young lady, the worst spanking of your whole life!"

The child issues an elaborate shrug and strides off in a huff.

"I love you," says Stephen, removing the pillow from his privates like a chef lifting the lid from a stew pot.

Again they press together, throwing all they have into it, every limb and gland and orifice, no holds barred, no positions banned.

"Unpardonable," Kate groans.

"Unpardonable," Stephen agrees. He's never been so excited. His entire body is an appendage to his loins.

"We'll be damned," she says.

"Forever," he echoes.

"Kiss me," she commands.

"Farewell, friends," says Xallibos. "And keep those kiddies coming!"

→ ⊕ ←

Wrestling the baptismal font from the trunk of his car, Connie ponders the vessel's resemblance to a birdbath—a place, he muses, for pious sparrows to accomplish their avian ablutions. As he sets the vessel on his shoulder and starts away, its edges digging into his flesh, a different metaphor suggests itself. But if the font is Connie's Cross, and Constitution Road his Via Dolorosa, where does that leave his upcoming mission to Angela Dunfey? Is he about to perform some mysterious act of vicarious atonement?

"Morning, Father."

He slips the font from his shoulder, standing it up upright beside a fire hydrant. His parishioner Valerie Gallogher weaves amid the mob, dressed in a threadbare woolen parka.

"Far to go?" she asks brightly.

"End of the block."

"Want help?"

"I need the exercise."

Valerie extends her arm and they shake hands, mitten clinging to mitten. "Made any special plans for Saint Patrick's Day?"

"I'm going to bake shamrock cookies."

"Green?"

"Can't afford food coloring."

"I think I've got some green—you're welcome to it. Who's at the end of the block?"

"Angela Dunfey."

A shadow flits across Valerie's face. "And her daughter?"

"Yes," moans Connie. His throat constricts. "Her daughter."

Valerie lays a sympathetic hand on his arm. "If I don't have green, we can probably fake it."

"Oh, Valerie, Valerie–I wish I'd never taken Holy Orders."

"We'll mix yellow with orange. I'm sorry, Father."

"I wish this cup would pass."

"I mean yellow with blue."

Connie loops his arms around the font, embracing it as he might a frightened child. "Stay with me."

Together they walk through the serrated March air and, reaching the Warren Avenue intersection, enter the tumbledown pile of bricks labeled No. 47. The foyer is as dim as a crypt. Switching on his penlight, Connie holds it aloft until he discerns the label *Angela Dunfey* glued to a dented mailbox. He begins the climb to apartment 8-C, his parishioner right behind. On the third landing, Connie stops to catch his breath. On the sixth, he puts down the font. Valerie wipes his brow with her parka sleeve. She takes up the font, and the two of them resume their ascent.

Angela Dunfey's door is wormy, cracked, and hanging by one hinge. The mere act of knocking swings it open.

They find themselves in the kitchen–a small musty space that would have felt claustrophobic were it not so sparely furnished. A saucepan hangs over the stove; a frying pan sits atop the icebox; the floor is a mottle of splinters, tar paper, and leprous shards of linoleum. Valerie sets the font next to the sink. The basin in which Angela Dunfey washes her dishes, Connie notes, is actually smaller than the one in which the Church of the Immediate Conception immortalizes infertiles.

He tiptoes into the bedroom. His parishioner sleeps soundly, her terrycloth bathrobe parted down the middle to accommodate her groggy, nursing infant; milk trickles from her breasts, streaking her belly with white rivulets. He must move now, quickly and deliberately, so there'll be no struggle, no melodramatic replay of 1 Kings 3:26, the desperate whore trying to tear her baby away from Solomon's swordsman.

Inhaling slowly, Connie leans toward the mattress and, with the dexterity of a weasel extracting the innards from an eggshell, slides the barren baby free and carries her into the kitchen.

Beside the icebox Valerie sits glowering on a wobbly three-legged stool.

"Dearly beloved, forasmuch as all humans enter the world in a state of depravity," Connie whispers, casting a wary eye on Valerie, "and forasmuch as they cannot know the grace of our Lord except they be born anew of water"–he places the infant on the floor near Valerie's feet–"I beseech you to call upon God the Father that, through this baptism, Merribell Dunfey may gain the divine kingdom."

"Don't beseech *me*," snaps Valerie.

Connie fills the saucepan, dumps the water into the font, and returns to the sink for another load–not exactly holy water, he muses, not remotely chrism, but presumably not typhoidal either, the best the under-budgeted Boston Water Authority has to offer. He deposits the load, then fetches another.

A wide, milky yawn twists Merribell's face, but she does not cry out.

At last the vessel is ready. "Bless these waters, O Lord, that they might grant this sinner the gift of life everlasting."

Dropping to his knees, Connie begins removing the infant's diaper. The first pin comes out easily. As he pops the second, the tip catches the ball of his thumb. Crown of thorns, he decides, feeling the sting, seeing the blood.

He bears the naked infant to the font. Wetting his punctured thumb, he touches Merribell's brow and draws the sacred plus sign with a mixture of blood and water. "We receive this sinner unto the mystical body of Christ, and do mark her with the Sign of the Cross."

He begins the immersion. Skullcap. Ears. Cheeks. Mouth. Eyes. O Lord, what a monstrous trust, this power to underwrite a person's soul. "Merribell Dunfey, I baptize you in the name of the Father ..."

→ ⊕ ←

Now comes the nausea, excavating Stephen's alimentary canal as he kneels before the porcelain toilet bowl. His guilt pours forth in a searing flood–acidic strands of cabbage, caustic lumps of potato, glutinous strings of bile. Yet these pains are nothing, he knows, compared with what he'll experience on passing from this world to the next.

Drained, he stumbles toward the bedroom. Somehow Kate has bundled the older children off to school before collapsing on the floor alongside the baby. She shivers with remorse. Shrieks and giggles pour from the nursery: the preschoolers engaged in a raucous game of Blind Man's Bluff.

"Flaying machines," she mutters. Her tone is beaten, bloodless. She lights a cigarette. "Peeling the damned like ..."

Will more rum help, Stephen wonders, or merely make them sicker? He extends his arm. Passing over the nightstand, his fingers touch a box of aspirin, brush the preserved *Epigaea repens*, and curl around the neck of the half-full Arbutus bottle. A ruddy cockroach scurries across the doily.

"I kept Willy home today," says Kate, taking a drag. "He says his stomach hurts."

As he raises the bottle, Stephen realizes for the first time that the label contains a block of type headed "The Story of Trailing Arbutus." "His stomach *always* hurts." He studies the breezy little paragraph.

"I think he's telling the truth."

Epigaea repens. Trailing arbutus. Mayflower. And suddenly everything is clear.

"What's today's date?" asks Stephen.

"Sixteenth."

"March sixteenth?"

"Yeah."

"Then tomorrow's Saint Patrick's Day."

"So what?"

"Tomorrow's Saint Patrick's Day"—like an auctioneer accepting a final bid, Stephen slams the bottle onto the nightstand—"and Valerie Gallogher will be leaving Boston Isle."

"Roger's old teacher? Leaving?"

"Leaving." Snatching up the preserved flower, he dangles it before his wife. "Leaving ..."

→ ⊕ ←

"... and of the Son," says Connie, raising the sputtering infant from the water, "and of the Holy Ghost."

Merribell Dunfey screeches and squirms. She's slippery as a bar of soap. Connie manages to wrap her in a dish towel and shove her into Valerie's arms.

"Let me tell you who you are," she says.

"Father Cornelius Dennis Monaghan of Charlestown Parish."

"You're a tired and bewildered pilgrim, Father. You're a weary wayfarer like myself."

Dribbling milk, Angela Dunfey staggers into the kitchen. Seeing her priest, she recoils. Her mouth flies open, and a howl rushes out, a cry such as Connie imagines the damned spew forth while rotating on the spits of Perdition. "Not her too! Not Merribell! No!"

"Your baby's all right," says Valerie.

Connie clasps his hands together, fingers knotted in agony and supplication. He stoops. His knees hit the floor, crashing against the fractured linoleum. "Please," he groans.

Angela plucks Merribell from Valerie and affixes the squalling baby to her nipple. "Oh, Merribell, Merribell ..."

"Please." Connie's voice is hoarse and jagged, as if he's been shot in the larynx. "Please ... please," he beseeches. Tears roll from his eyes, tickling his cheeks as they fall.

"It's not *her* job to absolve you," says Valerie.

Connie snuffles the mucus back into his nose. "I know."

"The boat leaves tomorrow."

"Boat?" Connie runs his sleeve across his face, blotting his tears.

"A rescue vessel," his parishioner explains. Sliding her hands beneath his armpits, she raises him inch by inch to his feet. "Rather like Noah's Ark."

"Mommy, I want to go home."

"Tell that to your stepfather."

"It's cold."

"I know, sweetheart."

"And dark."

"Try to be patient."

"Mommy, my stomach hurts."

"I'm sorry."

"My head too."

"You want an aspirin?"

"I want to go home."

Is this a mistake? wonders Stephen. Shouldn't they all be in bed right now instead of tromping around in this nocturnal mist, risking flu and possibly pneumonia? And yet he has faith. Somewhere in the labyrinthine reaches of the Hoosac Docks, amid the tang of salt air and the stink of rotting cod, a ship awaits.

Guiding his wife and stepchildren down Pier 7, he studies the possibilities–the scows and barges, the tugs and trawlers, the reefers and bulk carriers. Gulls and gannets hover above the wharfs, squawking their chronic disapproval of the world. Across the channel, lit by a sodium-vapor searchlight, the *U.S. Constitution* bobs in her customary berth beside Charlestown Navy Yard.

"What're we doing here, anyway?" asks Beatrice.

"Your stepfather gets these notions in his head." Kate presses the baby tight against her chest, shielding him from the sea breeze.

"What's the *name* of the boat?" asks Roger.

"*Mayflower*," answers Stephen.

Epigaea repens, trailing arbutus, mayflower.

"How do you spell it?" Roger demands.

"M-a-y ..."

"... f-l-o-w-e-r?"

"Good job, Roger," says Stephen.

"I *read* it," the boy explains indignantly, pointing straight ahead with the collective fingers of his right mitten.

Fifty yards away, moored between an oil tanker and a bait shack, a battered freighter rides the incoming tide. Her stern displays a single word, *Mayflower*, a name that to the inhabitants of Boston Isle means far more than the sum of its letters.

"Now can we go home?" asks Roger.

"No," says Stephen. He has taught the story countless times. The Separatists' departure from England for Virginia ... their hazardous voyage ... their unplanned landing on Plymouth Rock ... the signing of the covenant whereby the non-Separatists on board agreed to obey whatever rules the Separatists imposed. "*Now* we can go on a nice long voyage."

"On *that* thing?" asks Willy.

"You're not serious," says Laura.

"Not me," says Claude.

"Forget it," says Yolanda.

"Sayonara," says Tommy.

"I think I'm going to throw up," says Beatrice.

"It's not your decision," Stephen tells his stepchildren. He stares at the ship's hull, blotched with rust, blistered with decay, another victim of the Deluge. A passenger whom he recognizes as his neighbor Michael Hines leans out a porthole like a prairie dog peering from its burrow. "Until further notice, I make all the rules."

129

Half by entreaty, half by coercion, he leads his disgruntled family up the gangplank and onto the quarterdeck, where a squat man in an orange raincoat and a maroon watch cap demands to see their ticket.

"Happy Saint Patrick's Day," says Stephen, flourishing the preserved blossom.

"We're putting you people on the fo'c'sle deck," the man yells above the growl of the idling engines. "You can hide behind the pianos. At ten o'clock you get a bran muffin and a cup of coffee."

As Stephen guides his stepchildren in a single file up the forward ladder, the crew of the *Mayflower* reels in the mooring lines and ravels up the anchor chains, setting her adrift. The engines kick in. Smoke pours from the freighter's twin stacks. Sunlight seeps across the bay, tinting the eastern sky hot pink and making the island's many-windowed towers glitter like Christmas trees.

A sleek Immortality Corps cutter glides by, headed for the wharfs, evidently unaware that enemies of the unconceived lie close at hand.

Slowly, cautiously, Stephen negotiates the maze of wooden crates–it seems as if every piano on Boston Isle is being exported today–until he reaches the starboard bulwark. As he curls his palm around the rail, the *Mayflower* cruises past the Mystic Shoals, maneuvering amid the rocks like a skier following a slalom course.

"Hello, Stephen." A large woman lurches into view, abruptly kissing his cheek.

He gulps, blinking like a man emerging into sunlight from the darkness of a copulatorium. Valerie Gallogher's presence on the *Mayflower* doesn't surprise him, but he's taken aback by her companions. Angela Dunfey, suckling little Merribell. Her cousin, Lorna, still spectacularly pregnant. And, most shocking of all, Father Monaghan, leaning his frail frame against his baptismal font.

Stephen says, "Did we...? Are you...?"

"My blood has spoken," Valerie Gallogher replies, her red hair flying like a pennant. "In nine months I give birth to our child."

Whereupon the sky above Stephen's head begins swarming with tiny black birds. No, not birds, he realizes: devices. Ovulation gauges sail through the air, a dozen at first, then scores, then hundreds, immediately pursued by equal numbers of sperm counters. As the little machines splash down and sink, darkening the harbor like the contraband tea from an earlier moment in the history of Boston insurgency, a muffled but impassioned cheer arises among the stowaways.

"Hello, Father Monaghan." Stephen unstraps his sperm counter. "Didn't expect to find *you* here."

The priest smiles feebly, drumming his fingers on the lip of the font. "Valerie informs me you're about to become a father again. Congratulations."

"My instincts tell me it's a boy," says Stephen, leaning over the rail. "He's going to get a second candy cane at Christmas," asserts the bewildered pilgrim as, with a wan smile and a sudden flick of his wrist, he breaks his bondage to the future.

→ ⊕ ←

If I don't act now, thinks Connie as he pivots toward Valerie Gallogher, I'll never find the courage again.

"Do we have a destination?" he asks. Like a bear preparing to ascend a tree, he hugs the font, pulling it against his chest.

"Only a purpose," Valerie replies, sweeping her hand across the horizon. "We won't find any Edens out there, Father. The entire Baltimore Reef has become a wriggling mass of flesh, newborns stretching shore to shore." She removes her ovulation gauge and throws it over the side. "In the Minneapolis Keys, the Corps routinely casts homosexual men and menopausal women into the sea. On the California Archipelago, male parishioners receive periodic potency tests and–"

"The Atlanta Insularity?"

"A nightmare."

"Miami Isle?"

"Forget it."

Connie lays the font on the bulwark then clambers onto the rail, straddling it like a child riding a seesaw. A loop of heavy-duty chain encircles the font, the steel links flashing in the rising sun. "Then what's our course?"

"East," says Valerie. "Toward Europe. What are you doing?"

"East," Connie echoes, tipping the font seaward. "Europe."

A muffled, liquid crash reverberates across the harbor. The font disappears, dragging the chain behind it.

"Father!"

Drawing in a deep breath, Connie studies the chain. The spiral of links unwinds quickly and smoothly, like a coiled rattlesnake striking its prey. The slack vanishes. Connie feels the iron shackle seize his ankle. He flips over. He falls.

"Bless these waters, O Lord, that they might grant this sinner the gift of life everlasting ..."

"Father!"

He plunges into the harbor, penetrating its cold hard surface: an experience, he decides, not unlike throwing oneself through a plate glass window. The waters envelop him, filling his ears and stinging his eyes.

We welcome this sinner into the mystical body of Christ, and do mark him with the Sign of the Cross, Connie recites in his mind, reaching up and drawing the sacred plus sign on his forehead.

He exhales, bubble following bubble.

Cornelius Dennis Monaghan, I baptize you in the name of the Father, and of the Son, and of the Holy Ghost, he concludes, and as the black wind sweeps through his brain, sucking him toward immortality, he knows that he's never been happier.

Apologue

The instant they heard the news, the three of them knew they had to do something, and so, joints complaining, ligaments protesting, they limped out of the retirement home, went down to the river, swam across, and climbed onto the wounded island.

They'd always looked out for each other in times gone by, and this day was no different. The ape placed a gentle paw on the rhedosaur's neck, keeping the half-blind prehistoric beast from stepping on cars and bumping into skyscrapers. The mutant lizard helped the incontinent ape remove his disposable undergarments and replace them with a dry pair. The rhedosaur reminded the mutant lizard to take her Prozac.

Before them lay the maimed and smoking city. It was a nightmare, a war zone, a surrealistic obscenity. It was Hiroshima and Nagasaki.

"Maybe they won't understand," said the rhedosaur. "They'll look at me, and all they'll see is a berserk reptile munching on the Coney Island roller coaster." He fixed his clouded gaze on the ape. "And you'll always be the one who shimmied up the Empire State Building and swatted at the biplanes."

"And then, of course, there was the time I rampaged through the Fulton Fish Market and laid my eggs in Madison Square Garden," said the mutant lizard.

"People are smarter than that," said the ape. "They know the difference between fantasy and reality."

"Some people do, yes," said the rhedosaur. "Some do."

The Italian mayor approached them at full stride, exhausted but resolute, his body swathed in an epidermis of ash. At his side walked a dazed Latino firefighter and a bewildered police officer of African descent.

"We've been expecting you," said the mayor, giving the mutant lizard an affectionate pat on the shin.

"You have every right to feel ambivalent toward us," said the rhedosaur.

"The past is not important," said the mayor.

"You came in good faith," said the police officer, attempting without success to smile.

"Actions speak louder than special effects," said the firefighter, staring upward at the gargantuan visitors.

Tears of remorse rolled from the ape's immense brown eyes. The stench filling his nostrils was irreducible, but he knew that it included many varieties of plastic and also human flesh. "Still, we can't help feeling ashamed."

"Today there is neither furred nor smooth in New York," said the mayor. "There is neither scaled nor pored, black nor white, Asian nor Occidental, Jew nor Muslim. Today there are only victims and helpers."

"Amen," said the police officer.

"I think it's clear what needs doing," said the firefighter.

"Perfectly clear." The mutant lizard sucked a mass of rubble into her lantern-jawed mouth.

"Clear as glass." Despite his failing vision, the rhedosaur could see that the East River Savings Bank was in trouble. He set his back against the structure, shoring it up with his mighty spine.

The ape said nothing but instead rested his paw in the middle of Cortlandt Street, allowing a crowd of the bereaved to climb onto his palm. Their shoes and boots tickled his skin. He curled his fingers into a protective matrix then shuffled south, soon entering Battery Park. He sat on the grass, stared toward Liberty Island, raised his arm, and, drawing the humans to his chest, held them against the warmth of his massive heart.

ƒucking Justice

His body was now a sacred place, a sentient temple of Solomonic wisdom, a flesh-and-bone altar at which the innocent would always find relief from persecution and the guilty be evermore called to account. His spinal column had acquired the precise arc of the rainbow with which God had sealed his covenant with Noah. His brain's two hemispheres bulged with the twin tablets of the Mosaic Law. The Code of Hammurabi gave ballast to the vessel of his heart.

Four days earlier, with the full enthusiasm of Andrew Jackson and the qualified endorsement of the Congress, Roger Brooke Taney had been sworn in as Chief Justice of the United States Supreme Court. After the ceremony had come a roundelay of dinners, balls, soirées, and, truth be told, visits to the Washington bordellos. Chief Justice Roger Taney had imbibed considerable quantities of wine from crystalline goblets and impressed large amounts of truth on callow journalists, all of them eager to hear what philosophical constructs he would bring to bear in interpreting the U.S. Constitution. An amazing interval—and yet as he stood on the dark chilly banks of the Potomac, the fog enshrouding the trees and the night wind gnawing his innards, he apprehended that the week's most memorable event was still to come.

The stranger had approached Roger at the bar of the Bellefleur Hotel, quite the most grotesque person he'd ever seen, a stumpish crookback whose sallow smile suggested a wooden fence from which every second picket had been removed. He identified himself as Knock the Dwarf. Although Roger's commitment to Aristotelian prudence had obliged him to give the wretch a portion of his time, his sense of propriety had deterred him from granting a full-blown interview. Their conversation was consequently pointed and brief.

"Our republic is young," Knock had said, "and yet already certain ancient and secret societies have established a presence on these shores–though of course such organizations are by definition hidden from view, which is why my employers assume that you are unacquainted with the Brotherhood of the Scales."

"Brotherhood of the Scales?" Roger said. "A musicians' league perhaps? A guild of fishermen?"

"Neither musicians nor fishermen."

Fishermen. Once again the familiar knot formed in Roger's throat, the tumor no surgeon's knife could ever ablate. The late Mrs. Taney was certainly no Catholic, and yet she'd insisted that their cook spend every Friday evening frying or baking or broiling some aquatic delicacy. It was surely Satan himself who'd spawned the fatal trout, arranging for one of its vertebrae to lodge in Mrs. Taney's gullet.

"Scales as in 'scales of justice,'" Knock explained, handing Roger a sheet of parchment, twice-folded and secured with a dollop of white tallow.

"Your employers are correct," Roger said. "I have not heard of the society in question. And now, if you will leave me to my privacy ..."

Knock tipped his ratty felt hat, bowed in a manner that seemed to Roger more insouciant than deferential, and scurried back to whatever moist and gloomy grotto served as this troglodyte's abode.

The message was succinct: a set of directions guiding the recipient to a particular willow tree on the Potomac's eastern shore, followed by four sentences.

> *A choice lies before you, Roger Taney, as momentous as any you will make whilst heading up the highest court in the land. You can either become the greatest Supreme Court Justice of this century, or you can add your name to that fat catalogue of judges orphaned by mediocrity and adopted by obscurity. We shall expect you at the stroke of midnight.*

The wind rushing off the black river put Roger in mind of his young nephew, Thomas, on whom he had recently lavished a wondrous toy frigate driven by flaxen sails and armed with four miniature brass cannons that, charged with a pinch of gunpowder, hurled glass marbles a distance of twenty feet. On Independence Day, Roger and Thomas had together enacted the Battle of Fort McHenry in a duck pond. As the frigate pounded the little mud-and-wicker garrison, man and boy had given voice to the stirring anthem recently composed by Roger's brother-in-law.

"And the rockets' red glare," they'd sung, "the bombs bursting in air, gave proof through the night that our flag was still there ..."

The ship now cruising up the river was nothing at all like Thomas's toy frigate. It was a thirty-foot shallop, the *Caveat* by name, as dismayed and forsaken as anything in "The Rime of the Ancient Mariner," her sails like moldering winding-sheets, her planks like worm-eaten wine casks, her rigging like the curtain-ropes in some unsavory theatre catering to sots and sensualists. The shallop sidled toward the bank. A gangway appeared, bridging the gap between rail and shore. Such a ship, Roger speculated, could only be crewed by pirates, and yet the instant he crossed over–for even a Chief Justice may act against his better judgment–it became obvious that, far from being a privateer, the *Caveat* was a kind of floating academy or waterborne monastery.

Her company, over twenty in number, all wore woolen robes, revealed by the full moon to be of varying hues, each beaky cowl offering Roger only the vaguest glimpse of the face beneath, rather the way his favorite sort of woman's gown provided an occasional flash of bosom. Perhaps these friars were the spiritual descendents of Saint Brendan, the seagoing cleric of Catholic legend. Or maybe their order had gone maritime in homage to *Les Trois Maries*–Mary Magdalene, Mary Salome, Mary Jacob–those pious women who, following the crucifixion, had traversed the Mediterranean and landed in Gaul.

No sooner had Roger stepped onto the weather deck than the tallest monk, swathed in red and radiating an agreeable floral fragrance, clasped his shoulder in a manner he found overly familiar but nevertheless ingratiating.

"You have made a wise decision, Judge Taney," the red monk said.

"How heartening to meet a man who will endure both apprehension and perplexity to increase the quantity of justice in the universe," the white monk said.

"I am indeed perplexed," Roger said, "and truly apprehensive."

"In matters metaphysical," the blue monk said, "confusion and fear walk hand-in-hand with enlightenment and grace."

"The ritual takes but an hour," the yellow monk said. "We shall have you back at the Bellefleur in time for breakfast."

137

"If you good friars were to lower your hoods," Roger asked, "would I perhaps recognize amongst you a familiar face or two?"

The red monk dipped his head and said, "You would be astonished to learn who belongs to the Brotherhood of the Scales."

⤳ ✾ ⤶

The voyage was short and uneventful. For an hour or so the *Caveat* flew southward from the city, then dropped anchor near a feature that the red monk identified as Janus Island, a gloomy forested mass rising from the bay like the shell of an immense sea turtle. Torches were lit. Lanterns glowed to life. A longboat was lowered, hitting the water with a sound like a beaver's tail slapping a mud bank.

Six monks clustered around Roger. Their sweet aroma and polyphonic humming gratified his senses. They directed him down a swaying rope-ladder to the longboat and positioned him in the stern, all the while chanting a song so beautiful he found himself wondering whether humankind might have done better to remain in the Middle Ages. The monks seized the oaks and rowed for Janus Island, the synchronous strokes providing their polyphony with a supplemental rhythm.

Attaining the beach, Roger's sponsors again took him in hand, their skin exuding olfactory choruses of rose and lavender. As the party advanced inland, the terrain became preternaturally dense, the trees packed so tightly together as to make the forest seem a collection of concentric stockades. Chirps and peals and whirrs of every sort poured from the darkness, an insect symphony as pleasing as the monks' sonorous voices.

The moon shone down more brightly still, its shimmering beams spilling through the trees like molten silver from a crucible. Roger shuddered with an amalgam of dread and fascination. His every instinct told him to break free of his sponsors, dive into the bay, and swim to the safety of the Maryland shore, and yet his curiosity kept him on the path, fixed on a destination whose nature he could not divine.

They had marched barely a mile when Roger realized that he and the monks were not alone. A female figure in a flowing gossamer gown darted here and there amongst the trees. She suggested nothing so much as a pagan dryad–though a true dryad, he decided, would enjoy greater freedom than this thrice-hobbled creature, who was freighted not only with a broadsword but also a pair of brass balance-scales and, as if she were about to be executed by a firing squad, a blindfold.

The red monk had evidently noticed the visitor as well, for he now turned to Roger and said, "No, Judge Taney, you are not going mad."

"Nor are you seeing a ghost," the white monk said.

The dryad awakened in Roger's soul a timeless and unfathomable yearning. Her hair was a miracle. The long undulating tresses emitted a light of their own, a golden glow that mingled with the moonbeams to form a halo about her head.

"This island is surely of the Chesapeake Bay variety," he said, "and yet it would seem we've landed in the Cyclades."

"You are most prescient, sir, for the creature in question is in fact the Greek deity Themis," the green monk said.

Even as Roger apprehended the visitor in all her splendor, radiant locks and ample hips and full bosom, she melted into the shadows. Themis? Truly? Themis herself, given flesh and essence through a power that only God and his monks could control?

"The ritual is simple, though burdened with a certain ambiguity," the red monk said. "Before dawn you will perform on Dame Themis an act of raw concupiscence."

"I don't understand," Roger said.

"You will subject the goddess to a vigorous carnal embrace," the orange monk said.

Revulsion coursed through Roger's frame like a wave of nausea. "I am determined to become the paragon of my profession," he said, his tone vibrant with incredulity and outrage, "but I shan't commit the sin of fornication to attain that goal."

"Fear not, novitiate," the white monk said. "Just as Christ is forever married to his Church, so are you now wed to Dame Themis, though for an interval considerably short of eternity."

"Nay, good friar, I am not married to anyone, as my dear Caroline passed away three years ago."

"We know all about it," the orange monk said.

"A bone in the throat," the green monk said.

"Your second wedding occurred last night," the red monk insisted. "The fact that you were nearly asleep at the time does not annul the marriage."

"I find all this most unpersuasive," Roger said, though he had to admit that the thought of conjugal congress with the dryad did not displease him.

"Perhaps you would care to see the relevant document," the green monk said.

From his robe he produced a small leather valise, then flipped it open and retrieved a paper that in the combined light of moon and lantern appeared to indeed consecrate a circumscribed marriage between Roger Taney of Baltimore and Dame Themis of Athens. Their union had commenced twenty-four hours earlier and would terminate at cockcrow. Roger's signature featured his characteristic curlicues. The goddess's handwriting was likewise ornate, a marvel of loops and serifs.

"I am entirely astonished," Roger said.

"In metaphysics all things are possible," the yellow monk said.

"So this is in fact my wedding night?"

The red monk nodded. "Your bride awaits you."

For the remainder of the journey Roger fixed his eyes on that nebulous zone where the glow of the torches and the light of the moon shaded to black. He scrutinized the shadows, studied the breaching roots, fixed on the wisps of fog. Dame Themis was nowhere to be seen. Perhaps she had retired to her private quarters, that she might prepare for the coming consummation.

A shot-tower loomed out of the darkness, a crumbling pile of stone whose calculated verticality had probably not cooled a cannonball since the War of Independence. Roger's sponsors led him inside, then guided him up a helical staircase that curled along the inner wall like a viper lying dormant in a hollow tree. A door of oak and iron presented itself. The red monk pushed it open.

Never before had the Chief Justice beheld so sumptuous a bedchamber, its windows occluded by velvet curtains, its walls hung with tapestries depicting hunting scenes, its floor covered with an Oriental carpet as thick and soft as Irish moss. Dame Themis's sword of justice stood upright in the far corner. The brass balance-scales rested on the window ledge, one carriage holding a daisy-chain, the other a garland of lilies.

Roger's bride was utterly naked, stripped of both her blindfold and her gown. She lay supine on the mattress, her luminous hair flowing across the pillow, her concavity beckoning like a portal to Paradise, whilst east of Eden her firm and noble breasts canted in opposite directions, one north, the other south. Her eyes, unbanded now, were as large and golden as Spanish doubloons.

What most caught Roger's attention was neither his bride's face, nor even her form, but rather the way the monks had presumed to compromise her powers of speech with a silken gag and constrain her limbs through an elaborate network of shackles, chains, and locks held fast to the floor by iron cleats.

The Chief Justice was quick to bring a complaint before his sponsors.

"We can assure you that the chains are essential," the red monk replied.

"In the throes of passion, Dame Themis is known to grasp her lover's windpipe and squeeze," the blue monk elaborated. "Your strangulation would be no less deadly for being unintended."

"And the silken kerchief–likewise necessary?" Roger said.

"Before we added it to the ritual, Dame Themis's ardor would often drive her to bite off her lover's ear," the orange monk said.

"Good friars, I am appalled," Roger said. "How can you imagine I would assent to know my wife in so barbaric a manner?"

"For many centuries the Brotherhood sought a gentler method of instructing its novitiates," the blue monk said. "Alas, they discovered that a certain theatricality is the *sine qua non* of a proper initiation."

"Tonight you will learn exactly how it feels to violate justice," the red monk said, "so that you will never commit such a transgression in the future."

"I would never have a woman against her will," Roger asserted.

"Against her will?" the red monk said in an amused tone. "As you set about acquiring this carnal knowledge, your bride may indeed groan and whimper in apparent distress. Please know that these noises are all for show, the better to impress the event on your psyche."

"For show?" Roger said.

"Dame Themis is a consummate actress," the white monk said.

"My conscience rebels at this arrangement," Roger said.

"And now we leave you to your lesson," the red monk said, resting an affirming hand on Roger's shoulder for the second time that night. "We are confident you will learn it well."

Against all odds and defying his every expectation, the monks were but five minutes gone when Roger found himself in a condition of acute arousal. He fixed his gaze on the object of his desire. His mute bride bucked against the mattress, her chains clanking together with a discordant but oddly affecting music.

He got undressed as quickly as he could, his breeches snagging briefly on his manhood.

The evening unfolded as the monks had foretold, Dame Themis issuing unhappy sounds and muffled protests throughout the ritual. Roger closed his eyes and concentrated on the lesson, and when at last the spasm arrived he understood his seed to be a great gift, a numinous filament from Arachne's loom, perhaps, or a segment of the thread by which Theseus had solved the Labyrinth of Minos. Justice deserved no less.

It was only with the approach of dawn, as the *Caveat* blew back up the Potomac in thrall to a violent tempest, that Roger felt prepared to put his wedding night into words. Sitting with the red monk and the white in their private cabin, imbibing their wine and reveling in their conversation, he attempted to narrate his recent liaison in all its cryptic beauty.

"It truly seemed that my bride did not reciprocate my passion." Roger took a generous swallow from his goblet.

"Dame Themis plays her part with great skill," the red monk said.

"Her bleating still echoes in my ears," he said, recalling her impersonation of agony. "I am hoping this wine might silence it."

"If not the wine, then the passage of time," the white monk said.

The red monk stiffened his index finger and plunged it into the shadowy depths of his cowl, presumably to relieve an itching nose. "What matters is that you have absorbed every sensation that attends the abuse of Dame Themis. In the decades to come, whenever you begin to render a brutish opinion, the erotic fire you experienced last night will start coursing through your flesh."

"Whereupon you will summon all your inner strength and bank those terrible flames," the white monk said.

"With God as my witness, such a conflagration will never again prosper in my loins." Roger inhaled deeply, sucking in the orchid glory of the red monk, the honeysuckle elegance of the white. "I shall resist the enticements of injustice with every fiber of my being."

The white monk filled his third goblet of the evening. "But, ah, such felicitous enticements–yes?"

Roger heaved a sigh. "Felicitous. Yes."

"You can see how easily a jurist might become addicted to iniquity," the white monk said.

"I would never have expected it," said Roger. "I am not so well educated a man as I thought."

"Metaphysics can be as subtle as the serpent," the red monk said. "Welcome to the Brotherhood of the Scales."

⊰ 🏵 ⊱

In the interval stretching from his first Supreme Court case to the outbreak of the Civil War, Roger Brooke Taney made four separate journeys across the Chesapeake Bay in search of the place where he and Dame Themis had consummated their mayfly marriage. He never found the shot-tower–indeed, he never even found Janus Island. And yet he did not for an instant doubt that the Brotherhood of the Scales existed, or that the friars had sponsored his membership in that arcane organization, or that he had connected with a dryad sometime after midnight on April 23, 1836.

To his infinite satisfaction, not one of the opinions Roger wrote during the first twenty-two years of his career was accompanied by the concupiscent symptoms that the friars had taught him to recognize. Had the despoilment of Dame Themis wrought a cure so complete as to purge pettiness and ignorance from his psyche forever? Or was his congenital sense of justice so acute that he'd never needed the ritual in the first place? In any event, it seemed clear that the name of Taney would be handed down to history as a synonym for integrity, an antonym for malice, and the very definition of fairness.

There were two cases in particular for which he believed he might be revered. The first traced to a suit brought by the Charles River Bridge Company, which charged travelers a small fee to cross its eponymous bridge, against a nascent competitor, who permitted pedestrians, horsemen, and carriages to pass over the same watercourse for free. The plaintiffs contended that their original charter from the Commonwealth of Massachusetts had granted them a monopoly, but the Taney Court took a different view. The charter in question, noted the majority, did not use the word "monopoly." Ergo, the ambiguity would be resolved in favor of the public. Roger Taney: man of the people, guardian of toll-free bridges.

Then there was the controversial and distasteful business of the Negro. Dred Scott was a black African slave whose peripatetic master, an army surgeon named John Emerson, had moved first from Missouri to Illinois, and thence to Fort Snelling in the Wisconsin Territory, and finally back to Missouri. In 1846 Dr. Emerson died, whereupon Dred Scott sued Irene Emerson, the doctor's widow, for his freedom. Because Illinois had always been a free state, ran the plaintiff's specious and naïve logic, and because slavery had been banned from the Wisconsin Territory under the Missouri Compromise, he had spent much of his life in a condition other than bondage, and therefore he could no longer be regarded as chattel. For some perverse reason Dred Scott had won his suit in a lower St. Louis court, but then the Missouri State Supreme Court had wisely overturned the earlier decision.

In their characteristic arrogance Scott and his Negro-loving confreres had refused to quit, and eventually they found a way to make a federal case of the matter. For it so happened that the legal administrator of Irene Emerson's property–her brother, J.F.A. Sanford–was a resident of New York, not Missouri, which meant that technically the whole affair lay beyond the jurisdiction of either state. After losing in a U.S. District Court, Scott appealed to the highest court in the land, whose Chief Justice was only too happy to set the plaintiff straight concerning the nature of chattel slavery in America–the plaintiff, the black race, the infernal abolitionists, the troubled republic, and, indeed, the whole world.

In *Scott v. Sanford*, Roger and six other justices ruled that any entity whose ancestors had ever been sold as slaves could never enjoy the rights of a federal citizen, most especially the right to bring a suit in court. Dred Scott and his kind were in fact pieces of property, as befitting the "inferior order" to which they belonged. Negroes, Roger averred, were "altogether unfit to associate with the white race." As for the nefarious practice of chopping up the republic into slave zones and free zones, the Taney Court concluded that Congress had no power to prohibit slavery in the territories. The Missouri Compromise was, in a word, unconstitutional.

If Roger had been forced to make a choice, he would have guessed that future generations would venerate him more for his opinion in

Scott v. Sanford than for the Charles River Bridge decision. But the issue of the bridge mattered too. It was one thing to earn an honest profit, and quite another to stifle the freedom of a competing corporation.

⌘

How strange, this darkness. As usual he'd gone to bed at ten o'clock. Now he was fully awake, ready to hear the arguments in *Torrance v. Ashton*–and yet not a single ray of light pierced his room. Could it be that he'd slept for an entire day? Was his characteristic vigor finally failing? Perhaps he should take his nephew's advice and step down from the bench before the year was out.

He dropped his head back on the pillow and brooded. An insect chorus reached his ears, a noise that made even less sense than the darkness. He had shut all his windows before retiring and, besides, since when had Delaware Avenue become a gathering-place for cicadas and crickets?

His attempt to rise from the mattress perplexed him even more than either the darkness or the insects. Manacles encircled his wrists and ankles, the concomitant chains snaking across his body and disappearing beneath the bed. Whenever he moved, the links of rusted iron gave forth a sound suggesting a bullfrog in pain.

A door swung open. A flickering light filled the bedchamber. The red monk entered, holding aloft a torch, followed by Knock the Dwarf.

"How long has it been?" the red monk said. "A quarter century? No, longer. Twenty-eight years."

Roger glanced in all directions. Dame Themis's broadsword lay in the corner. Her balance-scales rested on the window ledge, although the daisy-chain and the garland of lilies had long since disintegrated and blown away.

"Good friar, you must set me free," he gasped.

"The Brotherhood has been following your career with great interest," the red monk said. "Alas, I'm afraid we are disappointed with your performance on the bench."

"I've done nothing to deserve these chains," Roger said, straining against the shackles.

"My employers disagree," the dwarf chimed in.

"Did I bring an unconsidered populism to the Charles River Bridge decision?" Roger asked. "Is that it?"

The dwarf snickered. The red monk smirked.

"Perhaps I committed an error or two whilst serving on the bench," Roger continued, "but I always held fast to my principles."

"Dozens of errors," the red monk said. "The first occurred the very week you were sworn in, when you decided that a greater good might come from ravishing Dame Themis."

Anger and indignation boiled up in Roger's blood. "That was your decision, not mine!"

"No, Judge Taney–yours."

"You forced me to ravish her!" Roger cried.

"Shut up!" the dwarf demanded, and then, as if he doubted Roger's ability to carry out the directive, he pulled a silk kerchief from his trousers and used it to render the Chief Justice mute.

Lantern in hand, the white monk strode into the bedchamber, accompanied by a middle-aged man dressed far too foppishly for his years: blue velvet dressing gown embroidered with golden peacocks, red calfskin slippers, pomaded curls.

The white monk pointed toward Roger and said, "Behold Apollo, avatar of wisdom and probity."

"I was expecting someone younger," the coxcomb said.

"Tonight you will learn exactly how it feels to violate Apollo," the white monk informed the coxcomb, "that you might avoid such a lapse in your coming career."

Roger made every effort to accuse the monks of deception, but the intervening kerchief turned his sentences into absurdities.

"How can a god be so elderly?" the coxcomb asked.

"Metaphysics rarely follows a predictable course." The white monk installed his lantern on the nightstand and headed for the open door. "Cleave to the ritual, and all will be well," he added, marching through the jamb.

"Apollo is a *young* man," the coxcomb protested.

"Don't be deceived by appearances," the red monk said. "Your job is not to estimate Apollo's age but to abuse his flesh as emphatically as possible."

Roger tried to scream, *You have no right!*

The red monk pivoted ninety degrees and marched out of the room, taking his torch with him.

"As emphatically as possible," echoed the coxcomb in a tone of consternation.

146

Roger wanted to shout, You must show pity!

"Might I make a suggestion?" the dwarf inquired.

"Indeed," the coxcomb said.

Knock approached Dame Themis's broadsword and, seizing the handle, brought it before the coxcomb. "What better way to violate Apollo than to excise his virility?"

Have mercy!

"To become a great judge, I shall do whatever is required of me," the coxcomb told the dwarf.

Hear me, sir! I am not a god! I am a citizen of the United States! I am a human being!

The coxcomb went to work, and when he was done the balance-scales of Dame Themis had achieved Platonic equipoise, both loads of equal weight and identical mass, each carriage in perfect harmony with the other.

⇜ ✦ ⇝

In 1857, one year after Roger Taney wrote the majority opinion in Scott *v.* Sanford, Irene Emerson of Missouri remarried. Her new husband, Calvin Chaffee, was a devout abolitionist, and so the former Mrs. Emerson sold Dred Scott, his wife Harriet, and their two daughters to the sons of the late Peter Blow, Scott's first owner.

The Blow brothers, childhood friends of Scott's who had paid his legal fees over the years, immediately manumitted the African and his family. For nine months, the interval of a human gestation, Dred Scott lived a free man in the city of St. Louis, succumbing to tuberculosis at the age of fifty-nine.

Initially Scott's remains were laid to rest in Wesleyan Cemetery, but in 1867 the burial ground was closed and his body placed beneath a blank slab in Section 1, Lot No. 177 of Calvary Cemetery. A commemorative marker was added in 1957, giving the facts in the case, and the grave now bears an inscription: "In memory of a simple man who wanted to be free."

ısabella of castile
answers Her Mail

to you, Don Cristóbal Colón, our Admiral of the Ocean Sea, Viceroy and Governor of all the Islands to be found by you on your Great Voyage of Discovery, greetings and grace ...

What a beautiful and welcome sight was your albatross messenger, swooping out of the skies like a new soul arriving in Heaven! How your letter raised my failing hopes and lifted my sagging spirits! O brave mariner, I am confident that the seagoing gardens of which you spoke, those vast floating mats of sargasso weed, signify that your fleet has at last drawn near the Indies. By the time these words appear before your eyes, you will have walked the bejeweled streets of Cathay and toured the golden temples of Cipangu.

Dearest friend, I should like to know your opinion about a troublesome matter. Do you have any views on the Jewish Question? Predictably enough, my Edict of General Expulsion has proven controversial here at Court. Our Keeper of the Privy Purse–I speak now of Santángel, perhaps the loudest of all those voices championing your expedition–became distressed to the point of tears, though as a *converso* he is doubtless biased by his Hebrew heritage. The clergy was divided. Whereas Friar Deza called the measure vital to the future of the Church, Friar Perez began quoting the Sermon on the Mount. But it was my old confessor Father Torquemada who used the strongest words. As long as unbelievers live among us, the Inquisitor explained, there can be no blood purity, no *limpieza de sangre*, in Spain.

And yet, three nights ago, a disquieting dream came to me. I no longer wore the Crown of Castile but the war helmet of Rameses II.

Am I the new Pharaoh? In banishing Spain's Jews, have I called divine disfavor upon my head? O Cristóbal, my heart feels like one of the great iron anchors you will soon drop into the waters off Asia.

Written in the City of Sante Fe on this 27th day of August, in the year of Our Lord Jesus Christ 1492.

I, THE QUEEN

→ ✠ ←

TO YOU, ISABELLA, by the Grace of God Queen of Castile, León, Aragón, Granada, Sicily, Sardinia, and the Balearics, greetings and increase of good fortune ...

Alas, we passed through the Sargasso Sea without sighting the Indies, a situation that so dismayed my officers and men they begged me to turn back. I was comforting them as best I could, pointing out that we had not yet gone two thousand miles (though in truth we had gone twenty-eight hundred), when the Ocean Sea began suddenly to swell, its waves rising high as battlements–as watchtowers–as the Pyrenees themselves. We rode those rollers, my Queen, plummeting inexorably from crest to cavity and back again. Terror-struck at first, we soon realized that God Himself had sent this cataclysm to speed us toward the Moluccas. Such a miracle has not occurred since Egypt's chariots gave chase to the Children of Israel!

You spoke of Spain's own Jews. By curious coincidence, the same tide that bore the *Niña*, the *Pinta*, and the *Santa María* out of port also carried what I took to be a contingent of your General Expulsion. As we followed the Rio Saltés to the sea, our way was blocked by every sort of vessel imaginable, their holds jammed with refugees clutching kettles, crockery, toys, lanterns, and other meager possessions. Initially this scene aroused in your Admiral an unequivocal pity (the weeping, the wailing, the old ones jumping overboard and crawling onto the rocks to die, the rabbis beseeching Yahweh to part the waters of the Mediterranean and lead the people dry-shod to a new Promised Land), but then Father Hojeda invited me to see it in a different light. "By driving the infidels from its cities, towns, and fields," Hojeda explained, "the Crown has made room for the pagan hordes we shall soon be ferrying to Spain from the Orient, thousands upon thousands of unbaptized souls yearning to embrace the Holy Faith."

So do not despair, Sovereign Queen. Your edict has served a divine plan.

I must rest my pen. A cry of "*Tierra!*" has just gone up from the lookout stationed atop our mainmast. *Gloria in excelsis Deo*–the impossible is accomplished! We have sailed West and met the East!

Written aboard the caravel *Santa María* on this 2nd day of September, in the year of Our Lord Jesus Christ 1492.

I, The Admiral

⇥ ✠ ⇤

TO YOU, DON CRISTÓBAL COLÓN, our Admiral of the Ocean Sea, Viceroy and Governor of all the Islands to be found by you on your Great Voyage of Discovery, greetings and grace ...

For five whole days I brooded upon the sobering news from North Africa–racking rumors of Jews cast naked into the sea by the captains we had hired to deport them, wrenching accounts of those very exiles starving on forgotten shores, grisly tales of these same refugees being eviscerated by Turkish mobs in quest of swallowed coins. Then came your letter of the 2nd.

O noble navigator, you have surely delivered your Queen from madness! I now see that the true and final purpose of our expedition is not to plot a new route to the Indies, nor is it to forge an alliance with the Great Khan, nor is it to build a bastion from which we might attack the Turkish rear and win back Constantinople (though these are all worthy aims). I now see that its true and final purpose is to lead all Asia to the Holy Faith. Not since my correspondence with Sixtus IV–through which he so kindly allayed my fears that in reducing the children of heretics to beggary the Inquisition overstepped its mandate–has my conscience known such release. Is it blasphemous for a Queen to compare her Admiral with her Pope? Then may God forgive me.

So, courageous conquistador, you have found the Moluccas at last. In your subsequent missives you may, if so inclined, make mention of the following matters: gold, silver, rubies, sapphires, diamonds, emeralds, precious silks, rare spices. But speak to me first and foremost of the spiritual condition of the Indian people. Do they seem well disposed to receive the Gospel? Does Father Hojeda wish to perform

151

all the baptisms himself, or shall I send a company of priests in your wake?

Written in our City of Sante Fe on this 7th day of September, in the year of Our Lord Jesus Christ 1492.

I, The Queen

To You, Isabella, by the Grace of God Queen of Castile, León, Aragón, Granada, Sicily, Sardinia, and the Balearics, greetings and increase of good fortune ...

How can mere words convey the miracle that is the Indies? How can I begin to describe the mysteries and marvels that have dazzled us in recent days? Vast glittering palaces! Mighty minarets belching smoke and fire! Ships that sail without benefit of wind! Coaches that move without a single horse in harness! Carriages that fly through the air on featherless wings!

After slipping beneath the largest bridge I have ever seen, a mile-long passageway stretching over our heads like a bronze rainbow, our fleet sailed up a dark and oily strait and anchored off what we took to be one of the lesser Moluccas. Dominating the island was an iron idol rising a hundred and fifty feet at least, surmounting a pedestal of almost equal height. I forthwith gathered together an exploration party consisting of Father Hojeda, Captain Pinzón, and myself, plus our translator Luis de Torres and our master-at-arms Diego de Harana. We came ashore in the dinghy of the *Santa María*, assembled in the shadow of the idol, and, thrusting the royal standard of Castile into the grassy soil, claimed the island for the Crown.

A most astonishing fact: there is no *limpieza de sangre* in Asia. Everywhere we turned, our eyes beheld a different fashion in flesh–dark, light, rough, coarse–and our ears rang with the greatest confusion of tongues since the Tower of Babel collapsed. We saw Moors. We saw Nubians. We saw Greeks and Slavs and Jews. From amid the general cacophony, Torres claimed he could discern not only Portuguese, Arabic, Yiddish, and Polish, but also the language of my native Genoa, though I caught no such syllables myself. Surprisingly, we soon encountered a sizable percentage of Indians for whom a peculiarly cadenced Castilian is the medium of choice. (I must confess, I was not aware that your Highness's overland mercantile endeavors had placed so many Spaniards in the Orient.) But the greatest shock, surely, was the omnipresence of English, not only in the mouths of the Indians but on the plethora of public signs, banners, mottos, and decrees.

"Give me your weary, your indigent, your huddled multitudes seeking to breathe without hinderance, the miserable garbage of your crowded beaches ..." So began Torres's uncertain rendering of the incantation that accompanies the idol. (English is not his *forte*.) "Send these, the homeless, typhoon-buffeted to me," he continued. "I lift my lantern beside the portal of gold."

The idol's form is female, and she evidently embodies something called *libertad*–a difficult idea to explicate, but Torres has inferred it means "giving free rein to your worst instincts and basest impulses." No doubt the "huddled multitudes" are sacrifical victims. Some are probably burned to death–hence the firebrand in the idol's right hand. Others are impaled alive–hence the seven dreadful spikes that decorate her crown.

With the setting of the sun I directed my party back to the caravels, dined alone on ham and beer, and began the present epistle. We are uncertain of our next move. From the Indians' chatter, Torres has surmised that other Moluccas lie in our vicinity–the Spice Island of Ellis to the north, the Spice Island of Governors to the east, the Spice Island of Manhattan to the northeast–and we are strongly inclined to explore them. But, O my Queen, this idol of *libertad* vexes us most sorely. The very sight of her looming over the fleet prickles our flesh and troubles our bowels. Might you perchance be willing to dispatch a regiment of soldiers to the Indies, so we can undertake to baptize this cult without fear of immolation? Eagerly I await your reply.

Written aboard the caravel *Santa María* on this 12th day of September, in the year of Our Lord Jesus Christ 1492.

I, The Admiral

TO YOU, DON CRISTÓBAL COLÓN, our Admiral of the Ocean Sea, Viceroy and Governor of all the Islands to be found by you on your Great Voyage of Discovery, greetings and grace ...

Frankly, my Admiral, we don't quite know what to make of your Spice Islands and their polyglot aborigines. As with the Jewish Question, the Court is of several minds. Santangel thinks you may have stumbled upon the Lost Tribes of Israel. The clergy believes you have sailed clear past the Indies and landed in one of these secret colonies set up by Europe's escaped convicts and fugitive mutineers.

In any event, we cannot send you infantry support. Now that Granada is ours, we have demobilized the army, leaving in uniform only our border troops, our palace guards, and our Santa Hermandad. But even if an extra regiment did lie at our disposal, we would not ship it across the Ocean Sea. Dearest Cristóbal, have you forgotten the sheer power of Scripture? Do you doubt the potency of Truth? Once Father Hojeda tells them the whole story, from the Virgin Birth to the Resurrection, this *libertad* cult will surely abandon its wicked, pagan, persecuting ways. So say Friars Deza and Perez.

This is not a happy time for the Queen of Castile. My daughter still grieves for her husband, the Crown Prince Alfonso, killed last month in a riding accident, and she evinces no romantic interest in his successor. Day in, day out, the Infanta skulks about the castle, dressing in black, singing bawdy ballads, and, worst of all, threatening to join the Holy Sisters in Toledo. Let her marry our Lord Jesus Christ in the next life–at the moment her duty is to marry Portugal!

Yet another lady-in-waiting has acquiesced to Ferdinand's advances. As soon as her transgression became apparent, I hurried the harlot and her nascent babe off to the nearest convent, though in truth I would have preferred to hurry the king off to the handiest monastery. (It is quite enough to make me regret that you and I behaved so honorably last April in my Segovian rose garden.) If there were chastity belts for men, I would this very night slip one over my husband's lecherous loins, lock it up, and hide the key where I alone can find it.

I am bored, sir. Nothing amuses me. Yesterday I attended a bullfight–an unrelievedly gory and grotesque spectacle. I have half a mind to outlaw the entire sport. This morning's *auto-da-fé* was equally jejune. Of the nineteen heretics paraded through the streets in *sanbenitos*, eleven repented, seven went to the stake, and one dropped dead from fright. I left before the burnings, the weather having turned rainy and cold.

Cristóbal, you and you alone can relieve my tedium. You must visit these other Moluccas, teaching the Indians about eternal life, searching out the golden portals, and having many beguiling adventures. And then, when you are finished, you must pick up your pen and excite me with your exploits.

Written in our City of Sante Fe on this 17th day of September, in the year of Our Lord Jesus Christ 1492.

I, The Queen

✦ ✠ ✦

To You, Isabella, by the Grace of God Queen of Castile, León, Aragón, Granada, Sicily, Sardinia, and the Balearics, greetings and increase of good fortune ...

Following your directive of the 17th, we have spent the past fourteen hours in quest of souls and gold, and I must tell you at the outset that never did a man endure a more perplexing day.

The *Niña* has always been my favorite among the fleet, and certainly the ship best designed for exploring coasts, so with dawn's first light I transferred my flag to her, leaving Pinzón and his brothers in charge of the *Santa María* and the *Pinta*. Once Torres, Harana, and Father Hojeda were aboard we took off, eventually dropping our anchor perhaps sixty yards off Manhattan. Setting out in the dinghy, we disembarked at a place called "Battery Park," unfurled our standard, and acquired the island for Spain.

We were immediately struck by the large number of beggars in our midst, men and women with dirty faces, torn clothing, hollow eyes, and vacant bellies. Poor as heretics' children, they carried all their earthly belongings about in sacks (rather like the Jews I noted traveling down the Saltés), and we quickly identified them as the "homeless, typhoon-buffeted" creatures mentioned on the idol's plaque. An infinite remorse gripped me as I realized they were all destined to be skewered on the spikes of *libertad* and consumed by her flames.

Torres tried several times to start a conversation with these wretches, asking why they did not flee from Battery Park to whatever monasteries, convents, and sanctuaries might grace the interior. Their responses were invariably a crude idiomatic expression to the effect that Torres should become a hermaphrodite and experience sexual congress with himself.

As if sensing our communication difficulties, a bold young Indian approached, offering his services as both interpreter and guide. Born

155

Rodrigo Menendez, he said he was raised in the distant Spanish-speaking land of "Cuba-man." Though formidable in appearance, with a tiny gold ring through his right nostril, a dark blue kerchief tied around his forehead, and a shirt inscribed BEAM ME UP, SCOTTY, THERE'S NO INTELLIGENT LIFE DOWN HERE, he assured us he was of the Holy Faith, attending Mass regularly as well as something called "Cardinal O'Connor High School-man," situated on the Twenty-third Street. We offered to pay him in the various trinkets that appeal so profoundly to the African peoples with whom the Crown barters: red felt caps, glass necklaces, little brass bells. He was not interested. When we displayed the cask of vintage Marques de Cacares that Father Hojeda had so cleverly brought ashore, however, the youth's eyes lit up like votive candles, and for this good consideration he entered our employ.

A tour of "Lower Manhattan," Rodrigo assured us, typically begins with "the New York Stock Exchange." From his description, we surmised it was a principal meeting place of the *libertad* cult. Steeling ourselves, we followed the youth east along the "Wall" road, site of many grand citadels and lofty towers. The passing Indians fairly dripped of gold–gold bracelets, gold wedding bands, gold chains about their necks, gold pebbles in their teeth.

We entered the temple in question. Believe me, your Highness, rarely has a faith excited such zeal. Those who attend the New York Stock Exchange celebrate with a frenzy I have never seen before. They run around like lunatics and shout like the Apostles at Pentecost. It did not take Father Hojeda long to decide that these stock exchangers are nowise ready to hear about Jesus Christ, so tenacious are their present beliefs. I am inclined to concur.

As we left the temple, the utter strangeness of the surrounding city prompted me to speculate we might have reached the fabled waterbound kingdom of which Marco Polo wrote. I asked Rodrigo if we could possibly be on one of the Cipangu Islands.

He said, "The which?"

"Cipangu Islands. You know–the Japans."

Whereupon the youth explained that Cipangu indeed possessed many "holdings" on Manhattan, including treasuries, trading posts, and money-lending houses plus something called "Rockefeller Center-man." However, while these assorted enterprises evidently make Manhattan a kind of colony of Cipangu, Rodrigo reckoned the actual Kingdom of Japan to be some considerable distance away.

"If we're not in Cipangu, have we perhaps found Cathay?" asked Father Hojeda.

"Huh? Cathay?"

"Do you call it Quinsay? China, perhaps?"

"Ah–you want to see Chinatown!"

The youth guided us to an enclave consisting primarily of places to eat. It took us but a moment to realize that "Chinatown" is no more contiguous with Cathay than the money-lending houses are contiguous with Cipangu. We did, however, enjoy an excellent lunch of pork, rice, and bamboo shoots. Rodrigo paid for this food using the local currency, a debt we agreed to cover with a second cask of Marques de Cacares.

"Our fervent hope was to form an alliance with the Great Khan," I explained to the youth, making no effort to hide my disappointment over the disparity between Chinatown and Cathay. "We bear a royal letter of recommendation from the king and queen of Spain."

"The closest we've got to a khan is the mayor," the youth answered, "but I don't think he worries a whole lot about where he stands with the king and queen of Spain."

Through further questioning of Rodrigo, we learned that this "mayor" claims an African heritage, whereupon Father Hojeda and I decided it was probably most accurate to regard him as a local chieftain. Rodrigo offered to take us to the ruler's headquarters, a "City Hall-man" lying perhaps a half mile south of Chinatown. We accepted. As we set out on our diplomatic mission, however, the youth casually mentioned that a previous such Chief of Manhattan had been of Jewish descent. Naturally I was not about to open negotiations with any realm whose throne has held the avaricious assassins of Christ–not without explicit orders from your Highness.

"We would like to see the sources of the gold," I said to Rodrigo.

The youth replied, "Gold? Yeah, sure, I can show you some gold."

"We would also like to see the gems," added Harana.

"And the spices," added Torres.

"And the precious fabrics," added Father Hojeda.

"We go uptown-man," said the youth. "We take the subway, eh?"

So we did. These "subways" proved to be machines most terrible and terrifying: self-propelled coaches linked in serpentine configurations, racing through underground passageways at demonic speeds. All during the trip, Rodrigo engaged in a long, rambling, unsolicited speech to the effect that, while he doesn't question the sanctity of marriage, he is just as glad his parents got divorced, and while he admits the wrongfulness of thwarting semen on its journey, he would never leave home without a pocketful of manhood sheaths, and while he understands that extracting fetuses from the womb is a sin, he doesn't know how he'd react if his girlfriend Martina ever became pregnant by him. O my dearest Isabella, it would seem that, before we attempt to convert this city's Indians to Catholicism, we must first seek to convert its Catholics to Catholicism.

Reaching the "Pennsylvania" station via the "Seventh Avenue Local," we climbed back to the surface and followed our guide north to a place where he promised we would see the precious fabrics. He spoke the truth. All the way from the Thirty-fourth Street to the Fortieth, nimble Indian peasants transported silks, satins, cashmere, velvet, gossamer, chenille, damask, and a hundred other exotic cloths (including a wrinkleproof material known as "polyester"), shuttling them about in the form of both uncut bolts and finished suits. At the moment, I cannot say exactly what trading opportunities this bazaar may offer Spain. We saw many Jews.

"What about the gold?" asked Harana.

"This way," said Rodrigo, pointing north. "Gold, silver, gems."

He took us to "the Jewelry District," on the Forty-seventh Street near "the Avenue of the Americas." Again, the youth knew whereof he spoke. Treasure lay on all sides, nearly all of it under the jurisdiction of Jews wearing dreadlocks, grotesque hats, and long black coats. We must not take anything, Rodrigo cautioned us. If we tried to remove the gold, the *policía* would intervene, presumably cutting off our hands and feet in the manner, my Queen, of your Santa Hermandad.

"Are the spices near?" asked Harana.

"Bit of a hike," said the youth. "You up for it?"

Our party traveled west, then north on the "Broadway" road to "Columbus Circle," locus of an idol bearing a singularly pleasing countenance, then higher still to the Eighty-first Street, where we found ourselves at the source of the spices. Even from the sidewalk we could smell them: cloves, nutmeg, anise, cinnamon, thyme, ginger, basil—a thousand and one Oriental delights, wafting into our nostrils like the expirations of angels.

Then we saw the name.

Zabar's.

"Jews?" I inquired.

"Jews," the youth confirmed.

We did not go inside.

Dearest Isabella, could it possibly be that your Second Exodus beat us across the Ocean Sea? Did your ministers by some strange quirk equip the exiled infidels with ships faster even than the *Niña*, the *Pinta*, and the *Santa María*?

I am back in my cabin now, scribbling by the light of a full moon, a perfect sphere that sails the sky like a burning pomegranate. The tide is rising in Upper New York Bay, lifting the *Santa María* up and down on her hawser like a ball riding atop the snout of Bronx Zoo seal. The harbor air scrapes my throat, burns my chest, and brings tears to my eyes.

You must advise us, Sovereign Queen. These Spice Islands confound our minds and confuse our souls. Should we confiscate the gold? Lay claim to the silks and spices? Present our credences at City Hall-man? Attempt to convert the stock exchangers? What?

Written aboard the caravel *Santa María* on this 22nd day of September, in the year of Our Lord Jesus Christ 1492.

I, The Admiral

✦ ✠ ✦

TO YOU, DON CRISTÓBAL COLÓN, our Admiral of the Ocean Sea, Viceroy and Governor of all the Islands to be found by you on your Great Voyage of Discovery, greetings and grace ...

Forgive my tardiness in answering, but we have recently uprooted the Court, the food supplies in Sante Fe having become depleted and its latrines full, with the result that your communiqué of the 22nd went momentarily astray.

What twisted wind, what perverted current has brought you to the city of which you speak? How are we to account for such a mad and upside-down dominion, this Manhattan where Jews prosper, prevail, and place themselves upon thrones? You are not in Asia, Cristóbal.

A consensus has emerged here. My King, my councilors, and my heart all agree. You must not linger another moment in that Satanic place. Leave, friend. We have no use for Manhattan's filthy gold. We do not seek its tarnished silver, tainted gems, rancid spices, rotten silks.

Predictably, Santángel offers a voice of dissent. He wants you to stay on Manhattan and learn how a city without *limpieza de sangre* has accomplished so many marvels. I believe it is the Jew in him talking. No matter. My wish, not his, is your command.

Take the next tide, Admiral. Pull up your anchor, sail south, and don't stop till you've found a world that makes some sense.

Written in our City of Barcelona on this 1st day of October, in the year of Our Lord Jesus Christ 1492.

I, The Queen

⤳ ✠ ⤶

To You, Isabella, by the Grace of God Queen of Castile, León, Aragón, Granada, Sicily, Sardinia, and the Balearics, greetings and increase of good fortune ...

It is my supreme pleasure to report that your royal intuitions were correct. We quit New York within an hour of your letter's arrival, returning to the Ocean Sea and heading due south as you so wisely instructed. Once again the waves became like mountains, and once again we followed them to our destiny. On October twelfth, after a journey of six days, an exhilarating cry of *"Tierra!"* issued from my lookout.

The island we found that afternoon bore little resemblance to Manhattan. It had no citadels, subways, beggars, or Chinese inns. We came ashore on a pristine expanse of gleaming white coral, beyond which lay a jungle so lush and green we thought immediately of Eden before the Fall. When the natives appeared, at first simply peering out from among the trees, then walking down to the beach to greet us, we were further reminded of the Golden Age. They were gentle beyond telling, peaceful beyond belief, and naked as the day God made them. Unlike Rodrigo back on Manhattan, they eagerly accepted our gifts, placing the red felt caps on their heads, draping the glass necklaces atop their bare bosoms, and jangling the little brass bells like children. They call their world Guanahaní, but we forthwith named it San Salvador after Him whose infinite mercy brought us here.

Have we at last reached Asia? I cannot say. There are many beautiful islands in this part of creation. We have given them all Spanish names–Hispaniola, Santa María la Antigua, Puerto Rico, Trinidad, Santa Cruz–so God will know from which nation this Holy Endeavor proceeds. In every case, the natives have proven as docile and prelapsarian as those on San Salvador. They are ignorant of horse and ox, innocent of wheel, plow, and musket. Beyond the occasional juju clutched in a brown fist or amulet slung about a sunbaked neck, we find no evidence of religion here. Say the word, and Father Hojeda will begin the baptisms.

At the moment I am on Hispaniola, watching a dozen maidens frolic in the clear blue waters of a bay called Acul. As the sun descends, it turns the girls' bare skin the very color of the bronze swords with which we shall keep these people in check. Have I arrived in Paradise, my Queen?

Written aboard the caravel *Santa María* on this 17th day of October, in the year of Our Lord Jesus Christ 1492.

I, The Admiral

TO YOU, DON CRISTÓBAL COLÓN, our Admiral of the Ocean Sea, Viceroy and Governor of all the Islands to be found by you on your Great Voyage of Discovery, greetings and grace ...

Friar Deza says Spain is now "on the threshold of a grand and glorious age." Father Torquemada thinks we stand "on the verge of a Thousand Year Empire such as the world has never known."

They may be right. Six days ago, Emanuel I of Portugal asked for the Infanta's hand in marriage, and she dutifully accepted. The day after that, the Islamic King Boabdil surrendered the keys to the Alhambra, and our victory over the Moors became complete. Then, twenty-four hours later, your missive arrived from Hispaniola.

O my Admiral, the belief here is that, if you are not in the Indies, you have come upon something no less valuable for Spain, a great pool of unclaimed souls both ripe for conversion and ready to relieve Castile of all strenuous and unseemly labor. When I read your letter to my councilors, a cheer resounded throughout the castle, and before long we were all drinking the same vintage of Marques de Cacares with which you bargained in Manhattan.

Santángel did not join our celebration. He says Torquemada's Thousand Year Empire will last no more than a few centuries. "In fleeing Manhattan, Spain has made a fatal mistake," he insists. "By running away to Hispaniola, Don Cristóbal has merely bought the

Crown some time."

Last night a violent and frightening vision afflicted my sleep. Like the Golem of Jewish folklore, the idol of *libertad* had by some miracle come to life, and had by no less a miracle betaken herself to Europe. So heavy were her footfalls that the very mountains of Spain commenced to tremble, then to crack apart, then to collapse upon themselves like ancient Atlantis sinking into the waters beyond the Pillars of Hercules.

What do you make of my dream, Cristóbal? Could it be that Santángel is right, and the best you can do for Spain is buy her some time? Very well. Amen. Empire is the art of the possible.

So baptize those brown natives, dear sailor. Put them to work. Punish those who cling to their fetishes and rites. And buy Spain some time, O my Admiral. Buy her some time.

Written in our City of Barcelona on this 23rd day of October, in the year of Our Lord Jesus Christ 1492.

I, THE QUEEN

The zombies of Montrose

Darkness. The living room of Arabella LeGrand, a suburban voodoo queen residing in the fictitious town of Montrose, Pennsylvania. Coffee table, loveseat, bookcase, rug, floor lamp. The bookcase holds a candelabrum, two mixing bowls filled with dirt, and a portable radio from which issues a distressing melody, perhaps something from Mussorgsky's "Pictures at an Exhibition." A large spoon extrudes from each mixing bowl.

Two candleholders with red tapers occupy the coffee table, and a woman's shoulder bag lies on the floor. As the action progresses, we'll be invited to imagine three doors in the vicinity, one granting access to the front foyer, one leading to the kitchen, and one opening onto the cellar stairwell.

Enter ARABELLA LeGRAND, dressed in a Gypsy skirt with large pockets. She is a high-spirited woman of strong philosophical convictions and impressive metaphysical capabilities.

Lights up as Arabella switches off the radio and begins igniting the candles. She speaks directly to the audience.

> ARABELLA: I'll never forget the first time I brought somebody back from the dead. I could've practiced on any old corpse, but for my trial zombie I picked Lloyd, my late husband. Car crash. Forty-five years

old. Poor Lloyd. *(beat)* He wasn't particularly grateful when I resurrected him. In fact, he was annoyed. "Damn it, Arabella, now what?" I could see his point, but I needed somebody to lay the new linoleum in the kitchen.

The moan of a returning zombie briefly distracts her.

ARABELLA: *(cont'd)* Right away, Lloyd wanted a new name. He made me call him Jacques. "Jacques," "Lloyd," no matter—it wasn't like I really had him back. My kitchen floor looks great though.

A second moan throws her out of the reverie. She recovers.

ARABELLA: *(cont'd)* Lloyd's gone now. Malnourishment. A zombie can't digest anything except the dirt you removed from his grave when you exhumed him. Eventually you run out, and the corpse drops dead, and you have to go revive somebody else.

A third moan. She can't ignore it.

ARABELLA: *(cont'd)* Maurice? Come on in!

MAURICE shuffles into the living room from the foyer. His face is pale, black circles under his eyes. He holds a weed puller in one hand, a cantaloupe in the other.

MAURICE: *(zero affect)* If I were alive, I'd be feeling mighty hungry now.

Arabella removes a bowl of dirt from the bookcase and proffers it to Maurice. The zombie receives his dinner.

MAURICE: Dirt. Yum.

ARABELLA: Did you finish weeding Mrs. Barlow's vegetable garden?

MAURICE: *(waves weed puller)* The cabbages are almost ripe. The lettuce is ready for picking. *(tosses cantaloupe to Arabella)* She sent you her biggest cantaloupe.

ARABELLA: Tomorrow she hopes you'll pull the worms off her tomatoes.

MAURICE: *(non sequitur)* I miss the desires themselves more than I miss their fulfillment.

Still holding his dirt, Maurice exits toward the kitchen. As before, Arabella speaks directly to the audience.

ARABELLA: When a person has the power to raise the dead, she develops a strong sense of obligation to the living. In the old days, a zombie queen would use her corpses to help out the workers in the sugarcane fields and the tin mines.

Arabella hefts the cantaloupe.

ARABELLA: *(cont'd)* Mary Barlow can barely afford to buy groceries, so I've started sending Maurice over to help her raise a few vegetables. Poor old Horace Bickle used to get up at five every morning to deliver the *Montrose Daily Times.* It took me all day to teach Marguerite his route, but so far we haven't had a single dissatisfied customer.

Maurice returns with his dirt bowl and a canister of whipped cream.

ARABELLA: *(cont'd)* Clarence Tucker used to spend all his spare time licking and stuffing envelopes, so I started lending him Françoise. She's dead, but she has an excellent tongue.

Maurice pulls the cap off the whipped cream canister.

ARABELLA: *(to Maurice)* Whipped cream?

MAURICE: I can't taste it. *(shrugs)* The TV commercial is very persuasive.

Once again Arabella speaks directly to the audience.

ARABELLA: Patty Ambrose's eyesight got so bad she almost lost her job driving the school bus, but now Jean-Louis does it for her. Patty still goes along, riding in the front seat, helping the kids on and off.

Maurice attempts to frost his dirt with whipped cream. The canister delivers nothing but stale air.

MAURICE: Faugh. Empty.

ARABELLA: Listen, Maurice, some people are coming over tonight–the Montrose Public Safety Committee. Be nice to them. They're not sure zombies are a good idea. They might want to ban you.

MAURICE: I can pull eighty weeds in less than an hour, roots and all!

ARABELLA: They say they're concerned about sanitation issues, but I'll tell you what *really* bothers them. They're furious because I won't loan my zombies to wealthy people.

MAURICE: Ah.

ARABELLA: If I start letting the rich have zombies, the poor won't get their fair share.

MAURICE: Metaphysical socialism.

ARABELLA: Exactly.

MAURICE: Dialectical immaterialism.

ARABELLA: Indeed.

MAURICE: Voodoo economics.

Still holding his dirt, Maurice starts toward the kitchen in quest of a new whipped cream canister.

MAURICE: *(cont'd)* Such a dreamer you are, Arabella. Try being a corpse some time. It will make you a realist.

Exit Maurice. Arabella addresses the audience.

ARABELLA: The situation's getting out of hand. I've received insider tips from stockbrokers, new cars from bank presidents, diamond necklaces from brain surgeons. They think it would be so chic having a zombie around the mansion–cleaning the swimming pool, serving the canapés, tending the roses, walking the yorkie. I won't squander the dead that way.

Someone knocks on the front door.

ARABELLA: *(cont'd)* It's open!

Enter SUSAN WINGROVE, the mayor of Montrose, a middle-aged, no-nonsense politico whose conscience routinely informs her that she has selected the wrong line of work.

ARABELLA: *(cont'd)* Hello, Mayor Wingrove.

SUSAN: Ms. LeGrand. *(shakes Arabella's hand)* Are the others here yet?

ARABELLA: No.

SUSAN: *(mildly conspiratorial)* I came a little early

on purpose. I'm hoping I might speak with Herman privately. In his new ... condition.

ARABELLA: *(to Susan)* You mustn't expect too much.

SUSAN: He was a good husband. A little stuffy, but good. Made his own breakfast, built us a patio–he even managed my last campaign. Poor Herman.

ARABELLA: A skiing accident, right?

SUSAN: Broke his neck.

ARABELLA: He'll want you to call him Gaston.

SUSAN: What? *(American pronunciation)* Gaston?

ARABELLA: *(French pronunciation) Gaston.* Call him *Gaston.*

SUSAN: Gaston.

Maurice returns from the kitchen, bearing his dirt and a new canister of whipped cream. He sits on the loveseat, sprays some whipped cream into the bowl, and begins spooning the dirt into his mouth.

SUSAN: *(indicating Maurice)* That one looks familiar.

ARABELLA: Maurice used to work at the supermarket.

MAURICE: Paper, or plastic?

Finding a slug in his food, Maurice attempts to mimic revulsion.

MAURICE: *(cont'd)* Oh, yuck. A slug.

He pulls the slug free, dangles it in the air—and suddenly eats it.

MAURICE: *(cont'd)* Yum. I mean yuck.

ARABELLA: His name was Eddie Watkins. Lung cancer.

SUSAN: Oh, dear.

MAURICE: *(shoving bowl toward Susan)* Would you like some dirt?

SUSAN: No, thank you.

ARABELLA: Time for bed, Maurice.

MAURICE: *(rising, to Susan)* Would you like to see my coffin?

SUSAN: Not right now. *(to Arabella)* We might want to interview Maurice later. Will it be hard to wake him up?

ARABELLA: *(shaking head)* Zombies can't sleep–but they do need their rest.

MAURICE: Once you've experienced ontological oblivion, insomnia doesn't seem so bad.

ARABELLA: *(to zombie)* Big day tomorrow, Maurice, deworming all those tomatoes.

MAURICE: May I read in bed?

ARABELLA: *(assenting)* Lights out by 9:30 .

A moan signals the return of another zombie.

ARABELLA: *(cont'd)* Come in, Gaston!

Maurice removes Heidegger's Being and Time *from the bookcase and, still gripping his dinner, exits toward the cellar stairs.*

> ARABELLA: *(cont'd)* Now that you've seen what they're like, do you still want to...?
>
> SUSAN: I'm not going to enjoy it, but ... yes, I want to meet him.

Susan's resurrected husband, now called GASTON, enters from the foyer: pale face, black eyes, shambling gait. He wears ragged clothes and a torn felt hat.

Gaston takes the second dirt meal from the bookcase, flops down on the loveseat, and speaks. His voice is toneless, but we still detect a note of exasperation.

> GASTON: God, what a day! "Gaston, read us a story." "Gaston, tie my shoes." "Gaston, give me a horsy-back ride."

Gaston spoons dirt into his mouth.

> ARABELLA: *(to Susan)* Gaston baby-sits for Mrs. Fishbine every day, so she can work the cash register at Home Depot.
>
> GASTON: "Gaston, I have to go potty." "Gaston, we want to see *Toy Story.*"
>
> SUSAN: Hello, Herman. *(American pronunciation)* Gaston.
>
> GASTON: *(French)* Gaston.
>
> SUSAN: *(French)* Gaston.

Gingerly, she joins him on the loveseat.

> GASTON: Susan? Is that you?

SUSAN: Uh-huh.

ARABELLA: I'll leave you two alone.

Still holding cantaloupe, Arabella exits toward the kitchen.

GASTON: So ... how's life?

SUSAN: I'm doing okay.

GASTON: "Doing okay." That's *good*, isn't it?

SUSAN: Our daughter's about to graduate from Villanova.

GASTON: *(straining to feel)* Well, *well.* *(beat)* You appear to be *quite healthy*, Susan.

SUSAN: I feel great. They found a lump in my breast last month, but it was benign.

GASTON: My, my. *(proffers bowl)* Would you like some dirt?

SUSAN: I just had dinner. *(earnest)* Tell me what it's like.

GASTON: Dirt?

SUSAN: Death.

GASTON: A phenomenologist might put it this way, "There is nothing that being dead is like."

SUSAN: *(feigning comprehension)* I see.

GASTON: *(indicating candle)* I can tell you this candle is red, but I don't experience the redness. *(touches Susan's cheek)* I know your cheek is soft, but the softness doesn't register. My reality is devoid of sensation. All qualia are absent. I think this suggests that consciousness is not supervenient on the physical, but reflects an as yet undiscovered property of the universe, wouldn't you agree?

SUSAN: *(perplexed)* Yes. *(beat)* But do you feel *exploited*, Herman?

GASTON: Gaston.

SUSAN: Gaston.

GASTON: Exploited?

SUSAN: Some people think zombies should be outlawed in Montrose. Last week the Borough Council appointed a Public Safety Committee. We're meeting with Ms. LeGrand tonight: me ... and Reverend Larkin ... and–

GASTON: Reverend Larkin? Yuck. *(mimicry)* "Now *you too* can be part of our wonderful new expedition to find the Holy Grail. Just send your hard-earned cash to Radio Station WQRX."

SUSAN: *(chagrined)* He gives the Committee a certain moral authority. Whatever we decide, the Borough Council will go along with it.

GASTON: "It is easier for a poor man to pass through the eye of a needle than for a rich camel to enter the Kingdom of Heaven." *(to Susan)* Who *else* is coming over? Richard Nixon?

Susan blanches slightly: Ben Grigsby is not a comfortable topic.

SUSAN: The County Health Inspector. You know, Ben Grigs–

GASTON: Ben Grigsby? That chucklehead got re-elected? He stuffed the ballot box all over again?

SUSAN: Ben never stuffed the ballot box. That was just a rumor...

GASTON: Maybe I wasn't the ideal campaign manager, Susan, but I never recruited any voters for you in Greenbriar Cemetery.

SUSAN: ... and the second time around, there was no controversy at all. Ben earned every vote he got. *(uncertain)* I'm sure of it.

GASTON: You mean the people actually *wanted* him? That's even worse! If I was alive, I'd be glad I didn't live to see it.

SUSAN: *(confused)* Yes. *(beat)* Ben believes he can prove that zombies are a public health hazard.

GASTON: I'll be honest, Susan: I used to worry that you and Ben had a thing for each other–back when you were both on that Sewer Study Task Force. Imagine that.

SUSAN: *(forced sincerity)* Imagine that.

GASTON: You were so *dedicated* to that task force.

SUSAN: Montrose has a lot sewers.

GASTON: You know something? Ben's wife had the same suspicions I did.

SUSAN: How ... suspicious of her. *(the subject must change)* So your preference would be for Ms. LeGrand to stay in business, right?

GASTON: The dead have no preferences.

SUSAN: If you could persuade her to let *everybody* in Montrose have a zombie ... even wealthy people ... I'm sure the Public Safety Committee would–

Arabella enters, sans cantaloupe. Her sudden appearance cuts Susan off. Gaston yawns.

GASTON: That was a yawn, wasn't it? I must be tired.

ARABELLA: Your coffin's waiting.

GASTON: *(to his wife, portentously)* You have much to think about, Susan.

Gaston rises from the loveseat and, grasping his dirt bowl, stumbles toward the bookcase. He removes a copy of Immanuel Kant's Critique of Pure Reason.

GASTON: *(cont'd)* Goodnight, everyone.

SUSAN: Goodnight, *Gaston.*

ARABELLA: No reading after 9:30.

Dirt and philosophy in hand, Gaston exits toward the cellar stairs.

Someone knocks on the front door. Suddenly galvanized, Arabella rushes toward the loveseat, lifts a cushion, and pulls out a cloth voodoo doll.

SUSAN: What's *that?*

ARABELLA: I made it in the likeness of your friend Commissioner Grigsby. *(pointedly)* Your *good* friend Commissioner Grigsby.

She removes a pair of scissors from her shoulder bag.

ARABELLA: *(cont'd)* All I need is a DNA sample.

Another round of knocking. Arabella puts the doll and the scissors in her skirt pocket.

SUSAN: None of your cheap voodoo tricks, Ms. LeGrand. This case must be decided on its merits alone.

ARABELLA: No case is ever decided on its merits alone. That's why there's a Susan Wingrove Campaign Fund. *(responds to knocking)* Come in!

BEN GRIGSBY, the smooth and opportunistic County Health Inspector, sweeps into the room holding a black satchel.

BEN: An open sewer, right in the middle of Montrose! A pest hole of filth and contagion! *(notices Susan)* Hello, Susan. *(forced professionalism)* Mayor.

Ben and Susan trade freighted glances.

SUSAN: Hello, Ben. Ms. LeGrand, this is Ben Grigsby, County Health Inspector.

ARABELLA: So I gather. Would you like some dirt, Inspector?

Ben frowns, sets his satchel on the coffee table, and takes out four jars, each filled with a colored liquid reagent.

BEN: *(to Susan)* Our paths don't seem to cross much these days, Susan.

SUSAN: Whose fault is that?

Maurice enters from the cellar stairwell, carrying his copy of Being and Time, *which he evidently found impenetrable. He approaches the bookcase, reshelves the Heidegger, and selects Nietzsche's* Beyond Good and Evil. *As he starts back toward the cellar, Ben blocks his path.*

BEN: Stop, dead man! Don't move!

Maurice freezes. Ben sniffs the zombie head to foot.

BEN: *(cont'd)* Just as I suspected–he *smells bad!* *(to Susan)* A breeding ground for plague!

Ben returns to the coffee table and removes four tools from his satchel: syringe, tweezers, medicine dropper, Q-Tip.

BEN: *(cont'd)* A walking toxic-waste dump!

ARABELLA: His name is *Maurice*.

SUSAN: Do you have any tea, Ms. LeGrand? It's going to be a long evening.

ARABELLA: Everything's in the kitchen. Help yourself.

Susan heads into the kitchen. Nietzsche in hand, Maurice starts to exit.

BEN: Stay right there *Maurice*. This scientific investigation has barely begun.

A brief comedic ballet follows as Ben collects four samples from Maurice and transfers them to the reagent jars.

BEN: *(cont'd)* Let's see: we'll need *(wields syringe)* two cc's of blood ... *(uses tweezers)* a skin sample ... *(inserts medicine dropper)* an ounce of saliva ... *(swizzles Q-Tip)* and a bit of ear wax.

Taking out her scissors, Arabella sneaks up behind Ben and snips off a lock of his hair.

BEN: *(to Maurice)* Okay, dead man, you're done.

As Maurice shuffles out of the room, Arabella retrieves a bottle of rubber cement from her shoulder bag and surreptitiously affixes the lock to the doll. She slips the cement and the doll into her skirt. Ben meanwhile seizes the first reagent jar and shakes it.

BEN: *(cont'd)* This reagent will tell the tale. Organic chemistry never lies.

He holds the jar up to the light.

BEN: *(cont'd)* Hah! Just as I suspected, Ms. LeGrand! Your zombies are carrying amoebic dysentery!

Arabella turns away from Ben, takes out the doll, and proceeds to tickle it. Though obviously perplexed by the sensation, Ben can't help giggling.

Regaining his composure, he sets down the dysentery experiment, holds up the second reagent jar, and shakes it.

BEN: And here we have ... Asiatic cholera!

Arabella extends her index finder and jabs it into the doll's stomach.

Ben suddenly clutches his belly and gasps. Despite his confusion, he manages to set down the second reagent jar, grab the third, and examine it.

BEN: *(cont'd)* Jackpot! African sleeping sickness!

As Ben sets down the jar, Arabella puts the doll through a series of bizarre gyrations. Wholly against his will, Ben mimics the doll's convulsive dance.

Susan enters carrying a tea tray: pot, cups, sugar, cream. For an instant she simply stands in place, perplexed by Ben's antics. Sizing up the situation, she sets down the tray and yells at Arabella.

SUSAN: Stop that, Ms. LeGrand! You stop that!

Arabella returns the doll to her skirt pocket. Ben regains control of himself. He glances in all directions, trying to discover the source of his recent spasms.

SUSAN: *(cont'd)* Ben, this woman is devious!

A knock on the door.

ARABELLA: Come in!

Ben holds up the fourth reagent jar, shakes it, and prepares to pronounce on the result.

REVEREND JEREMIAH LARKIN strides into the room. He is an imposing man whose worldview derives largely from St. Paul's First Letter to the Republicans.

SUSAN: Hello, Reverend Larkin.

BEN: Syphilis!

JEREMIAH: What?

ARABELLA: *(to Ben, angry)* Oh, *please* let's be honest, Inspector. The minute I let you have one of your own, you'll decide my zombies aren't a health hazard after all. But I won't do it. No zombie for Ben Grigsby, who inherited *one million dollars* from his Uncle Alex. *(points to Susan)* No zombie for Mayor Wingrove, who pulls in an extra *two hundred thousand* a year as the landlord of Skyview Terrace. *(points to Jeremiah)* No zombie for Reverend Larkin, whose radio station clears an annual profit equal to the budget of Guatemala.

JEREMIAH: Costa Rica.

BEN: *(to Jeremiah)* You're late.

JEREMIAH: Sorry. I decided to walk. *(rubs his chest*

and winces) Doctor Merrick said it's good for the heart. *His* heart maybe, not mine. *(gasps)* Christ had the Via Dolorosa. I have a cholesterol count of 345.

As Susan pours Jeremiah a cup of tea, he staggers into the loveseat and pulls out a pill bottle. The minister removes a pill, lobs it into his mouth, and washes it down with tea.

BEN: *(indicating fourth jar)* The proof is irrefutable. These corpses are harboring four different epidemic diseases. The Borough Council will have no choice but to ban them!

Gaston shuffles in from the cellar stairwell, wearing a sour expression and clutching his copy of Kant's Critique of Pure Reason. *He reshelves it and selects Heidegger's* Being and Time *instead.*

Transcending his pain, Jeremiah rises from the loveseat and blocks the zombie's path.

JEREMIAH: Herman? Herman Wingrove? Remember me? Your minister?

GASTON: I'm Gaston now.

JEREMIAH: Tell me honestly, Herman. Wouldn't you be better off dead?

GASTON: I *am* dead.

JEREMIAH: Dead and *buried*, I mean.

GASTON: All phenomenological experience is beyond me.

Jeremiah confronts Arabella with a full measure of his wrath.

JEREMIAH: How *evil* of you, Arabella LeGrand! How *cruel*! To create beings who are incapable of (*mispronounces*) phomenalogical experience!

GASTON: It's not so bad. I used to get migraines.

JEREMIAH: I'll bet Mrs. Wingrove could have an adulterous love affair right in front of Mr. Wingrove, and he wouldn't feel one tittle of jealousy!

BEN: (*joining in*) Somebody could kiss Mrs. Wingrove *right now*, and Mr. Wingrove wouldn't even *care*.

GASTON: Ben Grigsby? Is that really you? (*to Arabella*) This is the man I was telling you about, the one who gets corpses to vote for him.

BEN: Susan, I think we should put Reverend Larkin's theory to the test.

He sweeps Susan into his arms and kisses her passionately. Against her better judgment, Susan reciprocates.

Gaston's only response is to decide against the Heidegger volume. He reshelves it. Jeremiah studies Gaston's impassive face.

JEREMIAH: Not a twitch!

Ben pulls Susan onto the loveseat, and they engage in a bizarre variety of necking, half passionate, half clinical. Jeremiah leads the impassive Gaston toward the couple.

JEREMIAH: (*cont'd*) Not a twinge! Not a flicker! Not a blip! (*to Arabella, indicating Gaston*) Do you realize what you've done, Arabella LeGrand? Shame on you! You've stolen this man's *soul*! In a Godless age, who will protect the rights of the undead?

Jeremiah climbs onto the coffee table, the better to study the whole group. Inspired by his newfound elevation, he behaves as if commanding a pulpit.

JEREMIAH: *(cont'd)* But the Lord, he shall come in a cloud of flame, and then shall the wicked know his wrath! He shall scourge the atheists and the idolaters *(points at Arabella)* and the *enchantresses* and the flag burners and the gun controllers and the adulterers *(glances at Susan and Ben, realizes he's condemning them)* and certain adulterers and the sodomites and the Darwinists and the *(pain sears his chest)* environmental ... alarmists ... and ... and ... and–

Jeremiah clutches his shoulder and falls on the floor, dead. His demise gets the attention of Ben and Susan. They rise from the loveseat and stand over Jeremiah's body.

SUSAN: Good heavens, is he ... dead?

GASTON: A reasonable supposition.

Arabella bends over Jeremiah, grasps his wrist, and feels for a pulse.

BEN: Leave this to me. I'm the professional here.

Arabella stands aside. Ben pulls a mirror from his satchel and holds it over Jeremiah's mouth. He checks the glass for condensation.

BEN: *(cont'd)* He's dead.

Ben looks at himself in the mirror. He smoothes back his hair.

ARABELLA: Gaston, give me a hand.

Together, Gaston and Arabella pick up Jeremiah's body and carry it out of the room, toward the cellar stairs. Ben and Susan are now alone.

SUSAN: Poor old Jeremiah. At least he fell in the line of duty.

BEN: Kiss me again.

SUSAN: Ben, we have to talk.

BEN: My marriage is over. This time I mean it.

SUSAN: I don't care.

BEN: No. Really. Karen and I are through.

SUSAN: Ben, everybody knows there were some irregularities the *first* time you got elected, but the *second* time around, you earned every vote, right?

BEN: What does *that* have to do with anything?

SUSAN: I need an honest answer. How many dead people voted for you in last year's election?

BEN: Susan—

SUSAN: How many?

BEN: This isn't—

SUSAN: *How many?*

BEN: Three hundred and thirty. But they were all *recently* dead.

SUSAN: I thought so .

BEN: I'm definitely leaving Karen.

SUSAN: Not for me you aren't.

BEN: Let's save that discussion for tomorrow. Right now we've got to block those zombies. I now call to order the first meeting of the Montrose Public Safety Committee!

SUSAN: No, Ben. The meeting's over. *(under her breath)* Everything's over.

BEN: Come on, Susan! It's you and me against the dead!

SUSAN: I don't think so.

BEN: *(to Susan)* How can you blithely ignore major disease vectors? *(points to reagent jars)* Amoebic dysentery, Asiatic cholera, African sleeping sickness–

SUSAN: None of those are *airborne* diseases. You can't catch them from a zombie unless you eat it or have sex with it.

BEN: *(to Susan, angry)* Since when did *you* get elected County Health Inspector?

SUSAN: Since when did *you?*

An otherworldly moan issues from the cellar stairwell.

BEN: Damn it, Susan, we have to present a *united front.* I mean, now that the Public Safety Committee is down to just two ...

Jeremiah staggers into the room: pale face, dark eyes—a zombie.

JEREMIAH: *(zero affect)* No, friends, there are still *three* of us.

SUSAN: Jeremiah! You're ... back.

JEREMIAH: Pierre.

SUSAN: Pierre.

JEREMIAH: *(philosophical)* It was a most congenial

funeral. Short, but congenial. They dug me a cozy little hole in the cellar. I have a clean, well-lighted grave.

Arabella and Gaston re-enter the room.

JEREMIAH: *(cont'd)* I'll say one thing for death—it gives you a new point of view. From my present perspective, I would argue that there's nothing inherently wrong with using resuscitated corpses for charitable purposes.

GASTON: *(to Jeremiah)* Of course, charity by itself is insufficient. We must also commit ourselves to basic civil liberties and economic egalitarianism.

JEREMIAH: Charity is always optional.

GASTON: Whereas justice never is.

ARABELLA: Have you been reading Karl Marx, Gaston?

GASTON: Dear Abby.

JEREMIAH: *(paraphrasing previous exchange)* "And if a man comes to you and asks, 'May I borrow your zombie for a day?', say unto him, 'He's yours to keep, brother.'"

BEN: I'm sorry, Jeremiah, but dead people can't testify before the Borough Council.

SUSAN: *(to Ben)* If they can *vote*, they can *testify*.

JEREMIAH: *(to Arabella, admiringly)* "And what voodoo queen, if she finds that one of her hundred zombies has gone astray, does not leave the ninety and nine and seek the one who is lost?"

SUSAN: Gaston, the Committee will almost certainly recommend that Ms. LeGrand be allowed to stay in business.

BEN: Over my dead body.

GASTON: A wise decision, Susan.

JEREMIAH: Good for you, Mrs. Wingrove.

BEN: This is insane!

Arabella pulls the doll from her skirt and holds it in front of Ben. She tickles it. Ben giggles. She folds its arms across its chest. Ben involuntarily assumes a straitjacket posture.

The two of them exchange ferocious stares: everything is now clear to Ben. Slowly, deliberately, Arabella drops the doll. Ben collapses.

SUSAN: Give up, Ben. Vote for the zombies.

As Arabella picks up the doll, Ben slowly rises to his feet. He continues to face these hopeless odds with a bizarre sort of nobility.

Suddenly Arabella chokes the doll—not severely, but enough to momentarily shut off Ben's air supply. Gagging, he collapses once again.

Ben rises, ready for another round. Susan snatches the doll from Arabella.

SUSAN: *(cont'd)* You've had your fun, Arabella. *(beat)* Now I'm going to have mine.

BEN: I shall not sacrifice my principles!

Susan steps toward the bookcase and holds the doll's crotch near the candle flame. She and Ben trade knowing glances.

BEN: Especially my dearest principles. *(beat)* You win, Susan.

SUSAN: It's for the best, Ben.

Susan returns the doll to Arabella, then walks over to Gaston and hugs him.

SUSAN: *(cont'd)* Keep up the good work, Gaston.

GASTON: Mrs. Fishbine's children run me ragged, but I've finally found my calling in life. It was nice to see you again, Susan.

SUSAN: It was nice to see you again, Gaston. *(to Jeremiah)* Coming, Pierre?

JEREMIAH: I belong *here* now. *(pulls small hedge trimmer from his pocket)* Tomorrow I'm helping old Mr. Colby with his yard-work business.

BEN: *(beat)* You'll find it very satisfying.

JEREMIAH: See you at the Council meeting.

SUSAN: I'm looking forward to it.

Susan begins to exit.

BEN: Wait, Susan. I'll walk you to your car.

SUSAN: *(pointedly)* I took the bus. *(brightens)* Goodnight, everyone.

Susan marches into the foyer. Friendless and confused, Ben looks around, then smiles weakly and addresses Arabella.

BEN: You've got my vote, Ms. LeGrand, but give me that damn doll.

Arabella hands Ben the doll. As an experiment, he tickles it, which triggers an involuntary giggle.

JEREMIAH: Goodnight, Ben.

GASTON: Pleasant dreams, sir.

Exit Ben. Gaston and Jeremiah stumble toward the bookcase. They respectively select Descartes's On Method *and Hegel's* Phenomenology of Spirit, *then exit toward the cellar stairs.*

Alone now, Arabella turns on the radio and addresses the audience. A misterioso organ theme plays under her speech.

ARABELLA: I've been reviving the dead for nearly three years now, but I still don't understand them. And yet we need the dead, don't we? Without the dead, the living would become much too impressed with themselves.

She moves slowly around the room, blowing out each candle. As the room darkens, she directs her voice toward the whole Kingdom of Thanatos.

ARABELLA: *(cont'd)* Do you hear me, all you corpses out there? Listen, I know how hard it is for you. Worms, grave robbers, ungrateful descendents. But I'm on your side. You have a friend in Arabella LeGrand.

She lowers her voice and resumes speaking to the audience.

ARABELLA: *(cont'd)* As for the rest of you ... neighbors, citizens, future cadavers ... when you go to die, hang a sign around your neck–DO NOT RESUSCITATE UNTIL DOOMSDAY–and I promise to leave you alone. But before you hang that sign, remember one thing. I'm offering you a second chance to make yourself useful in this world.

She turns off the radio and quenches the last candle.

ARABELLA: *(cont'd)* You won't get a third.

The room goes dark.

The cat's pajamas

"ALL POLITICS IS LOCAL POLITICS."
—*Tip O'Neill*

The eighteenth-century Enlightenment was still in our faces, fetishizing the rational intellect and ramming technocracy down our throats, so I said to Vickie, "Screw it. This isn't for us. Let's hop in the car and drive to romanticism, or maybe even to preindustrial paganism, or possibly all the way to hunter-gatherer utopianism." But we only got as far as Pennsylvania.

I knew that the idea of spending all summer on the road would appeal to Vickie. Most of her affections, including her unbridled wanderlust, are familiar to me. Not only had we lived together for six years, we also worked at the same New Jersey high school–Vickie teaching American history, me offering a souped-up eleventh-grade Humanities course–with the result that both our screaming matches and our flashes of rapport drew upon a fund of shared experiences. And so it was that the first day of summer vacation found us rattling down Route 80 in our decrepit VW bus, listening to Crash Test Dummies CDs and pretending that our impulsive westward flight somehow partook of political subversion, though we sensed it was really just an extended camping trip.

Despite being an *épater le bourgeois* sort of woman, Vickie had spent the previous two years promoting the idea of holy matrimony, an institution that has consistently failed to enchant me. Nevertheless, when we reached the Delaware Water Gap, I turned to her and said, "Here's a challenge for us. Let's see if we can't become man and wife by this time tomorrow afternoon." It's important, I feel, to suffuse a relationship with a certain level of unpredictability, if not outright caprice. "Vows, rings, music, all of it."

"You're crazy," she said, brightening. She's got a killer smile, sharp at the edges, luminous at the center. "It takes a week just to get the blood-test results."

"I was reading in *Newsweek* that there's a portable analyzer on the market. If we can find a technologically advanced justice of the peace, we'll meet the deadline with time to spare."

"Deadline?" She tightened her grip on the steering wheel. "Jeez, Blake, this isn't a *game*. We're talking about a *marriage*."

"It's a game and a gamble–I know from experience. But with you, sweetheart, I'm ready to bet the farm."

She laughed and said, "I love you."

⇨ ✦ ⇦

We spent the night in a motel outside a pastoral Pennsylvania borough called Greenbriar, got up at ten, made distracted love, and began scanning the yellow pages for a properly outfitted magistrate. By noon we had our man, District Justice George Stratus, proud owner of a brand new Sorrel-130 blood analyzer. It so happened that Judge Stratus was something of a specialist in instant marriage. For a hundred dollars flat, he informed me over the phone, we could have "the nanosecond nuptial package," including blood test, license, certificate, and a bottle of Taylor's champagne. I told him it sounded like a bargain.

To get there, we had to drive down a sinuous band of dirt and gravel called Spring Valley Road, past the asparagus fields, apple orchards, and cow pastures of Pollifex Farm. We arrived in a billowing nimbus of dust. Judge Stratus turned out to be a fat and affable paragon of efficiency. He immediately set about pricking our fingers and feeding the blood to his Sorrel-130, which took only sixty seconds to endorse our DNA even as it acquitted us of venereal misadventures. He faxed the results to the county courthouse, signed the marriage certificate, and poured us each a glass of champagne. By three o'clock, Vickie and I were legally entitled to partake of connubial bliss.

I think Judge Stratus noticed my pained expression when I handed over the hundred dollars, because he suggested that if we were short on cash, we should stop by the farm and talk to Andre Pollifex. "He's always looking for asparagus pickers this time of year." In point of fact, my divorce from Irene had cost me plenty, making a shambles of both my bank account and my credit record, and Vickie's fondness for upper-middle-class counterculture artifacts, solar-powered trash compacters and so on, had depleted her resources as well. We had funds enough for the moment, though, so I told Stratus we probably wouldn't be joining the migrant worker pool before August.

"Well, sweetheart, we've done it," I said as we climbed back into the bus. "Mr. and Mrs. Blake Meeshaw."

"The price was certainly right," said Vickie, "even though the husband involved is a fixer-upper."

"You've got quite a few loose shingles yourself," I said.

"I'll be hammering and plastering all summer."

Although we had no plans to stop at Pollifex Farm, when we got there an enormous flock of sheep was crossing the road. Vickie hit the brakes just in time to avoid making mutton of a stray ewe, and we resigned ourselves to watching the woolly parade, which promised to be as dull as a passing freight train. Eventually a swarthy man appeared gripping a silver-tipped shepherd's crook. He advanced at a pronounced stoop, like a denizen of Dante's Purgatory balancing a millstone on his neck.

A full minute elapsed before Vickie and I realized that the sheep were moving in a loop, like wooden horses on a carousel. With an impatience bordering on hysteria, I leaped from the van and strode toward the obnoxious herdsman. What possible explanation could he offer for erecting this perpetual barricade?

Nearing the flock, I realized that the scene's strangest aspect was neither the grotesque shepherd nor the tautological roadblock, but the sheep themselves. Every third or fourth animal was a mutant, its head distinctly humanoid, though the facial features seemed melted together, as if they'd been cast in wax and abandoned to the summer sun. The sooner we were out of here, I decided, the better.

"What the hell do you think you're doing?" I shouted. "Get these animals off the road!"

The shepherd hobbled up to me and pulled a tranquilizer

pistol from his belt with a manifest intention of rendering me unconscious.

"Welcome to Pollifex Farm," he said.

The gun went off, the dart found my chest, and the world turned black.

⚜ ✿ ⚜

Regaining consciousness, I discovered than someone–the violent shepherd? Andre Pollifex?–had relocated my assaulted self to a small bright room perhaps twelve feet square. Dust motes rode the sunlit air. Sections of yellow wallpaper buckled outward from the sheetrock like spritsails puffed with wind. I lay on a mildewed mattress, elevated by a box spring framed in steel. A turban of bandages encircled my head. Beside me stood a second bed, as uninviting as my own, its bare mattress littered with artifacts that I soon recognized as Vickie's–comb, hand mirror, travel alarm, ankh earrings, well-thumbed paperback of *Zen and the Art of Motorcycle Maintenance*.

It took me at least five minutes, perhaps as many as ten, before I realized that my brain had been removed from my cranium and that the pink, throbbing, convoluted mass of tissue on the nearby library cart was in fact my own thinking apparatus. Disturbing and unorthodox as this arrangement was, I could not deny its actuality. Every time I tapped my skull, a hollow sound came forth, as if I were knocking on an empty casserole dish. Fortunately, the physicians responsible for my condition had worked hard to guarantee that it would entail no functional deficits. Not only was my brain protected by a large Plexiglas jar filled with a clear, acrid fluid, it also retained its normal connection to my heart and spinal cord. A ropy mass of neurons, interlaced with augmentations of my jugular vein and my two carotid arteries, extended from beneath my orphaned medulla and stretched across four feet of empty space before disappearing into my reopened fontanel, the whole arrangement shielded from microbial contamination by a flexible plastic tube. I was thankful for my surgeons' conscientiousness, but also–I don't mind telling you–extremely frightened and upset.

My brain's extramural location naturally complicated the procedure, but in a matter of minutes I managed to transport both myself and the library cart into the next room, an unappointed parlor bedecked in cobwebs, and from there to an enclosed porch, all the while calling

Vickie's name. She didn't answer. I opened the door and shuffled into the putrid air of Pollifex Farm. Everywhere I turned, disorder prospered. The cottage in which I'd awoken seemed ready to collapse under its own weight. The adjacent windmill canted more radically than Pisa's Leaning Tower. Scabs of leprous white paint mottled the sides of the main farmhouse. No building was without its unhinged door, its shattered window, its sunken roof, its disintegrating wall—a hundred instances of entropy mirroring the biological derangement that lay within.

I did not linger in the stables, home to six human-headed horses. Until this moment, I had thought the centaurial form intrinsically beautiful, but with their bony backs and twisted faces these monsters soon deprived me of that supposition. Nor did I remain long in the chicken coop, habitat of four gigantic human-headed hens, each the size of a German shepherd. Nor did the pig shed detain me, for seven human-headed hogs is not a spectacle that improves upon contemplation. Instead I hurried toward an immense barn, lured by a spirited performance of Tchaikovsky's Piano Concerto No. 1 wafting through a crooked doorway right out of *The Cabinet of Dr. Caligari.*

Cautiously I entered. Spacious and high roofed, the barn was a kind of agrarian cathedral, the Chartres of animal husbandry. In the far corner, hunched over a baby grand piano, sat a humanoid bull: blunt nose, gaping nostrils, a long tapering horn projecting from either side of his head. Whereas his hind legs were of the bovine variety, his forelegs ended in a pair of human hands that skated gracefully along the keyboard. He shared his bench with my wife, and even at this distance I could see that the bull man's virtuosity had brought her to the brink of rapture.

Cerebrum in tow, I made my way across the barn. With each step, my apprehension deepened, my confusion increased, and my anger toward Vickie intensified. Apprehension, confusion, anger: while I was not yet accustomed to experiencing such sensations in a location other than my head, the phenomenon now seemed less peculiar than when I'd first returned to sentience.

"I know what you're thinking," said Vickie, acknowledging my presence. "Why am I sitting here when I should be helping you recover from the operation? Please believe me: Karl said the anesthesia wouldn't wear off for another four hours."

She proceeded to explain that Karl was the shepherd who'd tranquilized me on the road, subsequently convincing her to follow him

193

onto the farm rather than suffer the identical fate. But Karl's name was the least of what Vickie had learned during the past forty-eight hours. Our present difficulties, she elaborated, traced to the VD screening we'd received on Wednesday. In exchange for a substantial payment, Judge Stratus had promised to alert his patrons at Pollifex Farm the instant he happened upon a blood sample bearing the deoxyribonucleic acid component known as QZ-11-4. Once in possession of this gene–or, more specifically, once in possession of a human brain whose *in utero* maturation had been influenced by this gene–Dr. Pollifex's biological investigations could go forward.

"Oh, Blake, they're doing absolutely *wonderful* work here." Vickie rose from the bench, came toward me and, taking care not to become entangled in my spinal cord, gave me a mildly concupiscent hug. "An external brain to go with your external genitalia–I think it's very sexy."

"Stop talking nonsense, Vickie!" I said. "I've been *mutilated*!"

She stroked my bandaged forehead and said, "Once you hear the whole story, you'll realize that your bilateral hemispherectomy serves a greater good."

"Call me Maxwell," said the bull man, lifting his fingers from the keyboard. "Maxwell Taurus." His voice reminded me of Charles Laughton's. "I must congratulate you on your choice of marriage partner, Blake. Vickie has a refreshingly open mind."

"And I have a depressingly vacant skull," I replied. "Take me to this lunatic Pollifex so I can get my brain put back where it belongs."

"The doctor would never agree to that." Maxwell fixed me with his stare, his eyes all wet and brown like newly created caramel apples. "He requires round-the-clock access to your anterior cortex."

A flock of human-headed geese fluttered into the barn, raced toward a battered aluminum trough full of grain, and began to eat. Unlike Maxwell, the geese did not possess the power of speech–either that, or they simply had nothing to say to each other.

I sighed and leaned against my library cart. "So what, exactly, does QZ-11-4 *do*?"

"Dr. Pollifex calls it the integrity gene, wellspring of decency, empathy, and compassionate foresight," said Maxwell. "Francis of Assisi had it. So did Charles Darwin, Clara Barton, Mahatma Gandhi, Florence Nightingale, Albert Schweitzer, and Susan B. Anthony. And now–now that Dr. Pollifex has started injecting me with a serum derived from your hypertrophic superego–now *I've* got it too."

Although my vanity took a certain satisfaction in Maxwell's words, I realized that I'd lost the thread of his logic. "At the risk of sounding disingenuously modest, I'd have to say I'm not a particularly ethical individual."

"Even if a person inherits QZ-11-4, it doesn't necessarily enjoy expression. And even if the gene enjoys expression"–Maxwell offered me a semantically freighted stare–"the beneficiary doesn't always learn to use his talent. Indeed, among Dr. Pollifex's earliest discoveries was the fact that complete QZ-11-4 actualization is impossible in a purely human species. The serum–we call it Altruoid–the serum reliably engenders ethical superiority only in people who've been genetically melded with domesticated birds and mammals."

"You mean–you used to be ... human?"

"For twenty years I sold life insurance under the name Lewis Phelps. Have no fear, Blake. We are not harvesting your cerebrum in vain. I shall employ my Altruoid allotment to bestow great boons on Greenbriar."

"You might fancy yourself a moral giant," I told the bull man, "but as far as I'm concerned, you're a terrorist and a brain thief, and I intend to bring this matter to the police."

"You will find that strategy difficult to implement." Maxwell left his piano and, walking upright on his hooves, approached my library cart. "Pollifex Farm is enclosed by a barbed-wire fence twelve feet high. I suggest you try making the best of your situation."

The thought of punching Maxwell in the face now occurred to me, but I dared not risk uprooting my arteries and spinal cord. "If Pollifex continues pilfering my cortex, how long before I become a basket case?"

"Never. The doctor happens to be the world's greatest neurocartographer. He'll bring exquisite taste and sensitivity to each extraction. During the next three years, you'll lose only trivial knowledge, useless skills, and unpleasant memories." "Three years?" I howled. "You bastards plan to keep me here *three years?*"

"Give or take a month. Once that interval has passed, my peers and I shall have reached the absolute apex of vertebrate ethical development."

"See, Blake, they've thought of *everything,*" said Vickie. "These people are *visionaries.*"

"These people are Nazis," I said.

"Really, sir, name calling is unnecessary," said Maxwell with a snort. "There's no reason we can't all be friends." He rested an affirming hand on my shoulder. "We've given you a great deal of information to absorb. I suggest you spend tomorrow afternoon in quiet contemplation. Come evening, we'll all be joining the doctor for dinner. It's a meal you're certain to remember."

꒓ ✹ ꒱

My new bride and I passed the night in our depressing little cottage beside the windmill. Much to my relief, I discovered that my sexual functioning had survived the bilateral hemispherectomy. We had to exercise caution, of course, lest we snap the vital link between medulla and cord, with the result that the whole encounter quickly devolved into a kind of slow-motion ballet. Vickie said it was like mating with a china figurine, the first negative remark I'd heard her make concerning my predicament.

At ten o'clock the next morning, one of Karl's human-headed sheep entered the bedroom, walking upright and carrying a wicker tray on which rested two covered dishes. When I asked the sheep how long she'd been living at Pollifex Farm, her expression became as vacant as a cake of soap. I concluded that the power of articulation was reserved only to those mutants on an Altruoid regimen.

The sheep bowed graciously and left, and we set about devouring our scrambled eggs, hot coffee, and buttered toast. Upon consuming her final mouthful, Vickie announced that she would spend the day reading two scientific treatises she'd received from Maxwell, both by Dr. Pollifex: *On the Mutability of Species* and *The Descent of Morals*. I told her I had a different agenda. If there was a way out of this bucolic asylum, I was by-God going to find it.

Before I could take leave of my wife, Karl himself appeared, clutching a black leather satchel to his chest as a mother might hold a baby. He told me he deeply regretted Wednesday's assault—I must admit, I detected no guile in his apology—then explained that he'd come to collect the day's specimen. From the satchel he removed a glass-and-steel syringe, using it to suck up a small quantity of anterior cortex and transfer it to a test tube. When I told Karl that I felt nothing during the procedure, he reminded me that the human brain is an insensate organ, nerveless as a stone.

I commenced my explorations. Pollifex's domain was vaster than I'd imagined, though most of its fields and pastures were deserted. True to the bull man's claim, a fence hemmed the entire farm, the barbed-wire strands woven into a kind of demonic tennis net and strung between steel posts rising from a concrete foundation. In the northeast corner lay a barn as large as Maxwell's concert hall, and it was here, clearly, that Andre Pollifex perpetuated his various crimes against nature. The doors were barred, the windows occluded, but by staring through the cracks in the walls I managed to catch glimpses of hospital gurneys, surgical lights, and three enormous glass beakers in which sallow, teratoid fetuses drifted like pickles in brine.

About twenty paces from Pollifex's laboratory, a crumbling toolshed sat atop a hill of naked dirt. I gave the door a hard shove–not too hard, given my neurological vulnerability–and it pivoted open on protesting hinges. A shaft of afternoon sunlight struck the interior, revealing an assortment of rakes, shovels, and pitchforks, plus a dozen bags of fertilizer–but, alas, no wire cutters.

My perambulations proved exhausting, both mentally and physically, and I returned to the cottage for a much needed nap. That afternoon, my brain tormented me with the notorious "student's dream." I'd enrolled in an advanced biology course at my old alma mater, Rutgers, but I hadn't attended a single class or handed in even one assignment. And now I was expected to take the final exam.

꒰ ◉ ꒱

Vickie, my brain, and I were the last to arrive at Andre Pollifex's dinner party, which occurred in an airy glass-roofed conservatory attached to the back of the farmhouse. The room smelled only slightly better than the piano barn. At the head of the table presided our host, a disarmingly ordinary looking man, weak of jaw, slight of build, distinguished primarily by his small black moustache and complementary goatee. His face was pale and flaccid, as if he'd been raised in a cave. The instant he opened his mouth to greet us, though, I apprehended something of his glamour, for he had the most majestic voice I've ever heard outside of New York's Metropolitan Opera House.

"Welcome, Mr. and Mrs. Meeshaw," he said. "May I call you Blake and Vickie?"

"Of course," said Vickie.

"May I call you Joseph Mengele?" I said.

Pollifex's white countenance contracted into a scowl. "I can appreciate your distress, Blake. Your sacrifice has been great. I believe I speak for everyone here when I say that our gratitude knows no bounds."

197

Karl directed us into adjacent seats, then resumed his place next to Pollifex, directly across from the bull man. I found myself facing a pig woman whose large ears flopped about like college pennants and whose snout suggested an oversized button. Vickie sat opposite a goat man with a tapering white beard dangling from his chin and two corrugated horns sprouting from his brow.

"I'm Serge Milkovich," said the goat man, shaking first Vickie's hand, then mine. "In my former life I was Bud Frye, plumbing contractor."

"Call me Juliana Sowers," said the pig woman, enacting the same ritual. "At one time I was Doris Owens of Owens Real Estate, but then I found a higher calling. I cannot begin to thank you for the contribution you're making to science, philosophy, and local politics."

"Local politics?" I asked.

"We three beneficiaries of QZ-11-4 form the core of the new Common Sense Party," said Juliana. "We intend to transform Greenbriar into the most livable community in America."

"I'm running for Borough Council," said Serge. "Should my campaign prove successful, I shall fight to keep our town free of Consumerland discount stores. Their advent is inevitably disastrous for local merchants."

Juliana crammed a handful of hors d'oeuvres into her mouth. "I seek a position on the School Board. My stances won't prove automatically popular–better pay for elementary teachers, sex education starting in grade four–but I'm prepared to support them with passion and statistics."

Vickie grabbed my hand and said, "See what I mean, Blake? They may be mutants, but they have terrific ideas."

"As for me, I've got my eye on the Planning Commission," said Maxwell, releasing a loud and disconcerting burp. "Did you know there's a scheme afoot to run the Route 80 Extension along our northern boundary, just so it'll be easier for people to get to Penn State football games? Once construction begins, the environmental desecration will be profound."

As Maxwell expounded upon his anti-extension arguments, a half-dozen sheep arrived with our food. In deference to Maxwell and Juliana, the cuisine was vegetarian: tofu, lentils, capellini with meatless marinara sauce. It was all quite tasty, but the highlight of the meal was surely the venerable and exquisite vintages from Pollifex's cellar. After my first few swallows of Brunello di Montalcino, I worried that Pollifex's scalpel had denied me the pleasures of intoxication, but eventually the expected sensation arrived. (I attributed the hiatus to the extra distance my blood had to travel along my extended arteries.) By the time the sheep were serving dessert, I was quite tipsy, though my bursts of euphoria alternated uncontrollably with spasms of anxiety.

"Know what I think?" I said, locking on Pollifex as I struggled to prevent my brain from slurring my words. "I think you're trying to turn me into a zombie."

The doctor proffered a heartening smile. "Your discomfort is understandable, Blake, but I can assure you all my interventions have been innocuous thus far—and will be in the future. Tell me, what two classroom pets did your second-grade teacher, Mrs. Hines, keep beside her desk, and what were their names?"

"I have no idea."

"Of course you don't. That useless memory vanished with the first extraction. A hamster and a chameleon. Florence and Charlie. Now tell me about the time you threw up on your date for the senior prom."

"That never happened."

"Yes it did, but I have spared you any recollection of the event. Nor will you ever again be haunted by the memory of forgetting your lines during the Cransford Community Theater production of *A Moon for the Misbegotten*. Now please recite Joyce Kilmer's 'Trees.'"

"All right, all right, you've made your point," I said. "But you still have no right to mess with my head." I swallowed more wine. "As for this ridiculous Common Sense Party—okay, sure, these candidates might get my vote—I'm for better schools and free enterprise and all that—but the average Greenbriar citizen..." In lieu of stating the obvious, I finished my wine.

"What *about* the average Greenbriar citizen?" said Juliana huffily.

"The average Greenbriar citizen will find us morphologically unacceptable?" said Serge haughtily.

"Well ... yes," I replied.

"Unpleasantly odiferous?" said Maxwell snippily.

"That too."

"Homely?" said Juliana defensively.

"I wouldn't be surprised."

The sheep served dessert—raspberry and lemon sorbet—and the seven of us ate in silence, painfully aware that mutual understanding between myself and the Common Sense Party would be a long time coming.

⊰ ✾ ⊱

During the final two weeks of June, Karl siphoned fourteen additional specimens from my superego, one extraction per day. On the Fourth of July, the shepherd unwound my bandages. Although I disbelieved his assertion to be a trained nurse, I decided to humor him. When he pronounced that my head was healing satisfactorily, I praised his expertise, then listened intently as he told me how to maintain the incision, an ugly ring of scabs and sutures circumscribing my cranium like a crown of thorns.

As the hot, humid, enervating month elapsed, the Common Sense candidates finished devising their strategies, and the campaign began in earnest. The piano barn soon overflowed with shipping crates full of leaflets, brochures, metal buttons, T-shirts, bumper stickers, and porkpie hats. With each passing day, my skepticism intensified. A goat running for Borough Council? A pig on the School Board? A bull guiding the Planning Commission? Pollifex's menagerie didn't stand a chance.

My doubts received particularly vivid corroboration on July 20th, when the doctor staged a combination cocktail party and fund-raiser at the farmhouse. From among the small but ardent population of political progressives inhabiting Greenbriar, Pollifex had identified thirty of the wealthiest. Two dozen accepted his invitation. Although these potential contributors were clearly appalled by my bifurcation, they seemed to accept Pollifex's explanation. (I suffered from a rare neurological disorder amenable only to the most radical surgery.) But then the candidates themselves sauntered into the living room, and Pollifex's guests immediately lost their powers of concentration.

It wasn't so much that Maxwell, Juliana, and Serge looked like an incompetent demiurge's roughest drafts. The real problem was that they'd retained so many traits of the creatures to which they'd been grafted. Throughout the entire event, Juliana stuffed her face with canapés and petit-fours. Whenever Serge engaged a potential donor in conversation, he crudely emphasized his points by ramming his horns into the listener's chest. Maxwell, meanwhile, kept defecating on the living room carpet, a behavior not redeemed by the mildly pleasant fragrance that a vegetarian diet imparts to bovine manure. By the time the mutants were ready to deliver their formal speeches, the pledges stood at a mere fifty dollars, and every guest had manufactured an excuse to leave.

"Your idea is never going to work," I told Pollifex after the candidates had returned to their respective barns. We were sitting in the doctor's kitchen, consuming mugs of French roast coffee. The door stood open. A thousand crickets sang in the meadow.

"This is a setback, not a catastrophe," said Pollifex brushing crumbs from his white dinner jacket. "Maxwell is a major Confucius scholar, with strong Kantian credentials as well. He can surely become housebroken. Juliana is probably the finest utilitarian philosopher since John Stuart Mill. For such a mind, table manners will prove a snap. If you ask Serge about the Sermon on the Mount, he'll recite the King James translation without a fluff. Once I explain how uncouth he's being, he'll learn to control his butting urge."

"Nobody wants to vote for a candidate with horns."

"It will take a while–quite a while–before Greenbriar's citizens appreciate this slate, but eventually they'll hop on the bandwagon." Pollifex poured himself a second cup of French roast. "Do you doubt that my mutants are ethical geniuses? Can you imagine, for example, how they responded to the Prisoner's Dilemma?

For three years running, I had used the Prisoner's Dilemma in my Introduction to Philosophy class. It's a situation-ethics classic, first devised in 1951 by Merrill Flood of the RAND Corporation. Imagine that you and a stranger have been arrested as accomplices in manslaughter. You are both innocent. The state's case is weak. Even though you don't know each other, you and the stranger form a pact. You will both stonewall it, maintaining your innocence no matter what deals the prosecutor may offer.

Each of you is questioned privately. Upon entering the interrogation room, the prosecutor lays out four possibilities. If you and your presumed accomplice hang tough, confessing to nothing, you will each get a short sentence, a mere seven months in prison. If you admit your guilt and implicate your fellow prisoner, you will go scot-free–and your presumed accomplice will serve a life sentence. If you hang tough and your fellow prisoner confesses-and-implicates, *he* will go scot free–and *you* will serve a life sentence. Finally, if you and your fellow prisoner both confess-and-implicate, you will each get a medium sentence, four years behind bars.

It doesn't take my students long to realize that the most logical course is to break faith with the stranger, thus guaranteeing that you won't spend your life in prison if he also defects. The uplifting-but-uncertain possibility of a short sentence must lose out to the immoral-but-immutable fact of a medium sentence. Cooperation be damned.

"Your mutants probably insist that they would keep faith regardless of the consequences," I said. "They would rather die than violate a trust."

"Their answer is subtler than that," said Pollifex. "They would tell the prosecutor, 'You imagine that my fellow prisoner and I have made a pact, and in that you are correct. You further imagine that you can manipulate us into breaking faith with one another. But given your obsession with betrayal, I must conclude that you are yourself a liar, and that you will ultimately seek to convert our unwilling confessions into life sentences. I refuse to play this game. Let's go to court instead.'"

"An impressive riposte," I said. "But the fact remains ..." Reaching for the coffee pot, I let my voice drift away. "Suppose I poured some French roast directly into my jar? Would I be jolted awake?"

"Don't try it," said Pollifex.

"I won't."

The mutant maker scowled strenuously. "You think I'm some sort of mad scientist."

"Restore my brain," I told him. "Leave the farm, get a job at Pfizer, wash your hands of politics."

"I'm a sane scientist, Blake. I'm the last sane scientist in the world."

I looked directly in his eyes. The face that returned my gaze was neither entirely mad nor entirely sane. It was the face of a man who wasn't sleeping well, and it made me want to run away.

‡ ✹ ‡

The following morning, my routine wanderings along the farm's perimeter brought me to a broad, swiftly flowing creek about twelve feet wide and three deep. Although the barbed-wire net extended beneath the water, clear to the bottom, I suddenly realized how a man might circumvent it. By redirecting the water's flow via a series of dikes, I could desiccate a large section of the creek bed and subsequently dig my way out of this hellish place. I would need only one of the shovels I'd spotted in the toolshed—a shovel, and a great deal of luck.

Thus it was that I embarked on a secret construction project. Every day at about 11:00 A.M., right after Karl took the specimen from my superego, I slunk off to the creek and spent a half-hour adding rocks, logs, and mud to the burgeoning levees, returning to the cottage in time for lunch. Although the creek proved far less pliable than I'd hoped, I eventually became its master. Within two weeks, I figured, possibly three, a large patch of sand and pebbles would lie exposed to the hot summer sun, waiting to receive my shovel.

Naturally I was tempted to tell Vickie of my scheme. Given my handicap, I could certainly have used her assistance in building the levees. But in the end I concluded that, rather than endorsing my bid for freedom, she would regard it as a betrayal of the Common Sense Party and its virtuous agenda.

I knew I'd made the right decision when Vickie entered our cottage late one night in the form of a gigantic mutant hen. Her body had become a bulbous mass of feathers, her legs had transmuted into fleshy stilts, and her face now sported a beak the size of a funnel. Obviously she was running for elective office, but I couldn't imagine which one. She lost no time informing me. Her ambition, she explained, was to become Greenbriar's next mayor.

"I've even got an issue," she said.

"I don't want to hear about it," I replied, looking her up and down. Although she still apparently retained her large and excellent breasts beneath her bikini top, their present context reduced their erotic content considerably.

"Do you know what Greenbriar needs?" she proclaimed. "Traffic diverters at certain key intersections! Our neighborhoods are being suffocated by the automobile!"

"You shouldn't have done this, Vickie," I told her.

"My name is Eva Pullo," she clucked.

"These people have brainwashed you!"

"The Common Sense Party is the hope of the future!"

"You're talking like a fascist!" I said.

"At least I'm not a coward like you!" said the chicken.

For the next half-hour we hurled insults at each other—our first real post-marital fight—and then I left in a huff, eager to continue my arcane labors by the creek. In a peculiar way I still loved Vickie, but I sensed that our relationship was at an end. When I made my momentous escape, I feared, she would not be coming with me.

⇥ ⚙ ⇤

Even as I redirected the creek, the four mutant candidates brought off an equally impressive feat—something akin to a miracle, in fact. They got the citizens of Greenbriar to listen to them, and the citizens liked what they heard.

The first breakthrough occurred when Maxwell appeared along with three other Planning Commission candidates—Republican, Democrat, Libertarian—on Greenbriar's local-access cable channel. I watched the broadcast in the farmhouse, sitting on the couch between Vickie and Dr. Pollifex. Although the full-blooded humans on the podium initially refused to take Maxwell seriously, the more he talked about his desire to prevent the Route 80 Extension from wreaking havoc with local ecosystems, the clearer it became that this mutant had charisma. Maxwell's eloquence was breathtaking, his logic impeccable, his sincerity sublime. He committed no fecal faux pas.

"That bull was on his game," I admitted at the end of the transmission.

"The moderator was *enchanted*," enthused Vickie.

"Our boy is going to win," said Pollifex.

Two days later, Juliana kicked off her campaign for School Board. Aided by the ever energetic Vickie, she had outfitted the back of an old yellow school bus with a Pullman car observation platform, the sort of stage from which early twentieth-century presidential candidates campaigned while riding the rails. Juliana and Vickie also transformed the bus's interior, replacing the seats with a coffee bar, a chat lounge, and racks of brochures explaining the pig woman's ambition to expand the sex education program, improve services for special needs children, increase faculty awareness of the misery endured by gay students, and—most audacious of all—invert the salary pyramid so that first-grade teachers would earn more than high-school administrators. Day in, day out, Juliana tooled around Greenbriar in her appealing vehicle, giving out iced cappuccinos, addressing crowds from the platform, speaking to citizens privately in the lounge, and somehow managing to check her impulse toward gluttony, all the while exhibiting a caliber of wisdom that eclipsed her unappetizing physiognomy. The tour was a fabulous success—such, at least, was the impression I received from watching the blurry, jerky coverage that Vickie accorded the pig woman's campaign with Pollifex's camcorder. Every time the school bus pulled away from a Juliana Sowers rally, it left behind a thousand tear-stained eyes, so moved were the citizens by her commitment to the glorious ideal of public education.

Serge, meanwhile, participated in a series of "Meet the Candidates" nights along with four other Borough Council hopefuls. Even when mediated by Vickie's shaky videography, the inaugural gathering at Greenbriar Town Hall came across as a powerful piece of political theater. Serge fully suppressed his impulse to butt his opponents—but that was the smallest of his accomplishments. Without slinging mud, flinging innuendo, or indulging in disingenuous rhetoric, he made his fellow candidates look like moral idiots for their unwillingness to stand firm

against what he called "the insatiable greed of Consumerland." Before
the evening ended, the attending voters stood prepared to tar-and-
feather any discount chain executive who might set foot in Greenbriar,
and it was obvious they'd also embraced Serge's other ideas for making
the Borough Council a friend to local business. If Serge's plans came to
fruition, shoppers would eventually flock to the downtown, lured by
parking-fee rebates, street performers, bicycle paths, mini-playgrounds,
and low-cost supervised day care.

As for Vickie's mayoral campaign–which I soon learned to call
Eva Pullo's mayoral campaign–it gained momentum the instant she
shed her habit of pecking hecklers on the head. Vickie's commitment
to reducing the automobile traffic in residential areas occasioned the
grandest rhetorical flights I'd ever heard from her. "A neighborhood
should exist for the welfare of its children, not the convenience of its
motorists," she told the local chapter of the League of Women Voters.
"We must not allow our unconsidered veneration of the automobile to
mask our fundamental need for community and connectedness," she
advised the Chamber of Commerce. By the middle of August, Vickie
had added a dozen other environmentalist planks to her platform,
including an ingenious proposal to outfit the town's major highways
with underground passageways for raccoons, badgers, woodchucks,
skunks, and possums.

You must believe me, reader, when I say that my conversion to the
Common Sense Party occurred well before the *Greenbriar Daily Times*
published its poll indicating that the entire slate–Maxwell Taurus, Juliana
Sowers, Serge Milkovich, Eva Pullo–enjoyed the status of shoo-ins. I was
not simply trying to ride with the winners. When I abandoned my plan
to dig an escape channel under the fence, I was doing what I thought was
right. When I resolved to spend the next three years nursing the Pollifex
Farm candidates from my cerebral teat, I was fired by an idealism so
intense that the pragmatists among you would blush to behold it.

I left the levees in place, however, just in case I had a change of
heart.

The attack on Pollifex Farm started shortly after 11:00 P.M. It was
Halloween night, which means that the raiders probably aroused no
suspicions whatsoever as, dressed in shrouds and skull masks, they
drove their pickup trucks through the streets of Greenbriar and down

Spring Valley Road. To this day, I'm not sure who organized and paid for the atrocity. At its core, I suspect, the mob included not only yahoos armed with torches but also conservatives gripped by fear, moderates transfixed by cynicism, liberals in the pay of the *status quo*, libertarians acting out anti-government fantasies, and a few random anarchists looking for a good time. Whatever their conflicting allegiances, the vigilantes stood united in their realization that Andre Pollifex, sane scientist, was about to unleash a reign of enlightenment on Greenbriar. They were having none of it.

I was experiencing yet another version of the student's dream–this time I'd misconnected not simply with one class but with an entire college curriculum–when shouts, gunshots, and the neighing of frightened horses awoke me. Taking hold of the library cart, I roused Vickie by ruffling her feathers, and side by side we stumbled into the parlor. By the time we'd made our way outside, the windmill, tractor shed, corn crib, and centaur stables were all on fire. Although I could not move quickly without risking permanent paralysis, Vickie immediately sprang into action. Transcending her spheroid body, she charged into the burning stables and set the mutant horses free, and she proved equally unflappable when the vigilantes hurled their torches into Maxwell's residence. With little thought for her personal safety, she ran into the flaming piano barn, located the panicked bull man and the equally discombobulated pig woman–in recent months they'd entered into a relationship whose details needn't concern us here–and led them outside right before the roof collapsed in a great red wave of cascading sparks and flying embers.

And still the arsonists continued their assault, blockading the main gate with bales of burning hay, setting fire to the chicken coop, and turning Pollifex's laboratory into a raging inferno. Catching an occasional glimpse of our spectral enemies, their white sheets flashing in the light of the flames, I saw that they would not become hoist by their own petards, for they had equipped themselves with asbestos suits, scuba regulators, and compressed air tanks. As for the inhabitants of Pollifex Farm, it was certain that if we didn't move quickly, we would suffer either incineration, suffocation, or their concurrence in the form of fatally seared lungs.

Although I had never felt so divided, neither the fear spasms in my chest nor the jumbled thoughts in my jar prevented me from realizing what the mutants must do next. I told them to steal shovels from the toolshed, make for the creek, and follow it to the fence. Thanks to my levees, I explained, the bed now lay in the open air. Within twenty minutes or so, they should be able to dig below the barbed-wire net and gouge a dry channel for themselves. The rest of my plan had me bringing up the rear, looking out for Karl, Serge, and Dr. Pollifex so that I might direct them to the secret exit. Vickie kissed my lips, Juliana caressed my cheek, Maxwell embraced by brain, and then all three candidates rushed off into the choking darkness.

Before that terrible night was out, I indeed found the other Party members. Karl lay dead in a mound of straw beside the sheep barn, his forehead blasted away by buckshot. Serge sat on the rear porch of the farmhouse, his left horn broken off and thrust fatally into his chest. Finally I came upon Pollifex. The vigilantes had roped the doctor to a maple tree, subjected him to target practice, and left him for dead. He was as perforated as Saint Sebastian. A mattock, a pitchfork, and two scythes projected from his body like quills from a porcupine.

"Andre, it's me, Blake," I said, approaching.

"Blake?" he muttered. "Blake? Oh, Blake, they killed Serge. They killed Karl."

"I know. Vickie got away, and Maxwell too, and Juliana."

"I was a sane scientist," said Pollifex.

"Of course," I said.

"There are some things that expediency was not meant to tamper with."

"I agree."

"Pullo for Mayor!" he shouted.

"Taurus for Planning Commission!" I replied.

"Milkovich for Borough Council!" he shouted. "Sowers for School Board!" he screamed, and then he died.

₰ ✺ ₷

There's not much more to tell. Although Vickie, Juliana, Maxwell, and I all escaped the burning farm that night, the formula for the miraculous serum died with Dr. Pollifex. Deprived of their weekly Altruoid injections, the mutants soon lost their talent for practical idealism, and their political careers sputtered out. Greenbriar now boasts a mammoth new Consumerland. The Route 80 extension is almost finished. High-school principals still draw twice the pay of first-grade teachers. Life goes on.

The last time I saw Juliana, she was the opening act at Caesar's

Palace in Atlantic City. A few songs, some impersonations, a standup comedy routine–mostly vegetarian humor and animal-rights jokes leavened by a sardonic feminism. The crowd ate it up, and Juliana seemed to be enjoying herself. But, oh, what a formidable School Board member she would've made!

When the Route 80 disaster occurred, Maxwell was devastated–not so much by the extension itself as by his inability to critique it eloquently. These days he plays piano at Emilio's, a seedy bar in Newark. He is by no means the weirdest presence in the place, and he enjoys listening to the customers' troubles. But he is a broken mutant.

Vickie and I did our best to make it work, but in the end we decided that mixed marriages entail insurmountable hurdles, and we split up. Eventually she got a job hosting a preschool children's television show on the Disney Channel, *Arabella's Barnyard Band.* Occasionally she manages to insert a satiric observation about automobiles into her patter.

As for me, after hearing the tenth neurosurgeon declare that I am beyond reassembly, I decided to join the world's eternal vagabonds. I am brother to the Wandering Jew, the Flying Dutchman, and Marley's Ghost. I shuffle around North America, dragging my library cart behind me, exhibiting my fractured self to anyone who's willing to pay. In the past decade, my employers have included three carnivals, four roadside peep shows, two direct-to-video horror movie producers, and an artsy off-Broadway troupe bent on reviving *Le Grand Guignol.*

And always I remain on the lookout for another Andre Pollifex, another scientist who can manufacture QZ-11-4 serum and use it to turn beasts into politicians. I shall not settle for any sort of Pollifex, of course. The actual Pollifex, for example, would not meet my standards. The man bifurcated me without my permission, and I cannot forgive him for that.

The scientist I seek would unflinchingly martyr himself to the Prisoner's Dilemma. As they hauled him away to whatever dungeon is reserved for such saints, he would turn to the crowd and say, "The personal cost was great, but at least I have delivered a fellow human from an unjust imprisonment. And who knows? Perhaps his anguish over breaking faith with me will eventually transform him into a more generous friend, a better parent, or a public benefactor."

Alas, my heart is not in the quest. Only part of me–a small part, I must confess–wants to keep on making useful neurological donations. So even if there is a perfect Pollifex out there somewhere, he will probably never get to fashion a fresh batch of Altruoid. Not unless I father a child–and not unless the child receives the gene–and not unless the gene finds expression–and not unless this descendent of mine donates his superego to science. But as the bull man told me many years ago, QZ-11-4 only rarely gets actualized in the humans who carry it.

I believe I see a way around the problem. The roadside emporium in which I currently display myself also features a llama named Loretta. She can count to ten and solve simple arithmetic problems. I am enchanted by Loretta's liquid eyes, sensuous lips, and splendid form– and I think she has taken a similar interest in me. It's a relationship, I feel, that could lead almost anywhere.